Crunch Time

The Dream Traveler
Book Five

Ernesto H Lee

A Defining Moment
&
A Quote from the Movie, Catch Me If You Can.

Frank Abagnale Sr, "You know why the Yankees always win, Frank?

Frank Abagnale Jr, "Because they have Mickey Mantle?

Frank Abagnale Sr, "No, it's because no one can take their eyes off those damn pinstripes."

I'm not a baseball fan, so I'm in no position to judge if Frank Abagnale Sr, was entirely correct about the effect of the pinstripes on the opposition. But I do understand the power of a stunning first impression and, its infinite ability to create a defining moment in time*

Take for instance your dress of Emerald Blue that so quickly and easily took my breath away. So, effortless was your ability to mesmerize and enchant, that my heart was willingly given over to be held captive on the island of your love. And in a room so full of others, how was it possible that I could see only you? And how is it possible, that this single moment in time enchants me still?

Awake or asleep, the girl in the blue dress comes to me. Awake or asleep she calls to me. Awake or asleep she reveals to me, who I really am.

*A defining moment (noun) - *a point at which the essential nature or character of a person, group, etc., is revealed or identified, or* **defining moments** (plural noun) - *an event which typifies or determines all subsequent related occurrences.*

Ernesto H Lee
9th August 2020

Crunch Time

Table of Contents

Crunch Time

Preface

Under any other circumstance, the rescue of a colleague and the simultaneous recovery of twenty million pounds in gold bullion would have been cause for celebration. At minimum, it would have earned me the right to spend my evening relaxing.

But last night, celebration and relaxation for me were the furthest things from my mind. Catherine's discovery of my warrant card in Ashdown Forest, combined with the bitterness and raw emotion in her parting words, had been more than enough to quickly dispel any such thoughts of relaxation or self-congratulation.

Alone on the pavement watching her leave, I had been left reeling from the shock of her discovery and completely at a loss as to how to make things right.

To say that I now feel caught between a rock and a hard place would be a wholly inadequate summary of my current predicament. If I lie to Catherine again and she doesn't believe me, it will not only be the final nail in the coffin of our relationship—it will be the end of my career.

As far as Catherine is concerned, I have lied and shut her out one too many times. And who could really blame her? I know only too well that I'm out of second chances. I also know that if she gets even the faintest whiff of bullshit when I speak to her today, you can be damn sure that she will follow through with her threat to share her suspicions with DCI Morgan.

What, though, is my alternative? Tell the truth about how my warrant card ended up where it did and in that condition? As an option, that's hardly any better than choosing to lie again. The potential ramifications amount to very much the same thing when you consider who we are talking about.

Catherine Swain is not only a brilliant detective but one of the smartest and most logical people I know.

How could I possibly expect someone as well educated and rational as Catherine to believe something so far removed from society's definition of reality?

She wouldn't just think I was lying to her again. She would think that I had completely lost my marbles. Or worse, that I was deliberately making fun of her. This latter scenario is something that I don't even wish to contemplate. In this scenario, Catherine's reaction would be far from rational and far from pleasant.

So, a rock and a hard place doesn't even come close to where my head is right now. In fact, a rock and a hard place sounds quite a fun place to be in comparison.

All things considered then, what did I do last night to help myself out of this predicament? I'll tell you what I did. I watched the squad car leave and after staring hopelessly at the pavement for a few minutes, I went up to my apartment to take a long hot shower. After that, I did what I always do when my back is against the wall. I opened a new bottle of Jameson, buried my head in the sand, and somewhat predictably passed out on my sofa sometime around midnight.

With hindsight, of course, this wasn't one of my smartest moves ever. Friday morning has come around all too quickly, my head is pounding, and Catherine will want answers when I see her today.

For the second time in as many days, all I can think to say to myself as I brush my teeth is … "Fuck!"

Sean McMillan
May 4th, 2018

Present Day – Friday Morning, May 4th, 2018

In a lame attempt to delay the inevitable confrontation with Catherine, I get to Blackwell Station far later than I ordinarily would. My intention is to bypass our floor and head straight up to the morning briefing; but as I reach the security gate, the duty sergeant, Ted Morris, stands up to meet me.

"Sean, hang on there, mate. DI Gray wants to see you. She said you should go straight up as soon as you got here."

I smile and nod an acknowledgment. "Thanks, Ted, I'll catch her straight after the briefing. I guess she'll be leading it again tod–"

"No, the briefing is off today, Sean. You should go and see her right away. She was quite insistent about that."

Concerned that Catherine may have already spoken to DI Gray, I ask, "Did she say if she wanted me to bring DC Swain?"

Sergeant Morris shakes his head. "Nope, she just asked for you. Did you remember your access card today, or do you want me to buzz you in again?"

While he waits for an answer, I sheepishly reach into my jacket pocket to retrieve the wallet containing my faded warrant card and station access pass. When he sees the condition of the wallet and its contents, he laughs. "Christ almighty, Sean, have you been digging up spuds with that wallet? It looks almost as bad as you," he says, referring to my recent injuries. "Does that access card even still work, mate?"

I nervously place the card against the scanner. To my astonishment, the security gate opens, and I pass through. Surprised himself that the card is still working, Morris shrugs and says, "I'll request a new access pass and warrant card for you anyway. You can't be walking around with that in your pocket. Have a good day, mate. Oh, and good job, by the way, in getting DCI Morgan back."

■ ■ ■ ■ ■ ■ ■

Sarah Gray is preoccupied in her office reviewing a case file and doesn't immediately notice my arrival. I tactfully tap on the open door and she looks up and smiles as I take a seat. After putting the case file in her desk drawer, there is a short pause before she grimaces and points to my face.

"Those bruises look worse than they were yesterday, Sean. How are you feeling? That was a pretty traumatic couple of days for you both."

I self-consciously run my hand across the lump on the back of my head. "I'm fine, ma'am. This lump has gone right down and the bruises on my face look much worse than they are."

Unconvinced, Gray slowly nods. "Maybe so, but no one would blame you if you wanted to take a few days' personal time. There is no shame in it."

The last statement confuses me. "Sorry, ma'am, no shame in what?"

Addressing me in a way that suggests I should know the answer already, Gray says, "PTSD, Sean. Post-traumatic stress disord—"

"Yes, ma'am," I interrupt. "I know what PTSD is, and honestly, I'm fine. Besides, it's Friday and my only plan this weekend is to put my feet up and relax."

Gray nods again and smiles. "Okay, well that's good to hear. But if you do start feeling anxious or feel like you need some professional guidance, the Force's counselling service is there for that very reason. Just let me know and I can arrange for you to—"

Irritated at the continued intimation that I might need counselling, I interrupt again in the hope of closing down the subject, "Ma'am, I'm fine, honestly. I took a few knocks, that's all. Now, if it's okay, can we just leave it please?"

Reluctantly, Gray agrees to my request. "Okay, let's park this for now. But if you change your mind, you only have to say. In the meantime, it wouldn't do you any harm to take some leave. Why not take off until the 14th, like DC Swain has?"

My expression gives away my ignorance and leaves Gray looking slightly embarrassed. "Oh, don't you know? I'm sorry, I thought she would have already cleared this with you."

Not wishing to look stupid, I lie. "No, ma'am. I've a couple of missed calls from her. I was going to catch up with DC Swain this morning. You've spoken to her?"

"Yes, she called me at just after seven this morning to say she wasn't feeling great and asked to be excused duty today. I suggested some counselling to her and that she should take a short leave of absence. Like you, she declined the counselling, but she did accept the offer of leave."

I'm obviously concerned for Cath's welfare, but I also have something else on my mind. "Thank you, ma'am. I'll call her in a while to make sure she's okay. Did she say anything else?"

Sarah shakes her head. "No, just that she wasn't feeling well, which is hardly surprising. The boss said that she took a nasty fall into that pit yesterday."

I replay the scene in my mind and shudder slightly as I recall the sickening thud as she hit the ground. "Yes, ma'am, she did."

Gray stares directly at me for a few seconds and then asks, "Is everything alright? With you and, DC Swain, I mean."

"Yes. Yes, of course, ma'am. Like you said, just a tough couple of days for all of us."

To divert the conversation, I ask about DCI Morgan. "You've also spoken to the boss, ma'am? How is he?"

"Yes. I visited him in hospital last night. Considering what he's been through, he's doing fine.

"He'll be off work for at least a couple of weeks, but he did ask me to pass on his thanks for your part in his rescue. He also brought me up to speed with the details. I have to say, Sean, that using the Find My iPhone application was a stroke of genius."

Embarrassed, I shrug off the praise. "It was nothing, ma'am. I'm just glad everything worked out and Clive Douglas is back where he belongs."

My comment makes DI Gray frown slightly. "Take the praise while you can, Sean. I suspect that once the boss is back on his feet, you might be in for a bit of a bollocking for again involving a civilian in one of your cases. Perhaps you might want to reconsider that offer of some leave? It will do you good and give you some time to get your thoughts together."

Suddenly the offer of a leave of absence seems distinctly more appealing than it did earlier, and I gratefully accept.

"Thank you, yes. I think, I will. If it's okay with you, ma'am, I'll take the same leave as DC Swain and return to work on Monday 14th."

She of course agrees. I stand up to leave, but she asks me to wait. "Before you go, I have a couple of case updates that you might be interested in. This won't take long, Sean."

She gestures for me to retake my seat and then slides a sheet of paper across the desk. "The forensics boys pulled the remains of two adult males out of that hole last night. After being buried for so long, both bodies were fully decomposed, but there was enough uniform material and boot leather remaining for us to know with enough certainty that they had found two of our three missing security guards."

This is, of course, no surprise to me. And although I know who they have found, I ask anyway.

"That's good. Any luck in identifying which of the guards they are?"

Gray smiles and points to the bottom of the sheet. "Actually, yes. Whoever killed and buried them was either supremely confident that they would never be found, or they were just too lazy or too stupid to cover their tracks. The wallets of both men were still in their pockets."

I look to the bottom of the sheet and read aloud: "George John Benson and Peter Edwin Lane. So, ma'am, this just leaves Stuart Goldsmith unaccounted for?"

DI Gray takes back the sheet of paper. "Correct. Mr. Goldsmith remains as a person of interest in this case. But not as a suspect. Because of this fact and the length of time since his disappearance, it's doubtful that the Met are going to dedicate much time or many resources to trying to find him."

"But they will at least try?" I ask.

Gray nods, but her reply is less than reassuring. "I'm sure somebody will go through the motions of trying to find him. Let's be honest, though, Sean. Mr. Goldsmith had no known living relatives, no apparent friends, and nobody in the last thirty-five years has followed up on his disappearance. As cases go, finding him is not a priority."

I, of course, know exactly what happened to Stuart Goldsmith. Or I know at least up to the point where I forced him to leave his house to go into hiding. Even so, I'm still taken aback by the apparent lack of interest in getting to the bottom of what happened to him. Unreasonably and unfairly, I take out my frustration on Sarah Gray.

"Well, excuse me for thinking that's a cop-out, ma'am, but if determining the fate of Stuart Goldsmith is not a priority, then please tell me what is?"

To be sure that I have finished my short rant, Sarah waits for a couple of seconds before replying. Rather cleverly, she doesn't offer any kind of rebuke. Instead, she addresses me formally as a subtle form of restating her seniority.

"The priority, Sergeant McMillan, is to get Clive Douglas back to a high-security Category A facility as soon as possible.

"Secondary to that is getting Rosemary Pinois remanded in custody until her trial. Is that okay with you, Sergeant?"

Suitably chastised, I nod and apologize. "Yes, ma'am, of course. I'm sorry, I didn't mean to come across like th–"

Gray stops me mid-sentence. "Sean, it's fine. You had much more of a personal interest in this case than I did. You have every right to feel aggrieved at the lack of interest in finding Mr. Goldsmith. It is what it is, though. Let's just focus on what we can do, shall we?"

I nod my agreement. "Understood, ma'am. So, what are the next steps with Clive Douglas and Rosemary Pinois? Where are they both currently being held?"

"They have Rosemary Pinois in the holding cells over at Leeson Street," Gray replies. "She's due in court at two this afternoon for her initial remand hearing. Given the circumstances of her arrest, I'm not expecting there to be any surprises. And all things being equal, I'm expecting her to be remanded in custody without any credible objection from her legal counsel."

"Bronzefield Prison?" I ask.

"Yes, I think that's the most likely destination for her. It's the nearest prison set up to handle Category A females, following the permanent closure of HMP Holloway."

I shake my head in disgust. "It was a real shame they closed Holloway. It was a cold, unforgiving and soulless place. A woman like Rosemary Pinois would have fitted right in."

Sarah nods with a wry smile and says, "You're right about that, Sean. And let's face it, if Holloway was good enough for the likes of Myra Hindley, it would certainly have been good enough for our Rosemary.

"Don't feel too disappointed, though. I hear that Bronzefield is no holiday camp either. I'm sure the guards there will give her the kind of welcome she deserves."

"Let's hope so, ma'am. And what about Clive Douglas? What's the plan for him?"

Gray stands up, checks her watch, and smiles. "In about two hours, I have the pleasure of picking up ex-Detective Superintendent Clive Douglas from Meerholt Prison and personally escorting him back to HMP Yarwood. I've spoken to the Yarwood Prison governor this morning and he assures me that Douglas will be held in the isolation wing for the foreseeable future. I trust that meets with your approval, Sean?"

"Yes, ma'am. It's still better than he deserves. But it's a good start. May I ask who will be joining you on the escort?"

"You're concerned for my safety?"

"This is Clive Douglas we're talking about, ma'am. We know only too well that he shouldn't be underestimated. If he sees even the smallest opportunity to escape, you can be sure that he will take it."

Gray smiles and touches my arm. "Sean, I know how personal this is to you, but we have our bases fully covered on this one. Mike Thurgood will be accompanying me on the escort with one of his teams. You need to trust me that we have everything under control. I suggest now that you go home and put your feet u–"

"But how many vehicles in the convoy and how many armed officers, ma'am?"

Annoyed at my interruption and questioning of the arrangements, Gray holds up her hand and protests, "Sean, enough please. We know exactly who we are dealing with here. Standard protocol is for a three-vehicle convoy. The prisoner will be in the armored transfer vehicle with pairs of armed officers in rapid response vehicles to the front and rear.

"And I'll be riding shotgun with Clive to keep him company on the trip north. Good enough?"

"So, four armed officers plus yourself and the driver of the armored vehicle?"

"Correct. Now, please go home and take some well-deserved leave, Sean. I'll message you when we get to Yarwood. Okay?"

I nod and turn to leave, but then hesitate at the door and turn back around. "I want to come with you, ma'am. I want to be there on the escort."

Gray, who by now has already sat down at her desk again, stands back up and angrily points to the door. "You are testing my patience, DS McMillan. Either go home willingly, or I will have you escorted home. What's it to be?"

For a moment I consider leaving, but my desire to personally see Clive Douglas returned to Yarwood is too strong to ignore. "Ma'am, I'm not doubting your arrangements for the escort. I know that Inspector Thurgood and his men are more than capable of handling anything that might happen."

Gray raises her hands in confusion and asks, "So, what is it then? Why is it so important for you to be there? Haven't you had a gutful of Clive Douglas by now?"

I hesitate to answer, and Gray asks again, "Well, what is it? Either spit it out or go home and let me get on with my job."

"It's … it's personal," I reply. "With Clive Douglas I mean. I blame myself for him getting out of Yarwood in the first place. I should have just ignored him from the first time he made contact. Maybe then the boss wouldn't have got hurt. Maybe then–"

Sarah Gray cuts me off mid-sentence. "Sean, you followed up on a line of enquiry, as you were meant to. Any other good copper would have done the same. And the boss losing his finger wasn't down to you.

"We all know that, with or without Clive Douglas, Rosemary was bound to have figured out the boss's connection to the death of her father eventually."

She's probably right, but I still can't help feeling somehow responsible. "Maybe, ma'am, but this is something I need to do. I need to look that bastard in the eye one more time. Call it closure. I need closure, ma'am."

Gray shakes her head, but when she speaks again her tone has softened. "Closure? That's what this is about?"

"Yes, ma'am. I can't just sit at home waiting and not knowing what is happening. I need to be there. Let me join the escort and, as soon as it's done, you have my word I'll take that leave of absence to recharge my batteries."

Reluctantly and probably against her better judgment, DI Gray agrees to my request. "I doubt you would let it rest anyway, DS McMillan. You can meet me outside Meerholt Prison at 10.45. The prisoner escort is due to leave at 11 am sharp. You can ride in with me and use the time on the way up to say your fond farewells to Douglas." Then with a smirk, "I'm sure he will appreciate your company."

I raise my eyebrows knowingly, "Thank you, ma'am. I'm not sure how much Douglas will enjoy the trip, but I damn well know I will."

Gray walks me to the door. "Good, that's settled then. Now, if there's nothing else, I have a few things to do before I leave for Meerholt."

"Actually, ma'am. There is one other thing."

"You're pushing your luck, Sergeant McMillan. What is it?"

Knowing that my request is minor in comparison to what I have already asked for, I smile and ask if I can hitch a lift with her to Meerholt. "Sorry, ma'am, my car is still in the workshop having the windscreen replaced," I explain.

In response, DI Gray shakes her head, but she also gives me a grudging smile. "You're a cheeky bastard, McMillan. Meet me at the reception in an hour. Oh, and shut the door on your way out please."

■ ■ ■ ■ ■ ■ ■

With less than an hour to kill, I make my way to the station canteen to catch the end of the breakfast service. Apart from me, there are just three diners present, which suits me perfectly.

I find a seat well away from anyone else and after wolfing down a bacon and egg sandwich I take out my cell phone and scroll through my contacts until I reach Catherine's number.

More than once I change my mind and put down the phone, until finally I pick it up again and say to myself, "Just bloody call her, Sean. What's the worst that can happen?"

I count to three, then I place the call. It connects but is cut off almost immediately.

"Okay, so I guess that answers the question of whether she is still pissed with me," I say to myself. "No harm trying again then I suppose."

I hit the redial button. After three rings, I'm hopeful that this time she might answer the call. When I hear her voice, my heart rate noticeably quickens. I'm about to apologize, when I realize that I'm listening to her voicemail.

"Hi, this is Detective Constable Catherine Swain. I can't take your call right now, but if you leave your name, your contact number, and a short message, I will get back to you as soon as I can."

I wait for the beep that signals the end of her message, before stuttering my way through my own message.

"Uh, Hi, Cath, this is Sean. Well. What I mean to say is … well, you know who I am. I was calling to see if you were okay.

Sarah Gray said she spoke to you and you weren't feeling so good. She also said that you were taking some leave. I'm going to take the same leave time as you, and I was hoping we could meet up as soon as you are feeling up to it. We need to talk, Cath. What I mean to say is … well, I need to talk. I need to explain to you what has been happening. You deserve to know what has been happening. It's not what you think, though, it's just complicat–"

Before I can finish, the second voicemail beep signals the end of my recording. The call is cut off, and I'm left cursing myself for sounding like I'm making excuses again. I consider calling back to finish what I was trying to say but decide to leave it until after delivering Clive Douglas back to HMP Yarwood.

I figure that, by waiting, the next time I call her I can start with some good news.

■ ■ ■ ■ ■ ■ ■

We arrive at Meerholt with twenty minutes to spare before the start of the escort and I'm pleased to see a familiar face waiting for us at the reception. I smile and introduce DI Gray to Senior Officer Bayliss.

"Good morning, Patrick. It's good to see you again. This is my boss, Detective Inspector Sarah Gray. She's in charge of today's escort detail."

Gray shakes Bayliss' hand. "It's good to meet you, Officer Bayliss. I hope your guest hasn't been giving you too much trouble?"

Bayliss smiles and shakes his head. "We haven't heard so much as a peep from him since he arrived yesterday. He really looks broken this time. I don't think he's going to be giving you any trouble. Are you ready for us to bring him out?"

Gray nods and asks if DI Thurgood and his men have arrived.

"Yes, ma'am. The rest of your escort party are assembled in the yard. Officer Tyler will show you the way.

Bayliss leaves us to get Clive Douglas while PO Tyler leads us out towards the prison yard. As soon as Bayliss is out of earshot, Gray turns to me and asks, "Do you agree with Bayliss, Sean, that Clive is going to be a good boy this morning?"

I shake my head and smirk. "I think when he sees who his escort is, he is going to be more than a little pissed off, ma'am."

"So, not a broken man?"

"No. Not a chance of it. If I know nothing else about Clive Douglas, it's that he will keep on fighting until the last breath leaves his body. You can be sure of it, ma'am."

In the prison yard, DI Mike Thurgood is busy briefing his team. We wait for him to finish before we join him next to the armored escort vehicle.

"All ready?" Gray asks him.

"Yep, all set, Sarah. PC Mark Jarvis is your driver. Two of my other lads will be up front and I'll take tail end Charlie behind the meat wagon with Bob Wilkins." Thurgood then looks at me. "How you feeling, Sean? I didn't know you were joining us this morning."

"Last minute change of plan," Gray responds on my behalf. "Sean wanted to finish what he'd started. He'll be riding in with me to keep Clive company."

Thurgood thinks about it for a second and then raises his eyebrows and nods. "Fair enough. I can understand that. Good to have you on board, Sean." He looks beyond us and smiles. "Right then—I think it's time to get this show on the road."

I turn to see Clive Douglas slowly shuffling towards us surrounded by half a dozen prison officers. Although he is doing his best to portray the broken man, he's fooling no one.

The moment he catches sight of me and DI Gray, his back straightens, and his expression instantly changes to something much more reminiscent of his usual arrogance.

Bayliss orders his escort team to a halt within a few feet of where we are waiting and DI Gray steps forward to introduce herself. "Clive Douglas, I'm Detective Inspector Sar–"

"I know who you are," Douglas interrupts with a snarl. "In person, you're even more underwhelming than I was expecting, Inspector Gray."

With his recent remark about under-achievers fresh in her mind, Sarah is momentarily stumped and struggles to find a fitting response. Pleased with his early victory, Douglas smirks and pushes his advantage.

"Did I hit a nerve, Sarah?"

Before she can respond, Patrick Bayliss does something that takes us all by surprise. He moves up behind Douglas and deftly jabs his nightstick into the small of his back. The strike to the kidneys is painful enough to knock the wind out of him and cause him to wince, but not enough to cause any serious or lasting damage.

Clive doubles over, and Bayliss yanks him back up by the handcuffs. "That is your first and last warning, Douglas. One more smart word, and you will be making this trip Hannibal Lecter style. Do we understand each other?"

With no wish to be gagged or strapped into a straitjacket attached to a board, Douglas gives a grudging nod and Bayliss releases his grip.

Ordinarily, use of force like this would have elicited some kind of protest or response from at least one of us.

On this occasion, however, and with this particular prisoner, it seems wholly appropriate. We all remain quiet and while Sarah Gray signs the transfer papers, I discretely congratulate Bayliss.

"Nice shot, Patrick. That should keep him quiet for a while."

Bayliss smiles and remarks that Douglas had it coming, before he turns and takes back the clipboard from DI Gray, "Okay, that all seems to be in order, inspector. He's all yours. Good luck."

Two of Mike Thurgood's officers step forward and take a firm grip of Clive's arms. We follow as they lead him to the back of the armored truck where PC Jarvis is waiting with the doors open. With Douglas firmly secured inside the internal cage, we take our seats and buckle in. Jarvis locks the rear doors and takes his own seat up front.

A few minutes pass without anything happening and I watch as Douglas stares impassively at the windowless side wall of his cage. Finally, and almost looking impatient to get going, he turns to me to say something but is interrupted as Sarah Gray's radio crackles to life.

"All call signs, this is alpha sierra one, confirmed ready to move. Alpha sierra two and three, your status please?"

Thurgood's second team respond, "Sierra two, good to go, boss."

Gray waits for them to finish before she adds, "Alpha sierra three, good to go."

∎ ∎ ∎ ∎ ∎ ∎ ∎

The escort convoy gets under way, and Douglas turns back to face the wall. The first ten minutes of our trip are made in complete silence. Somewhat predictably, Clive Douglas is the one to break the silence. He turns towards me with a grin and offers up his cuffed wrists. "I don't suppose you can remove these cuffs until we get to Yarwood, Sean?"

"You suppose right," Gray replies for me. "Now button it, unless you want us to gag you as well."

Douglas ignores her comment and smirks at me. "It's not like you to let the ladies do the talking for you, Sean. What's wrong? You're not in the mood for conversation with your old buddy Clive?"

DI Gray is about to cut him off, but I know she would be wasting her breath. "It's okay, ma'am. Where he's going, there will be precious little chance for conversation. Let him have his fun while he can. What's on your mind, Clive?"

Douglas stares at DI Gray intently for a moment before looking back at me. "I wasn't expecting to see you today, Sean. Surely you must be ready for a few days off by now?"

"What, and miss seeing you returned to solitary? No, Clive, I wouldn't have missed this little trip for the world."

Douglas chuckles slightly. "Well, enjoy it while you can. You know what they say about all good things coming to an end."

"Yes, I do. And so should you," I reply. "This is the end of the line for you, Douglas. No more games, no more chances. Just four walls and a small barred window to remind you of what you are going to be missing out on for the next forty to fifty years. Think on that, why don't you?"

Douglas sneers and shakes his head. "No, I don't think so. If it's all the same with you, I'd rather think about somewhere and something altogether more pleasant."

"Sure, knock yourself out, Clive. Positive thinking and pipe dreams like that will do you well in solitary. For the first five or six years at least. I hear that for most people five or six years is the tipping point."

"Yes, well, that's the difference between me and most people. And I include you amongst most people, Sean. You're a typical glass half-empty type, whereas my glass is always at least half-full."

DI Gray, who until now has been sitting quietly, leans forward to ask Clive, "So, you think you can make your own little piece of paradise in a nine by six segregation cell just by staying positive?"

"Anywhere can be a paradise with the right attitude, Sarah," Douglas responds with a shrug. Then turning back to address me, "Speaking of which, do I sense trouble in your own little paradise, Sergeant McMillan?"

I shake my head. "Sorry? I'm not following you."

"No partner today, Sean? I would have thought a trip like this would have been right up Catherine's alley. I do hope she's okay. That was a nasty fall she took yesterday."

I shake my head again. "Not that it's any of your concern, but DC Swain is taking a well-earned break. She did ask me to pass on her best wishes, though. I'm sure she'll come and see you the next time she has the urge to feel nauseous."

Douglas chuckles to himself again. "I'll look forward to that. And what about Maria and Benjamin? How are they?"

DI Gray shoots me a sideways glance, but I ignore it and instead remind Douglas to be careful what he says. "Don't push it, Clive. The Pintos are off-limits, as you well know."

He nods to me and then smirks at Sarah Gray. "Such a lovely family. You can understand his concern, can't you?"

Gray turns to me questioningly. "Sean?"

"Ignore him, ma'am. He's just trying to provoke a reaction. He knows that I'm friendly with the Pintos. He likes to play games with veiled threats, don't you, Clive?"

Douglas slowly shakes his head. "You should know by now, Sean, that I don't play games. Think what you want, though. It makes no difference to me. Where are we anyway? How long until we get there?"

Gray looks down at her watch. "Get comfortable, Clive. We've still at least another three and a half hours if the traffic remains clear. We'll be joining the M1 shortly, so why don't you just sit back and keep quiet? Question time is over."

"That's good, that's very good," Douglas says. "I should probably thank you now, Sean. Just in case I don't get the chance later."

Sarah and I exchange a troubled glance. "What the hell are you talking about?" I ask.

"Don't be so modest," Douglas replies with a wry smile. "I couldn't have got this far without your help, Sean. We really are a good team."

Now alarmed, Gray edges away from me. "Sean, what's going on? What's he talking about?"

"Ma'am, ignore him, he's playing his bloody mind games. It's what he does. Don't listen to him."

Unconvinced, Gray turns back to Douglas and starts to say, "What are you—"

"What am I talking about, DI Gray? I'm saying that DS McMillan has been a big help to me. And that … well, that it's only a matter of time now."

Finally realizing what could be happening, I go cold and blurt out, "Jesus Christ, we've been set up. You need to warn DI Thurgood, ma'am."

With a look of disbelief, DI Gray pushes even further away from me and reaches into her jacket for her sidearm. With it pointed squarely at my chest, she lifts her radio with her free hand and calmly sends a message to the other call signs.

"Alpha sierra one, alpha sierra two, this is alpha sierra three. Escort is believed compromised; I repeat escort is compromised. Advise immediate return to safe loca—"

Whether or not her message was heard by the other two call signs is a question for another day. What is certain is that our vehicle comes to an unexpected halt and a split second later the silence is shattered by the unmistakable and ungodly sound of metal striking metal and the shattering of glass.

It would later transpire that our pair of escort vehicles had been simultaneously rammed side on by a pair of stolen buses in a carefully coordinated ambush at the appropriately named Gallows Corner roundabout on the A12.

As the noise subsides, I unbuckle and try to stand up, but Gray orders me to sit back down. "I'm sorry, Sean. Until I know what the hell is going on, you need to stay there and keep your distance from me."

"Ma'am, you've got this all wrong," I protest. "He's trying to set me up." I turn towards Douglas who is sitting back with a smug look on his face. "Tell her, you bastard!"

Gray points her Glock at my face. "DS McMillan, I'm warning you. You need to keep quiet."

Then, keeping her weapon firmly pointed in my direction, she attempts to contact the other call signs. "All call signs, this is alpha sierra three, please advise your status. Sierra one, sierra two, please advise your status."

Predictably, there is no answer from either of the escort vehicles. DI Gray gets to her feet and nervously edges past me to tap on the driver's partition. "Jarvis, what's going on? What can you see?"

For a moment, PC Jarvis ignores the question. Then he slowly turns. A bead of sweat is snaking its way down the side of his face and his complexion is unnaturally sallow as he mumbles an apology, "I'm sorry, ma'am, I had no choice. I'm sorry."

He turns away, ignoring Gray's demands for him to explain what he means, and climbs down from the cab. Moments later we hear the key turning in the lock of the rear door.

As the sunlight filters in, Gray desperately tries to establish contact with base, until the sight of DI Thurgood and PC Wilkins on their knees at gunpoint stops her dead.

Both are flanked by a pair of heavily armed masked men. And both appear to be barely conscious.

One captor orders Sarah to drop her weapon and radio and hand over her cell phone. She immediately complies, and PC Jarvis nervously steps forward, proffering her a key. "They want you to open the cage and take his cuffs off, ma'am."

Gray takes a step back. "I'm sorry. I can't do that, PC Jarvis." Then, shaking her head at him in disapproval, "Can I ask why … Mark? It is Mark, isn't it?"

Unsure of what to do or say next, Jarvis hesitates to respond.

Clearly irritated by the delay, another of the masked men pushes Jervis aside and levels a sawn-off shotgun at Gray's chest. In a thick Northern Irish accent, he orders, "Unlock the cage and take his cuffs off. Do it now please, DI Gray. I won't be asking again so politely."

I know only too well what these kinds of men are capable of. But to my dismay, Gray dismisses my pleading look to open the cage. Instead she stubbornly stands her ground, telling him to open it himself.

Without a second's hesitation, the Irishman turns and points his shotgun towards Bob Wilkins' chest.

"Lift his fucking head up," he barks.

Wilkins' head is yanked back and in the split second before the blast, the terror in his eyes is clear for all to see. Mercifully, his fear is short-lived. The close-range shotgun blast rips his chest wide open. He slumps backwards onto the tarmac and bleeds out within seconds.

His executioner turns back to face us and takes the key to the cage from Jarvis, who is visibly shaking.

The Irishman places the key into Gray's trembling hands and calmly tells her, "I think we probably understand each other now, Sarah. Just do as you're told and nobody else needs to get hurt."

Gray appears to be rooted to the spot and it's clear that she is in shock. When she doesn't respond, the Irishman once more raises his voice to assert control, "Now get that fucking cage open before I use the other barrel on the inspector. Come on, bloody move yourself, woman!"

With her hands shaking uncontrollably, Gray fumbles to get the key into the lock. Her tormentor moves closer to steady and guide her hand. Douglas is already on his feet and is pushing at the door, even as the key is still turning in the lock. With the cage open, he pushes past his rescuer and holds his wrists out impatiently towards Gray.

"Bloody get these off, right now!"

The cuffs fall to the floor and Douglas rubs his wrists, before bending over to pick up DI Gray's sidearm and radio.

"What now?" the Irishman asks him.

Douglas steps down from the wagon and orders PC Jarvis into the cage. He then turns his weapon towards me and Gray, "On your bloody feet. Get in there with Jarvis."

Sarah Gray enters the cage and takes a seat next to PC Jarvis. I try to follow, but the Irishman stops me. He gestures towards Clive Douglas, who is smiling and shaking his head. "Not you, Sean," he says. "Not after everything you've done for me. You're coming with us. You can join the lads outside."

I turn back towards Gray to protest my innocence. "Ma'am, you have to believe me, Douglas is setting me up. This is what he does. You have to believe m–"

She cuts me off mid-sentence with a disgusted, "And is this what you meant by closure, Sean?"

"Save it, McMillan. We've a ride to catch and it won't wait," says the Irishman, punctuating his words with a vicious prod in the back from the butt of his shotgun, which ends our conversation and sends me careering towards the end of the wagon.

Douglas watches over me, while the Irishman secures the cage and kicks the key out of reach, under one of the seats.

He then slams shut the rear door and snaps off the key in the lock to further hinder any rescue attempt. Turning to Douglas, he quips, "I hope they bring a locksmith with them … or a little chunk of Semtex."

Douglas rewards the quip with half a smile, but his mind is elsewhere. Behind the crash site, cars have started to backup, and a small group of onlookers are moving cautiously towards us to find out what has happened.

The sight of the armed men and the sound of two shots being fired into the air from the Glock Douglas is holding is enough to halt their progress.

Nervously looking to the sky, Douglas grumbles, "Where the hell is it? It should be here by now."

The big Irishman tells him not to worry. Then he turns to scan the horizon. There is no need, however, for him to search too hard. The sound of incoming rotor blades is now apparent for all to hear. Just thirty seconds later, a sleek black chopper breaks through the low-lying clouds and descends rapidly onto the middle of the roundabout.

The Irishman orders his men to get aboard. The two holding onto DI Thurgood release their grip on his arms and take a seat next to the third man. Without support, the almost lifeless Thurgood slumps face-first to the ground with a sickening crunch.

I rush to help but am stopped by a warning from Douglas.

"Don't you bloody move, McMillan. Our business is not finished."

Bizarrely, he then offers me DI Gray's sidearm. "Here, take it."

I'm confused by his intentions, and Douglas gestures again for me to take the weapon.

Before I can say anything, the Irishman impatiently asks Douglas what he is playing at. "Clive, for fuck's sake, we need to get going. Just get it over with and get yourself on board before one of these gawkers tries to play the bloody hero."

Douglas dismissively waves the Irishman away. "Go on, you get aboard. I just need a minute. Go on, do as I tell you."

Reluctantly, the Irishman turns towards the chopper, but not before muttering something about all Englishmen being mad.

Alone with Douglas, I tell him that I'm not going to play whatever game he is playing. "I'm done with you, Clive. Just get on with it, whatever it is."

Douglas shakes his head. "No, Sean. You and me, we're never going to be done. I see a long and prosperous future for us on the horizon. I would, of course, love to stay to discuss it further with you, but, as I'm sure you can appreciate, time is against me right now. So, take the fucking gun and shake my hand."

"What? Why the hell would I shake your hand and what makes you think I wouldn't shoot you with that gun?"

"Because, Sean, we're surrounded by witnesses and you're not a cold-blooded murderer. And well … well, I guess I am."

Douglas drops to one knee and lifts DI Thurgood's head. He presses the muzzle of the Glock to Thurgood's temple and says, "And quite frankly if you don't take this weapon and shake my hand, I'll execute this piece of shit without a second thought. It's your choice. What's it to be, McMillan?"

I now know exactly what his game is but, faced with a choice that is no choice at all, I reluctantly take the weapon and offer my free hand to Douglas who enthusiastically shakes it with a self-satisfied nod.

"I knew you would see sense. It's always such a pleasure working with you, Sean. I'm just sorry that you can't come with us."

Then, pointing to the chopper, he adds, "It's only a six-seater. I'm sure you'll be fine, though. Until we meet again, DS McMillan."

He runs for the chopper and I watch helplessly as it slowly ascends, then turns towards the west. When I can no longer see it, I turn and, for the first time, am able to take in the full extent of the carnage around me.

The hijacked buses have only slight damage to the front bumpers, but both escort vehicles are on their sides and look like they have been in a full-on fight with a high-speed freight train.

The damage to them is so catastrophic that it's a miracle Thurgood and Wilkins even survived the impact. Reminded that at least Thurgood is still alive, I call out for help to the onlookers, before calling the emergency services on my cell phone.

The crowd cautiously move forward but are only sufficiently reassured when I tuck the pistol inside my jacket pocket and show them my warrant card.

"I'm a police officer and I need your help until the emergency services arrive." I point to where Thurgood is lying. "This officer needs urgent attention. But don't move him; he may have spinal injuries. And there are two other police officers in the vehicle in front. I don't know how badly they are hurt, but someone needs to check on them."

I leave them to get organized and return to the back of the meat wagon to check on Gray and PC Jarvis. Gray is banging on the side of the vehicle and shouting to attract attention.

"Hello! Can anyone hear me? I'm a police officer. Hello, is anyone there?"

I hammer on the side wall and shout, "Ma'am, it's Sean. Douglas and his thugs are gone. Just sit tight, help is on its way."

There is a short pause before I hear her speak again, "Oh, thank God. What about Mike Thurgood and his men? Please tell me they're alive, Sean."

"They're being looked after. Just sit tight, help is on the way. Ma'am, this wasn't how it looked. Douglas wants you to think I helped him get away. He wants you to–"

Concerned with more important things, Gray cuts me off and says, "Sean, listen to me. That can wait for now. Just get me out of here. If you have a weapon, shoot the lock out if you have to."

I don't immediately respond, and she calls out again, "DS McMillan, did you hear what I said? Shoot the lock out. That's a direct order."

"I'm sorry, ma'am. I can't do that. There's something that I need to do first. It's not what it looks like, though. I'm sorry."

I'm already walking at a fast pace towards the road, but the anger in Gray's words is not lost on me.

"McMillan! Get back here now. Get me out, or I swear to God I'll make it my personal mission to see you go down for life. You're finished, Sean. I swear to God, you're finished. You hear me, you bastard?"

I hear her loud and clear, but there is only one way I know to sort this mess out. I cross to the southbound side of the road and pull open the door to a stationary Blue Ford Fiesta.

I show my badge, but the elderly woman in the driver's seat still looks petrified. She obligingly gets out and I take her place behind the wheel. Feeling guilty for taking her car, I lower the window before leaving. "I'm sorry about this, love. It's a police emergency. I'll make sure you get your car back in one piece."

She may have smiled at my reassurance, but I can't be completely sure. Before I've finished speaking, I gun the engine and the old woman quickly fades from sight in my rear-view mirror as I make for home.

Although my apartment is the obvious first place that my colleagues will come looking for me, I need to travel, which means I need to sleep. I can't do that safely in my own home of course. But if I'm going to lie low somewhere for a few days, I'm going to need a few things. I'm also banking on having enough of a head start before Sarah raises the alarm and the boys in blue come knocking. It's not like I have another choice anyway.

I push the engine as hard as it will go and just after midday, I park the Fiesta opposite my apartment building.

Confident that everything is as it should be, I tuck the keys behind the sun visor and head inside. The young woman at the reception desk is tapping away at her cell phone and barely looks up as I pass her and enter one of the elevators.

Although it's highly unlikely that anyone could have got here ahead of me, I pause for a few seconds and press my ear to the door to my apartment. Satisfied that no one is inside, I unlock the door and go to the bedroom to retrieve a black leather carryall that I normally use on short trips.

Present Day – Friday Afternoon, May 4th, 2018

Working as quickly as I can, I stuff a change of clothes and my washbag into the carryall, along with my passport. Next, I take a bundle of cash from my desk drawer that I keep for moments like this. Better to be prepared than not, I always say.

The last thing I need to be sure of traveling quickly is in my front room. I take a bottle of Jameson Whisky from my bar cart and carefully place it in the top of the carryall.

Zipping it up, I'm completely unaware that I have company until the muzzle of a police-issue Glock pistol is pushed against the back of my head.

"Let go of the bag. Put your hands on your head, and then turn around slowly. You know the drill, Sean."

I release my grip on the carryall and slowly straighten up. "Cath, this is not how it looks. You have to listen to me."

Catherine pushes her sidearm harder against the back of my head and barks, "Shut your lying mouth, you bastard. I knew you were an arsehole—but this? How could you?"

"Cath, I was set up. Douglas set me up."

"You're a bloody liar," Catherine hisses. "And because of you, two good police officers are dead, and two more are fighting for their lives. Now be a man for once. Put your hands on your head and turn around to face me. And don't think for a moment that I won't bloody shoot you. You're a cop killer. I would probably get a medal. Or another commendation at the very least. Now, turn around. I'm not going to ask you again."

The revelation from Catherine that another of the escort team has died is a massive shock. Fully aware of how she must be feeling, I slowly raise my hands and place them on my head before turning to face her.

Although her face is set with a look of steely determination, the redness around her eyes gives away the fact that she has been crying.

"Cath, I was set up. I was only on that escort because I wanted to see Clive Douglas safely returned to Yarwood. His escape was nothing to do with me. I swear to yo–"

"And exactly why were you on that escort?" Cath interrupts me. "No, don't answer that. I already know. It was because you begged Sarah Gray. What was it? Some bollocks about closure. You're a liar, Sean. And not just about this. You've been lying to me about everything. Have you ever told me the truth about anything?"

"I promise you, Cath. Whatever you think I have done or what I am, you are wrong. I just need some time to put things right. You need to let me go. Let me go and I can put this right."

Catherine shakes her head and laughs. "Do you seriously expect me to believe anything that comes out of your mouth after what's happened today? For God's sake, you left Sarah Gray trapped in the back of that van and good men dying by the side of the road. Gray told me exactly what you di–"

I cut her off to say, "Gray is wrong, Cath. Douglas took advantage of my being there. If I was working with Clive Douglas, why the hell didn't I go with him? Why would I come back here?"

Cath gestures towards the carryall. "I don't know. Your passport maybe, or something else important?"

I shake my head, but before I can say anything, Catherine screams, "You're a bastard and a liar. You were seen, Sean. You were seen shaking Clive Douglas' hand before he got into the helicopter. Stand there now and tell me that didn't happen, I dare you."

My handshake with Douglas was seen by at least half a dozen witnesses, so denying it happened is pointless. I slowly shake my head again, and say, "He was going to kill DI Thurgood. I had no choice, Cath. It wasn't how it appeared. I had no choice; he was going to–"

My babbling declaration of innocence is abruptly cut off by a shouted command from outside, "Armed police. Is anyone inside the apartment?"

Still keeping her sidearm trained at my head, Catherine shouts over her shoulder, "This is DC Catherine Swain, I'm armed and have the suspect in my custody."

The Armed Response team cautiously enter the apartment. With three of them covering us, the fourth officer reaches into Catherine's jacket to retrieve her warrant card. Satisfied that she is who she says she is, he hands it back and orders his men to handcuff me.

Catherine lowers her own weapon and steps forward to search me. She pats me all over and then reaches into my jacket pocket and takes out Sarah Gray's service pistol. With everything going on, I had forgotten that I still had it. Catherine holds it up with her fingertips and asks, "DI Gray's?"

I nod and she tells one of the officers to bag it as evidence. She then turns to me and says, "This is becoming a bit of a habit, isn't it? Detective Sergeant McMillan, I am arresting you on suspicion of aiding an escape from custody and of being an accessory to murder. You do not have to say anything, but it may harm your defense if you do not mention when questioned something which you later rely on in court. Anything you do say may be given in evidence. Do you understand?"

Without waiting for a response, Catherine shakes her head in disgust and leaves me in the custody of the Armed Response team.

■ ■ ■ ■ ■ ■ ■ ■

By 2.30 pm, I've been booked in, processed and placed in one of the holding cells at Blackwell Station to wait for my legal representation to arrive. Being processed by my fellow officers at my home station is as embarrassing and uncomfortable for them as it is for me.

I've been through this before, though, so the looks of surprise at my arrest are now all too familiar.

Nobody is more surprised at the news than my solicitor. Thirty minutes after my call, the cell door opens and Sergeant Morris escorts her in.

"You've got five minutes, Sean. Don't keep them waiting. You're in deep enough shit already, mate."

Morris locks the door and I stand up to shake my solicitor's hand. "Thanks for coming so quickly, Jean. How are you?"

The last time I saw Jean Monroe was at my commendation ceremony, after taking down The Network. I'm sure on that occasion it would never have crossed her mind that she would next see me under these circumstances.

The shake of her head and frown confirms it. "What on earth have you done now, Sergeant McMillan?"

Before I can speak, she cuts me off with a warning. "And no lies please. If you want me to help, I need to know everything."

She points to the table and tells me to sit down. Joining me, she places her notepad and pen on the table. "Okay, we don't have long. So, please be as concise as possible."

Over the next few minutes, I give Jean a potted history of everything that has happened since my first visit to Clive Douglas in Yarwood Prison.

When I finish, Jean puts down her pen, sits back in her chair, and shakes her head. "That is quite a story, Sean."

"I know. But what do you think—you do believe me, don't you?"

In response she lowers her head slightly and peers across the top of her wire-framed glasses like a headmistress poised to talk down to a naughty schoolboy. "I'm your solicitor, Sean. Whether I believe you or not is neither here nor there. It's my job to defend you ... but ..."

"But what?" I prod.

"But, as I said, that is quite a story. And if it is true, then Sergeant Morris is correct. Unless you have a guardian angel, then you are well and truly in it up to your neck." She then raises her eyebrows and asks, "Do you have a guardian angel, Sean?"

"No guardian angel," I reply. "But I do have something I think we can use in my defense."

Jean shoots me a look of suspicion and asks me to explain. When I finish, she puts down her pen again and closes her notepad.

"Believe it or not, Sean, but that's not actually as crazy as it first sounded. Unless they have firm evidence linking you to the escape or to Clive Douglas, I can push that angle to have you bailed pending further enquiries. That would give you a much better chance of clearing your name than if you were remanded in custody."

I nod my agreement just as Ted Morris returns with two other officers to escort us to the interview room.

We stand to leave, but before we do Jean offers some advice, "Don't say or do anything stupid please, Sean. This is going to be hard enough as it is."

I give her a half-grin and raise my eyebrows, which causes her to frown again and shake her head. "I knew I shouldn't have answered the phone today," she says drily. "And this was going to be such a nice weekend."

■ ■ ■ ■ ■ ■ ■ ■

Seeing Catherine and DI Gray in the room is no real surprise, but it's a shock to see DCI Kevin Morgan. He's not in uniform and the seventy-two hours of stubble on his face does little to mask the effects of his recent trauma. His left hand is wrapped in a clean white dressing, and the presence of the hospital bracelet, still visible under his shirt-cuff, suggests an unplanned and hurried discharge from the hospital.

Under the circumstances, his attendance at this interview shouldn't be a huge surprise to me. But Morgan is clearly unwell, which only serves to add to my sense of guilt over what has happened. I awkwardly nod to each of my colleagues to acknowledge their presence, but they remain impassive.

DI Gray gestures for us to sit down.

For a few moments, we stare awkwardly at each other waiting for the other party to make the first move. Gray's expression gives nothing away; Catherine's eyes make no attempt to hide her contempt; and Morgan looks to be thinking carefully about what he is going to say. When he finally reaches for his glass of water, it's a familiar sign that he is ready.

He takes a sip from the glass, carefully places it back down, and clears his throat. "Ms. Monroe, before we begin this interview formally, there is something I would like to say to your client off the record. Is that acceptable?"

The reactions from Catherine and DI Gray make it obvious that they were unaware he was going to say this and have no idea what he is intending to say. He chooses to ignore their questioning looks and asks again, "DS McMillan, Ms. Monroe, is that okay with you?"

With nothing to lose, I nod and tell Jean that it's okay. She also nods her approval. Morgan half smiles and thanks us both, before firmly focusing his attention on me. He clears his throat for a second time, then begins.

"Things are not looking great for you, DS McMillan. We have multiple eyewitnesses to say that you shook hands with Clive Douglas before he made good his escape, and it is beyond doubt that you fled from a major crime scene leaving two police officers imprisoned, two dead, and two more seriously injured. This alone would be enou–"

I unwisely cut the boss off mid-sentence, "Sir, if you can let me explain. I can–"

My interruption is instantly silenced by a raised hand and a look of disapproval from DCI Morgan. "You'll get your chance, DS McMillan. But I strongly suggest for now that you keep quiet and listen very carefully to what I am saying."

Although it was not framed as a question, I nod my agreement anyway and Morgan continues, "As I was saying, in my opinion these two facts alone would be more than ample circumstantial evidence to gain Crown Prosecution Service approval to formally charge and remand you in custody, pending a full investigation and trial."

Morgan halts for a moment to let his last statement sink in. Then he takes a deep breath and continues, "I am, however, fully aware when it comes to you, Sergeant McMillan, that nothing is ever quite what it first seems. And more to the point, everyone in this room knows exactly what Clive Douglas is like and what he is capable of." Probably unconsciously, Morgan pulls his injured left hand towards his body as he says these words.

He quietly continues, "I'm also patently aware that but for your quick thinking I may well not have been here to tell you this. For these reasons and for these reasons alone, I'm going to cut you some slack today."

DI Gray starts to object but is stopped by a sideways glance from the boss. Unsure if he has finished or not, I look to Jean for guidance. In turn she looks to Morgan and asks, "Chief Inspector, I'm not quite sure where this is leading. Would you mind explaining what you mean when you say that you will cut my client some slack?"

The question is returned with a serious nod. Morgan explains, "Ms. Monroe, the nature of the allegations being faced by DS McMillan mean that ordinarily you and your client should now be sitting opposite a team from the Serious Crimes Squad instead of me and my team. The reason you are not is because I personally have gone out on a limb and cashed in more than a few overdue favors from my superiors to keep the investigation in-house.

"As a member of my team and as someone I consider to be a friend, I'm prepared to give Sergeant McMillan the benefit of the doubt at this time and accept until proven otherwise that he is innocent of any involvement in the murder of two police officers and the escape of Clive Douglas ... Does that answer your question?"

Jean confirms it does and Morgan turns his attention back to me. "I don't think I need to explain further what I've had to do to keep the Serious Crimes Squad at bay, but suffice to say, I've put myself on the line for you, DS McMillan. I sincerely hope my trust in you is not misplaced."

Massively relieved at this turn of events, I shake my head. "No, sir. It's not misplaced and I'm sincerely grateful for your support. I'm sure that once you've listened to my explanation, you'll be more than satisfied that I was not involved in any of this."

My comment elicits a scowl from Catherine that is plain for all to see, but DI Gray's expression continues to give nothing away. Morgan himself maintains direct eye contact with me for a few seconds before he slowly nods and says, "I really hope so, Sean. But I'm giving you fair warning. If I think you are lying to me, or I hear anything conclusive to link you to these murders or the escape, I won't hesitate to hand this case over to Serious Crimes.

"What's more, I will personally wash my hands of you and hang you out to dry. Do I make myself clear, DS McMillan?"

"Yes, sir. That's very clear."

"Good, and is there anything you would like to say before we start the interview?"

Unsure of whether it's appropriate, I nervously look at each of the faces opposite, before asking, "Sir, when I left … well, I mean, when I left the scene of the incident, PC Wilkins was dead, and Inspector Thurgood was badly injured. You said, though, that two officers were dead. May I ask who the second officer was and the condition of the other two officers?"

Before DCI Morgan can say anything, DI Gray leans forward and almost spits out a response, "You would know the answer to that question if you'd had an ounce of common decency in your body and stuck around to find out, DS McMillan. You left Bob Wilkins dead at the scene and Sergeant Alan Brady died on the way to hospital. The other two are both in …"

Gray's voice starts to falter and conscious that emotions are running high, DCI Morgan stops her and takes over.

"Alan Brady suffered catastrophic injuries in the collision. By the time the paramedics got to him, there was nothing they could do to save him."

Although this had nothing to do with me, the thought that I could have got help to him quicker still knocks me for six. After taking a moment to gather my thoughts, I ask, "And DI Thurgood and the fourth officer? I'm sorry, I don't recall his name, sir."

"PC Len Morris," DI Gray interjects. Her expression is no longer impassive. "He's in an intensive care unit. Fortunately for you, his condition has stabilized, and he is expected to pull through. DI Thurgood, however, is a completely different story. He's in …"

"He is in intensive care and in a very bad way," Morgan finishes for her. "He's currently in a medically induced coma, due to a massive bleed on the brain."

"But he'll be okay?" I nervously ask.

Morgan shakes his head. "It's too early to say at the moment. But it's not looking good." Morgan looks like he is about to say more, but he stops when DI Gray touches his hand.

Clearly impatient to turn the thumbscrews, she suggests to him that we should start the interview. Morgan checks the time on his watch and nods, "Yes, you're right, Sarah. Let's get on with this. DC Swain, start the recording please."

■ ■ ■ ■ ■ ■ ■ ■

Catherine cues the tape and after waiting for the indicator tone, DCI Morgan formally begins the interview.

"This interview is being recorded. For the benefit of the tape, the time now is 3.32 pm and the date is Friday, 4th May 2018. Present in the room are Detective Chief Inspector Kevin Morgan, Detective Inspector Sarah Gray, Detective Constable Catherine Swain, Detective Sergeant Sean McMillan, and DS McMillan's legal counsel Ms. Jean Monroe. DS McMillan, you are currently under arrest and being held on suspicion of aiding an escape from custody and of being an accessory to murder.

"The purpose therefore of this interview is to question you about these allegations and to establish if there is a case to answer that I can present to the Crown Prosecution Service. Do you understand?"

This is a more-than-familiar routine for me. I nod acknowledgment and for the benefit of the tape say, "Yes, sir. I understand."

"That's good," Morgan replies. "In that case, I'd like to start by asking you straight out if you had any involvement or prior knowledge of the plan to free Clive Douglas."

I shake my head and vehemently deny any involvement, "Absolutely not, sir. You know how much I despise that man. And you know what he put me through previously. It was mostly my work that put him away in the first place. Why on earth would I want to help him?"

"So, you deny any prior knowledge of the plan or any involvement in his escape?" DI Gray asks.

"That's right, ma'am. I know what Douglas said in the back of that escort vehicle, but it was all just opportunistic bullshit. He saw me there and simply took the opportunity to try to drop me in it."

"I think it worked," Gray responds with a sneer. "Remind me, what was it he said, DS McMillan?"

I shake my head. "I'm sorry, I don't remember exactly. I think it was something about thanking me for my help."

Gray leafs through her pocketbook and then says, "Let me refresh your memory. Oh yes, here it is. Douglas asked me where we were. I told him we were approaching the M1 and he responded by saying, That's very good. I should thank you now, Sean. Just in case I don't get the chance later. Do you recall that, DS McMillan?"

"Yes, ma'am, I do. I also recall asking him what the hell he was talking about."

Morgan looks to Gray and checks, "Is that correct?"

"Yes, sir. DS McMillan did ask that question. To which, Clive Douglas replied by telling DS McMillan not to be so modest. He then said, he could not have got this far without him and that they were a good team. I then asked again what he meant, and he restated that DS McMillan had been, a big help to him and that it was only a matter of time now."

"Which is exactly the kind of bullshit mind games he plays," I protest. "Sir, if I was in league with Clive Douglas, why on earth would he want to give up that fact to DI Gray? And why didn't I leave with him? None of it makes any sense. You have to believe that I did not help Clive Douglas escape and I'm not a murderer or an accessory to murder."

Morgan considers my statement for a moment, then says, "It does all seem rather unlikely, but this wouldn't be the first time that Clive Douglas has turned on one of his partners. I refer specifically to the fate of Paul Donovan."

Whether or not it's a deliberate attempt to test my reaction or not, his reference to the murder of Paul Donovan as a comparison to my own situation is enough for me to lose my composure.

"For crying out loud, sir, please don't compare me to that piece of shit. Donovan was at Clive's beck and call for years before he became a liability to him. I wouldn't piss on Clive Douglas if he was on fire. Surely after everything he put me through you must know that?"

Instead of answering my question, Morgan looks over to Gray's pocketbook and asks, "Why were you on that escort today, Sergeant McMillan? You weren't expected on duty and in fact you were offered a period of leave, which you turned down. DC Swain was also offered some leave. She took it happily. So, why then were you so reluctant to accept it, and why was it so important for you to be on that escort?"

Briefing Jean earlier, I hadn't thought to mention the offer of leave and my reason for being on the escort. She frowns and makes a note in her legal pad before nodding for me to answer the question.

"Actually, sir, I did accept the leave offered by DI Gray. I felt personally responsible, though, for what happened to you. So, before taking any leave, I wanted to see Clive Douglas being returned to Yarwood."

Pointing to her pocketbook, Gray says, "You said you wanted closure, DS McMillan." Her tone is sarcastic as she asks, "Did you get the closure you were looking for?"

Whilst we all know that I didn't, an answer is expected anyway. Up to now, Catherine has not said a word, but her eyes and facial expressions say exactly what she is thinking. When I answer, I address the entire room, but my eye contact is with her.

"No, ma'am. Far from it. And if there was anything I could have done to stop what happened, then, believe me, I would have done it."

Morgan makes some notes, which he shows to DI Gray. She nods and then asks, "If you're not working with Clive Douglas, why did he take you outside with him when he locked PC Jarvis and me in the cage? Why not leave you with us, if he had no intention of taking you with him?"

I know how it looks and if I was on the other side of the table, I would be asking the same questions. I shake my head again and say, "It was to add credibility to his bullshit, ma'am. If you had seen or heard what happened outside you would know that already and we wouldn't be wasting our time having this conversation instead of focusing our efforts on finding Douglas."

DCI Morgan nods and then says, "That brings us to the next question, Sergeant McMillan. We have half a dozen eyewitness statements that say that, just prior to the helicopter leaving, you were handed a sidearm by Clive Douglas and then you were seen to shake hands like old friends. Is that what happened?"

"It's not how it looked, sir."

"I didn't ask how it looked; I asked if that's what happened. Did Clive Douglas give you the service weapon taken earlier from DI Gray and did you shake hands with him?"

With the weight of statements confirming what I did, it is pointless to lie. I confirm that it did happen and try to offer an explanation.

"I was under duress, sir. Douglas was going to execute DI Thurgood if I didn't play along. Just prior to my shaking his hand, he dropped to his knees and had the gun to Thurgood's head."

"Perhaps this could be confirmed by some of your witnesses?" Ms. Monroe suggests to DCI Morgan. "If any of them were close enough to see this, it would go a long way to corroborating my client's version of events."

Morgan confers quietly with DI Gray, then says, "Thank you. Ms. Monroe, we'll arrange to speak with the witnesses again. I'm inclined to agree, though, that if it is true it would cast a different light on things. It wouldn't, however, explain why your client fled the scene of the incident leaving two colleagues trapped and, to his knowledge at the time, three colleagues seriously injured. Correct me if I am wrong, but that is not the normal response of an innocent man, Ms. Monroe."

Morgan than looks to me for an answer, but Jean steps in. "I've advised my client that for now he shouldn't make any comment around why he chose to leave the scene of the incident. We will, however, be prepared to make a comment as and when we feel it's appropriate to do so."

Morgan looks at me again. "Is that right, DS McMillan?"

"Yes, sir. I'm following the advice of my legal counsel."

"But you don't deny that you did in fact leave the scene of the incident knowing full well that two of your colleagues were trapped in the back of that vehicle and that three police officers were in desperate need of medical attention?"

"I'm sorry, sir. I can't comment on that at this time."

Any sympathy that Morgan may have had for me earlier is rapidly dissipating and he is now struggling to retain his composure. "For God's sake, Sean, I'm trying to help you. What kind of police officer runs out on his colleagues, refuses to answer questions, and then expects us to believe in his innocence? Did you or did you no–"

Jean Monroe straightens up in her chair and says firmly, "Chief Inspector, we have made it clear that we will not be providing any comment on this point at this time. I suggest you move along to your next question please."

Morgan and Monroe are old friends and long-time professional acquaintances, but when they are on opposing sides of the legal table, Kevin Morgan knows well enough that Jean will always place the interests of her clients first and that he should not take it personally. He makes a note to return to the question, then asks me what else Douglas said to me before leaving. "Did he give any indication where he might be heading? Did he say anything at all that might give us any lead to where we might find him?"

I shake my head. "He didn't say anything about where they were going, but if I was a betting man, I would say either Northern Ireland or more likely somewhere south of the border in the Republic."

"What makes you think that?" DI Gray asks.

"Two reasons, ma'am. The helicopter took off and headed west. Assuming they continued west, they could have been across the Irish Sea and outside of our jurisdiction within a couple of hours. It would be easy then to arrange onward passage for Douglas and his crew from there."

Morgan stops making notes and prompts, "You said two reasons. What's the second?"

DI Gray looks up from her own notes and asks, "The Irishman?"

"Yes, ma'am. I don't have a vast amount of experience or knowledge when it comes to the IRA, but this guy was a professional and there are very few other mobs that have the know-how or the ability to pull something like this off with such little notice."

"Meaning?" Morgan asks.

"Meaning, sir, that Clive Douglas was recaptured by us and sprung again within twenty-four hours. That's not the work of a hastily put together mob of amateurs. Have you checked the airspace records for this morning? We know where the chopper took off from and we know which direction it was heading. It should be easy eno–"

"Thank you, Sergeant McMillan," Morgan interrupts. "I have an officer already looking into that and there is already a working theory that Clive Douglas has had previous dealings with the IRA."

"So somewhere in Ireland is likely," I point out.

"Yes, that's a possibility, Sean," Morgan concedes in a more sympathetic tone, before switching back to a direct and more accusatory tone. "But after that we have no idea. So why don't you tell us where you were meant to meet him?"

"Sir, I was not involved in his escape, and I have no idea where he was planning to go. I can't say any more than I've said already about where he could be."

I'm taken by surprise when Catherine speaks for the first time. "You took the trouble to pick up your passport and cash. Why was that if you weren't planning on going somewhere?"

I look at Cath and shake my head before turning back to DCI Morgan, "Sir, I can't expl–"

"Actually, it's a valid question and I think we deserve to hear your explanation, DS McMillan. Why the urgent need to retrieve your passport if you weren't planning on going anywhere?"

Jean Monroe touches my arm and says quietly, "You don't need to answer that question, Sean." Turning to Morgan, she continues, "Chief Inspector, we've already made our views clear when it comes to events around my client leaving the scene of the incident. The same stance also applies to this aspect of his departure. We will comment on this as and when we deem–"

Morgan shakes his head in frustration. "Yes, yes, yes, as and when you deem appropriate. Tell me, Ms. Monroe, do you have any objection to my moving on to another line of questioning?"

"Is it relevant to the charges being leveled against my client, Chief Inspector?"

"I believe so," Morgan replies.

Jean looks to me for approval, but I'm as interested as she is to know what other line of questioning he might have, so of course I agree.

Turning back to face Morgan, Jean politely smiles and says, "Please, by all means, carry on, Chief Inspector."

DI Gray hands Morgan a sheet of paper that I know from experience will contain a list of prepared questions. He reads the list in silence and then places the sheet face-down on the table, before handing me the first page of a handwritten witness statement.

"Take a look at this please, DS McMillan. For the benefit of the tape, I have handed Sergeant McMillan an extract of a sworn statement given today by Detective Constable Catherine Swain.

"I would like to draw Sergeant McMillan's attention to the area highlighted in yellow. Do you see that part, Sergeant McMillan?"

Although I'm concentrating on reading the statement, I can feel Catherine's eyes burning into the side of my head. I read the entire page twice before looking back up and handing the statement to Jean and replying to Morgan, "Yes, sir, I can."

Morgan gives a satisfied nod. "Perhaps you would be good enough to read the highlighted part for me, DS McMillan."

With no objection forthcoming from Jean, I start to read aloud: "Part way through the drive to Kings Cross Station, Clive Douglas and Detective Sergeant McMillan were engaged in a conversation that I found to be very odd. Douglas suggested to DS McMillan that they would have made a great team. When DS McMillan objected to this, Douglas responded by saying words to the effect that – You might not admit it, but you're more like me than you realize. That head of yours is full of secrets, isn't it? Does your partner really know who you are? I, of course, asked DS McMillan what Douglas was talking about, to which DS McMillan replied – Nothing, Cath. He's talking out of his backside, as always. Shortly afterwards we arrived at Kings Cross Station, so nothing further was said on the subject."

I push the statement back across the table, but all I can think is, wow, Cath must really hate my guts to be prepared to give a statement against me. I'm also sure that I can guess what else might be coming later.

Morgan carefully places the statement back into its folder and then asks, "What were these secrets he was referring to, DS McMillan?"

I shake my head. "Sir, there are no secrets. It was nothing more than Clive Douglas trying to drive a wedge between me and Cath … I mean, DC Swain. This is classic Douglas through and through."

Jean leans forward. "If I may, Chief Inspector, I would like to ask Detective Constable Swain a question about her statement?"

Morgan nods his consent. "Of course. Go ahead, Ms. Monroe."

Catherine looks defiant; but, whilst I know her statement is accurate, I also know that deep down she will be worried about what she is going to be asked. Jean makes a show of checking through her notes and then gives Catherine a reassuring smile.

"DC Swain, you say in your notes that Clive Douglas said to my client – we would have made a good team. Or words to that effect. Is that correct?"

"It is," Catherine confidently replies.

Jean raises her hands and looks to both DCI Morgan and DI Gray before turning back to Catherine. "If that is indeed what was said, then I'm confused, DC Swain. My client is accused, amongst other things, of aiding and abetting in the escape of Clive Douglas and indeed of being part of his wider criminal organization. Surely saying – we would have made a great team would suggest that they weren't in fact working together. Quite the opposite, in fact. Wouldn't you agree, DC Swain?"

Jean has made an irrefutable point and Cath looks noticeably flustered as she tries to answer the question. To save her from further embarrassment, Morgan steps in. "Okay, you've made your point, which is duly noted, Ms. Monroe. DC Swain's comment will be removed from the record. Let's move on please."

I'm happy, of course, to have notched up this minor victory, but I'm feeling for Catherine. At some stage, I need to get her back on side and publicly embarrassing her like this is tantamount to hammering another nail in my coffin.

In a lame effort not to antagonize her any further, I deliberately focus my attention on DCI Morgan and DI Gray, who are quietly discussing their next move. With agreement reached, Morgan sits up straight in his chair and says, "DS McMillan, you've told us that you have no personal relationship with Clive Douglas and that you were not involved in his escape. Is that true?"

Ms. Monroe is quick to answer on my behalf. "DCI Morgan, my client has already answered that question and I think he has made it quite clear that he had no involvement or prior knowledge of any plan for Clive Douglas to escape.

"Equally, we've just heard a statement from DC Swain that would also suggest that my client and Clive Douglas were not working together. Unless you have some new information to indicate otherwise, I suggest that you move on with other matters. If you have any, that is."

In typical Kevin Morgan fashion, he ignores Jean's protest and keeps his eyes firmly focused on me.

"Okay, let's forget about Clive Douglas for the moment. What about Rosemary Pinois and Patrick Newman? Had you met either of them or had any personal relationship with them prior to your first trip to see Clive Douglas in Yarwood Prison with DC Swain?"

"Sir, I'd never even heard of them until we started investigating that case. It was Douglas that told us about Newman and Michael Davies. And my first contact with Rosemary Pinois was a few days later in the presence of DC Swain. Until then I'd never met the woman."

Morgan frowns and checks something on the paper in front of him before placing it back down.

"After we caught up with Rosemary Pinois in Ashdown Forest yesterday, she said something that makes me doubt that you only met her and Newman recently. Do you remember what she said?"

I remember almost word for word what Rosemary said in Ashdown Forest, because at the time it had sent a chill down my spine. I'd rather not admit to that, of course, so I shake my head and play dumb.

"I don't clearly recall, sir. There was a lot going on and, if you remember, Rosemary still had a gun in her hand."

In response, Morgan frowns and says sharply, "Of course I remember—that gun was pointing at me shortly afterwards. Let me remind you about what she said just before that."

He refers to his pocketbook, but there really is no need. He knows exactly what it says in his notes. Without referring to them again he recites word for word what was said in Ashdown Forest.

"For the benefit of the tape, when Rosemary Pinois approached us, she said and I quote: When you came to my home the first time, you reminded me of someone from my past. And not just me either. Paddy also thought he recognized you. The name was the same, but it's not possible. She then said: Perhaps your fath–, but she stopped herself. I think it is fair enough to assume that she was going to say 'father.' What do you think, DS McMillan? Is that a fair enough assumption?"

I look to Jean and then say, "Yes, sir. I think that would be fair."

"So, did your father know Rosemary or Patrick Newman?"

"No, sir. My father had no criminal connections whatsoever. He was a geography teach–"

DI Gray cuts me off to say, "Yes, we know. He was a primary school geography teacher. Were you named after him?"

"Ma'am?"

"Your name, DS McMillan. Rosemary said that the name was the same. Was your father also called Sean?"

It's clear that they have already checked my family details and my reply gives away my obvious annoyance. "You already know the answer to that, ma'am. His name was David. And in case you don't know, my mother's name is Janice, and our first family pet was a West Highland Terrier called Basil. Did I miss anything?"

Out of the corner of my eye, I can see that Jean Monroe is trying to stifle a smile. Morgan fails to see the humor.

"I suggest, Sergeant McMillan that you take this a little more seriously and save the wisecracks for another time. If you were to put yourselves in our shoes for a moment you would realize that this is a perfectly reasonable line of questioning, given what Rosemary said to you."

He's right, of course, and I now feel like a prize tool for responding like that when I know he is trying to help me. I apologize and Morgan nods before continuing.

"One final question on this subject before we move on. You possibly recall that I asked Rosemary what she meant?"

I nod. "Yes, sir. I do remember that."

"Good. I actually told her that she wasn't making any sense, and she replied: You're right. It doesn't make sense. It was a lifetime ago and it's nothing more than a coincidence. Only I don't think she was mistaken; and I don't think it was a coincidence. I think she stopped herself from saying more because you had met before and she was worried about blowing your cover. You had met Rosemary Pinois and Patrick Newman before. Isn't that right, DS McMillan?"

"No, sir. You're wrong. I'd never met or heard of either of them until the start of the case."

Morgan shakes his head. "No, I'm not buying it, Sergeant McMillan. You knew both of those characters from a good while back and by default that also means that you were in bed with

Clive Douglas. Christ, man, you've been bloody playing us from the first day you were assigned to this team."

I know this is a well-used tactic but being on this side of the table is no fun. Morgan knows that by pushing the right buttons, I will lose my cool again and I'm getting close.

"No, sir. I didn't know Pinois or Newman prior to this case and the first time I met Clive Douglas was shortly after your morning briefing a few months ago. My loyalty is to you and this department, sir."

Morgan mulls over my comment for a few moments and then adds his own. "If your loyalty really is to this department, then you have a strange way of showing it, Sergeant McMillan."

To calm things down, Jean asks, "Has Rosemary Pinois been interviewed since her arrest yesterday and has she provided any information to confirm that she knew my client prior to just a few days ago?"

DI Gray confirms that Rosemary was interviewed earlier today by officers from the Serious Crimes Squad. She then adds, "She wasn't specifically asked, though, about her relationship with DS McMillan."

Jean makes a brief note in her pad and comments, "So, DI Gray, Rosemary hasn't confirmed any link between her and my client other than his dealings with her in the execution of his duty?"

When DI Gray responds, it's clear from her tone that she is annoyed that Jean has them wrong-footed again.

"That is correct, Ms. Monroe. We will, though, be requesting to interview Rosemary ourselves and you can be sure we will be more direct in our questioning of any connection with your client."

"I would expect nothing less," Jean replies. "For now, though, all you have from Rosemary Pinois is a few words spoken in the middle of a highly stressful situation, which in your own words DCI Morgan made no sense.

57

"In fact, Chief Inspector, up to now you haven't presented anything that would justify charging my client or keeping him in custody a moment longer. In the interests of all, I would like to request his immediate release."

Kevin Morgan has been listening politely to Jean. When he's satisfied that she has finished, he smiles and carefully raises his left hand off the table. "That was a fine speech, Jean." Then, gesturing to his bandaged hand, adds, "You'll excuse me if I don't clap. You might well be right about Rosemary, but we are far from done with your client. If you will allow me to continue, there are still one or two items that I would like to ask DS McMillan about."

It's a rhetorical question of course. Morgan doesn't need permission from anyone to continue the interview. Without waiting for a response, he asks me, "Prior to yesterday, when was the last time you were in Ashdown Forest?"

If my instincts are right, I'm about to be shown the second part of Catherine's statement. But to admit to being in Ashdown Forest before will take me down a path that I would rather not go down.

Deliberately avoiding direct eye contact with Catherine, I take a deep breath and answer, "Until yesterday, I had never been to Ashdown Forest, sir."

My blatant lie is too much for Cath to stomach. Unable to stay quiet any longer, she shakes her head in disgust. "You're a bloody liar, Sean. How can you sit there and lie to us when you know damn well that we can prove you were there before? I used to have so much respect for you, but you're nothing but a liar and a coward. You disgust–"

The tirade of abuse is halted by Morgan asking Catherine to temper her language. "I appreciate that emotions are running high, DC Swain, but let's remember we are police officers please."

Catherine looks towards me and shakes her head again before apologizing to Morgan, "I'm sorry, sir. It won't happen again,"

He allows a moment for her to compose herself, then he continues with the interview.

"Although not presented exactly as I would have liked, I am inclined to agree with Detective Constable Swain. I think you are lying to us. I believe that you had been to Ashdown Forest before yesterday. And, more precisely, I believe that you'd also previously been to the part of Ashdown Forest where the missing gold and the bodies were recovered. Tell me I'm wrong, DS McMillan."

I shake my head and lie again. "You're wrong, sir. Yesterday was the first time that I'd ever set foot in Ashdown Forest. And don't forget the reason why I was there."

"I'm well aware of why you were there," Morgan replies. "And I've already mentioned how appreciative I am of that. But the fact remains that by lying or refusing to answer questions, you are making it very difficult for us to help you. You had been to Ashdown Forest before. You know it. We know it."

"No, sir. Yesterday was the first time. Until then I ha–"

"Then how did you know it was George Benson and Peter Lane buried in that hole?" Morgan interrupts me. "When you arrested Rosemary Pinois you only mentioned Benson and Lane. Why not the other missing guard, Stuart Goldsmith?"

"I uhm … I told you yesterday, sir. It was a mistake in the heat of the moment."

DI Gray interjects, "But it wasn't a mistake, was it, Sergeant McMillan? I told you this morning that the bodies of George Benson and Peter Lane were recovered from that hole and positively identified last night."

"You were also extremely confident yesterday that we would find them in that hole," DCI Morgan adds. "Why so sure, DS McMillan?"

"I wasn't sure," I reply. "It was just a hunch."

"Hunch or not, you were right about who and where we would find them," Morgan persists. "So, picking up on DI Gray's point, arresting Rosemary for the murders of just Benson and Lane wasn't a mistake, was it? You knew we would only find two bodies in that hole. You knew because this wasn't the first time you'd been to Ashdown Forest and it wasn't the first time you'd been near that hole."

Jean Monroe stops making notes and puts down her pen rather sharply. "Chief Inspector Morgan, do you actually have any real evidence to connect my client to the offences he was arrested for? Because all I have heard or seen up to now is entirely circumstantial and without substance. Nothing that has been discussed or presented today would be enough to convince the CPS to pursue a case against my client."

In response to Jean's question, Morgan smiles and reaches under the table for what I know already will be his ace in the hole. He places the transparent evidence bag down in front of me and says, "For the benefit of the tape, I am showing DS McMillan a sealed evidence bag marked with the reference FP4. Contained within the bag is a rather shabby black leather wallet containing a Metropolitan Police Warrant Card. Detective Sergeant McMillan, can you confirm that this is your warrant card and that it was taken from you during the booking-in process earlier today?"

The wallet has been placed in the bag with my warrant card and ID picture visible for all too see. Although the picture is badly faded there is no denying it is me. I confirm that the wallet is mine, then I push the bag back across the table.

Morgan holds up the bag and points to the wallet. "Would you explain to us how it got in this condition." Then he adds, "It almost looks like it was buried and recently dug up, DC McMillan."

This of course is something else that I failed to mention to Jean Monroe. We quietly confer for a moment before Jean says, "My client won't be making any comment on this point, DCI Morgan."

Morgan turns to me. "DS McMillan?"

"I'm sorry, sir. But no comment."

"Very well. Have it your way," Morgan responds. He then reopens the folder containing Catherine's witness statement and hands me the second page. "Feel free to read it. I suspect, though, that you already know what it says."

As feared, the second part of Catherine's statement describes how she found my warrant card when she was face-down in the hole in Ashdown Forest. She finishes her statement by describing her confrontation with me outside my apartment. I finish reading and hand the paper to Jean. She reads it carefully, then hands it back to DCI Morgan.

Morgan pauses for a few moments to gauge my reaction. When he gets none he refers to his notes and asks his next question, "Do you dispute DC Swain's assertion that she found your wallet in the very hole containing the bodies of George Benson and Peter Lane and that she later challenged you as to how and when it got there?"

Following Jean's earlier advice, I decline to comment.

"Okay, but you do agree that DC Swain's statement is accurate?" Gray asks.

"I'm sorry, ma'am. No comment."

"Being sorry is no good," Morgan snaps. "Being sorry isn't getting us anywhere. Is it, Sean? You've been lying to us from the moment we started this interview and the only reason you

61

don't want to comment is you know that we have you banged to rights. I wasn't joking earlier when I said your wallet and warrant card look like they had just been dug up. The reason I said it is because that is precisely what happened. Your wallet and warrant card ended up in that hole well before yesterday. I don't know how, and I don't know when, but I do know beyond doubt that you are lying about not being in Ashdown Forest prior to yesterday."

I try to protest but am quickly shut down by DCI Morgan. "I'm not finished, DS McMillan. DC Swain's discovery of your warrant card proves that you are lying about your earlier presence in Ashdown Forest, which in turn leads me to believe that you did know Pinois and Newman. It's reasonable then for me to surmise that you do have some connection to Clive Douglas, even if only by association."

"You're desperately fishing," Jean says. "And you know it, Chief Inspector. Nothing you've presented today is enough to hold my client. The presence or not of my client's credentials in that hole is not nearly enough to satisfy the CPS. Do you have anything else?"

Morgan is annoyed at the interruption, but he remains calm. "I disagree, Ms. Monroe. Your client has offered no explanation as to why his wallet was found at the scene of a double murder and I'm confident that this will be enough for the CPS to approve holding DS McMillan in custody pending further investigation by the Serious Crimes Squad. Now, unless you or your client have anything else to add, I think we are done here."

The odds of the CPS approving anything on the basis of today's interview are slim, but even if they do rule in my favor, it's not unusual for it to take up to two weeks to reach a decision, during which time I will remain in custody.

Desperate to stay out of prison, I whisper in Jean's ear that now is the time to play our hand. She politely smiles and says,

"Actually, Chief Inspector, I would like to address the matter of why my client left the crime scene and why he failed to assist his fellow officers."

This revelation leaves Morgan and Gray both looking surprised. Morgan checks his watch and then says, "Please. Go on, Ms. Monroe. I think we would all love to hear what you have to say on this subject."

"Thank you, Chief Inspector. Before I address that matter though, I would like to ask about the other police officer involved in this incident. The driver of the escort vehicle—PC Jarvis, wasn't it?"

"That's correct," Morgan replies. "What's your question?"

"I'd like to know if PC Jarvis was arrested and interviewed today,' Jean replies.

Morgan shakes his head. "No, he wasn't. There was no reason to arrest him."

"Really?" Jean asks with a puzzled expression. "My client informs me that PC Jarvis as much as admitted at the scene to having prior knowledge of the escape plan and that he took an active part in the escape itself. It was PC Jarvis who unlocked the back of the escort vehicle, wasn't it?"

"He was under duress," Gray replies.

"And so was my client," Jean says. "What kind of duress was PC Jarvis under that was so different from that of DS McMillan?"

"His wife and young child were being held in their home until after the job was completed," Morgan offers. "PC Jarvis was told they would be killed if he didn't help."

Jean shakes her head and frowns sympathetically. "That must have been a horrible experience for them. And under those circumstances it's perhaps understandable why PC Jarvis did what he did. I would ask you, though, to extend the same courtesy to my client who partly acted the way he did as a result of the extreme duress he was under."

"Partly?" DCI Morgan queries.

"Yes, Chief Inspector. DS McMillan was acting under duress during the escape. But I believe the primary reason for him leaving the crime scene was down to post-traumatic stress disorder. Given the–"

Gray interrupts to say, "PTSD? You have got to be kidding me."

"I'm not kidding at all, DI Gray. Didn't you yourself suggest to my client this morning that he might be suffering from PTSD and that he might want to speak to one of the Force counsellors if he was feeling anxious about anything."

Stumped for once, DI Gray stutters over her response. "Well, yes, but ... I mean, the offer of counselling is standard for all cases involving any level of trauma."

"You mean like being shot and assaulted numerous times in the last few months, DI Gray?

Well and truly on the offensive, Jean continues without allowing Sarah Gray the opportunity to respond, "Chief Inspector Morgan, if you continue with this charade and return my client to custody, I will not only be forced to register a complaint with the Police Ombudsman, I will also go public with how a recently decorated police officer was failed by his senior officers in their duty of care to him.

"Three months ago, DS McMillan was wrongly imprisoned and was subsequently shot by accomplices of the very man you are accusing him of now working with. Since then, he has been threatened and assaulted on numerous occasions and just a few short hours ago he was forced to witness the cold-blooded execution of a fellow officer.

I put it to you, DI Gray, that, as his senior officer, it was your responsibility to do more than merely suggest that DS McMillan see a counselor. You should have insisted on it."

Gray is now completely lost for words. She opens her mouth to speak, but then stops and closes it again. Morgan also knows well that any negative mention of my name in the press will stir up a shit storm that he can well do without.

He considers in silence what Jean has just said, before simply saying, "Anything else, Ms. Monroe?"

"No, Chief Inspector, I'm finished. For now."

Morgan shakes his head and gathers together his papers. "For the benefit of the tape, I am now pausing this interview for a short recess to confer with my colleagues. The time is 3.47 pm and DCI Morgan, DI Gray, and DC Swain are leaving the room."

Then, clearly annoyed at the latest turn of events, he barks at Catherine, "Turn the tape off please, DC Swain."

■ ■ ■ ■ ■ ■ ■

I wait for the door to fully close behind them before allowing myself a smile. "Jean, that was amazing. What do you think? They have to let me go, yes?"

"I think, Sean, that you could have helped yourself by availing me of all the facts when we spoke earlier. I assume that Catherine was telling the truth about your wallet?"

I confirm that she was, and Jean asks if I'm going to tell her how and when it ended up in the hole.

"I'd really love to," I reply. "But it's complicated."

Jean raises her eyebrows. "It always is with you, Sean, but it's probably best that you save that story for another time.

"From what I've heard today, though, I don't believe for a second that you are working with Clive Douglas or Rosemary Pinois."

I laugh. "Good. I'm glad to hear that. I would have had to fire you otherwise."

In a rare display of humor from Jean she raises both hands and says, "Oh no, that would be devastating. How could I possibly go on when my sole purpose in life is defending you, DS McMillan?"

We both laugh and then spend the next ten minutes discussing my chances of release. I'm quietly confident, but Jean is only cautiously optimistic. A few minutes later Morgan and the others return to the room.

■ ■ ■ ■ ■ ■ ■ ■

DCI Morgan himself starts the tape.

"Interview with Detective Sergeant Sean McMillan resumes at 4.02 pm. Still present in the room are DCI Morgan, DI Gray, DC Swain, DS McMillan, and legal counsel Ms. Jean Monroe."

Morgan now looks completely drained. He rubs his eyes and takes a deep breath before continuing, "Detective Sergeant McMillan, whilst I am far from convinced of your innocence in this affair, I am inclined at this time to concede that we don't have sufficient evidence to hold you in custody any longer."

Catherine and DI Swain look besides themselves with anger and disappointment. But they must surely understand the boss's reasoning for releasing me. I'm pleased at the result but have no intention of rubbing it in their faces. I remain steely faced as Morgan continues.

"I am now de-arresting you and am formally suspending you from duty pending further enquiries into your conduct. Your personal belongings will be returned to you, with the exception of your warrant card and your passport. Until advised otherwise, you are not permitted to enter this station, or to have contact with any of my officers. And under no circumstances are you allowed to represent yourself to anyone as a police officer. Is that understood, DS McMillan?"

"Yes, sir. Thank you, sir."

Morgan brushes off my thanks and says, "Good. Interview concluded at 4.04 pm. Turn off the tape please, DC Swain."

Without another word, Morgan gets up to leave, but I'm reluctant to let him leave thinking the worst of me.

"Sir, it's not how it looks. I had nothing to do with Douglas' escape or any of his other activities. I'm a good police officer and I intend to prove it."

Ignoring my statement, Morgan opens the door to leave, but at the last second, he changes his mind and turns to face me.

"I certainly hope so. But you're not making it easy for us to believe you. If you're as innocent as you say you are, you need to think very carefully about what you are going to say the next time we meet.

"Now if you don't mind, it's been a long day and I'd like to see my wife. Sergeant Morris will be along shortly to process you out. Don't make me regret releasing you today, Sean."

■ ■ ■ ■ ■ ■ ■

After completing the release formalities, Jean offers to take me home and we arrive outside my apartment building at just after 6 pm. I thank her for the lift, and we agree to meet again on Monday or Tuesday. Before getting out of the car, I thank her again.

"I mean it, Jean. I'm in your debt once again."

In response, Jean smiles and says, "Think nothing of it, Sean. It's my job. And besides, my bill will be in the post."

I laugh. "I'm sure it will. Have a good weekend, Jean."

"I think whether or not I have a good weekend will depend entirely on you," she responds with a frown.

"Sorry?" I ask.

"I mean, stay out of trouble, Sean. Relax and enjoy your weekend. Put your feet up, read a book, or splurge on Netflix. Do anything you want. Just don't try to get involved in the hunt for Clive Douglas and do not try to contact DC Swain. You're already walking on thin ice. Don't make things worse for yourself."

I nod my agreement, but my less-than-sincere expression gives away my intentions.

"I mean it, Sean. If you get arrested again this weekend, I will leave you to stew. The minute I get home, I'm turning my cell phone off and unplugging my landline."

I nod again and smile. "I promise, Jean. No trouble. I've got the new series of Peaky Blinders to catch up on. Thanks again for the lift. Go on. Go and enjoy your weekend."

■ ■ ■ ■ ■ ■ ■

Any normal person would follow Jean's advice to the letter. But I'm not a normal person and sitting around watching TV or reading a book all weekend is not an option for me. Clive Douglas has at least a six-hour head start, and whilst it would be easy enough for me to travel and end his escape attempt before it had even begun, it wouldn't necessarily solve my other problem.

Even if I provide information to foil Clive's escape attempt, I doubt it will be enough to convince Catherine that I am not somehow still involved in something criminal.

Her discovery of my warrant card in the same location as the remains of George Benson and Peter Lane is just too compelling for her to ignore. Regardless of any remaining loyalty she may have to me, it's almost certain that she would go ahead with her threat to take her suspicions to Morgan and Grey.

In her position I would probably do the same. But if this does happen, I will be back to square one as far as my own future is concerned.

I weight up my options over a couple of glasses of Jameson. Finally deciding on a drastic course of action, I do exactly what I was told not to do. I pick up my cell phone and call Catherine. The first four times, the call goes straight to her answerphone. On the fifth attempt she picks up and wastes no time in laying into me.

"Are you off your tiny bloody mind, Sean? What part of 'do not contact any of your colleagues' do you not understand?"

"Cath, please. If you just let me try to explain. I want to–"

"It's too bloody late!" Cath snaps. "You had your chance to explain earlier and you chose instead to tell a pack of lies. Fuck you, Sean! Don't call me again, or I'll have you arrested. Don't test me–"

"I'm ready to tell you the truth, Cath. Just give me a chan—"

"Don't make me laugh. You wouldn't know the truth if it walked up and slapped you in the face with a wet fish. You've told so many lies that you don't even know yourself what the truth is anymore. Why the hell should I believe you now?"

"Because I need you to believe that I had nothing to do with Douglas' escape or what happened to Mike Thurgood and his men. And the only way I can convince you of that is to come clean about everything else that has happened in the last few months. I promise you, Cath. Give me one chance to explain. If you don't believe me after that, then you can slap the cuffs on me. Please, Cath, just give me one more chance?"

For a few moments there is silence and then in a softer tone, Catherine says, "You don't know how much I want to believe you and God knows, I've given you so many chances to come clean before. Why should I believe it is going to be any different this time?"

"Because ... because this time the stakes are higher than ever before. Come and see me, Cath. I promise you won't regret it. Come now, I'll put the coffee on."

"What, you want me to come right now? No, Sean. I need time to think."

"That's okay. What about tomorrow?" I urge. "Come around twelve and I'll make us some lunch."

"No ... I mean, I don't know. I need time to think. Don't call me again, Sean."

The call abruptly ends, and I'm left none the wiser about whether Cath will come tomorrow. On balance I think her curiosity to hear what I have to say will get the better of her and she will come.

In hopeful expectation, I make another call. It's not late, but I have to call three more times before Ben picks up. He sounds tired and I tease, "Sleeping, were we?"

"Not that it's any of your business, but yes I was. What do you want, Dad?"

"I want your help and I've told you before, cut the dad shit."

Ben laughs and says, "Don't tell me. You want me to convince Mum that you're a good guy and that she should go out with you again?"

"No, nothing like that, Ben. We had a great night last week. It was so great in fact that she kissed me and asked if she could see me again. I'm sure she must have told you."

For the second time tonight, I hear the words fuck you. Then Ben asks, "So, what do you want if it's not Mum?"

"I've got a job for you, if you're still interested in helping me."

My offer of work piques Ben's interest and he enthusiastically responds, "Really?"

"Yes, really. Now listen carefully, and don't interrupt me, shithead."

I explain what I need him to do and he listens in silence until I finish. When he still doesn't say anything I ask, "What do you think?"

Ben chuckles to himself and says, "I think you're absolutely crazy and if you fuck this up, she's going to have your nuts on a plate."

"That's quite possible," I reply. "So, are you up for it?"

"I wouldn't miss it for the world." Ben laughs again. "What time do you want me there?"

"I told Catherine to get here for twelve, so get here for eleven. And don't forget the bloody camera. It's important."

"Yes, you've said. I won't forget it. Anything else?"

"Just don't be late and I repeat: don't forget the camera." Then before cutting off the call, I add sarcastically, "I'll see you tomorrow, son."

For the rest of the evening, I stalk Catherine's social media to find out as much as I can about her past life. Just after 11 pm, I save a picture from her Facebook timeline and run off a copy on my printer. Happy that I have a clear plan and exhausted from the day's events, I'm asleep as soon as my head hits the pillow.

Present Day – Saturday, May 5th, 2018

If I'm not nervous enough already about today, Ben arriving forty-five minutes late is an additional worry that I can well do without. I open the door to my apartment and angrily snatch the bag from his hands.

"What bloody time do you call this? I said eleven, Ben. Come on, get inside before she sees you."

I slam the door and follow him into my front room. Completely unconcerned, Ben drapes his jacket over the back of my sofa and takes a seat.

"The receipt's in the bag. You owe me sixty quid."

I take the Polaroid camera and receipt from the bag. "It's 52.99 actually. What about film?"

"It comes with two packs of ten in the box," Ben replies. "And it's sixty quid. You're paying my bus fare as well. And I don't take cheques or credit cards."

Ben holds out his hand expectantly and I wave him away. "You'll get your money when we're done. Now, are you sure you know what I need you to do?"

"I'm sure," Ben replies. "I still think you're bloody mad, though. Are you even sure she's coming?"

I nod. "She'll come. It's too tempting for her to ignore. Now grab your shit and wait in the bedroom until I tell you to come out. Oh, and make yourself useful. Get the camera ready to use."

Ben picks up his jacket and I hand him the camera, but instead of going to the bedroom, he ignores my instruction and goes into the kitchen. "I'm just going to grab a sandwich and a cup of tea," he calls. "Is that okay?"

Knowing it is pointless to argue, I shake my head. "Just get a move on. Make it and take it into the bedroom."

In typical Ben fashion, he ignores me again and takes his own sweet time.

"You stress too much, Pops. It's not like Catherine has a key anyway. I'll have plenty of time to hide after she gets here."

His logic is hard to ignore and I'm in no mood for a debate anyway. I tell him again to hurry up and then nervously keep an eye on the time as he proceeds to stuff his face with a triple-decker ham and pickle sandwich washed down with two cups of tea.

In the end, Ben was right not to be worried about the time. With no sign of Catherine and no contact from her by 1.15, he turns to me and says exactly what I'm thinking, "She's not coming, is she?"

Unconvincingly, I tell him that she is coming and to sit tight. But when the time gets to 1.45, I finally resign myself to the fact that she's going to be a no-show and I reluctantly hand Ben his jacket. "I'm sorry for wasting your time, mate. Go on, piss off and enjoy the rest of your weekend." He puts on his jacket and then cheekily reminds me that I still owe him for the camera.

"I would say you can pay me the next time you see me, but I'm just a poor student, remember, and well ... I don't trust you. Cough up, old man."

I reach for my wallet and call him a cheeky fuck, which breaks the tension and causes us both to laugh until a second later when our laughter is abruptly halted by the sound of my doorbell.

We both stare at each other and freeze. "Fuck!" I breathe. "She's here. Quick, grab the camera and make yourself scarce."

I push Ben towards the bedroom and warn him again to be quiet and to stay out of sight. "I'll come and get you when I need you."

Double-checking that the bedroom door is firmly closed, I walk slowly towards the front door, where I pause to take a deep breath to steady myself before opening it.

■ ■ ■ ■ ■ ■ ■

Even dressed casually, Catherine always manages to exude an air of professionalism and glamor. I smile and then nervously look over her shoulder.

"Hi, Cath. You're on your own?"

"Of course I am," she replies. "Who else were you expecting?"

"Nobody. What I meant to say … I mean, I wasn't sure if you would come or not," I stutter, her coolness increasing my nervousness.

"Cut the shit," Catherine says with a shake of her head. "You knew I would come. Now, are you going to leave me standing here or are we going to get on with this?"

Without waiting for an answer, Catherine comes in and I follow her towards the front room where she takes a seat. I offer to take her coat, but she impatiently declines the offer. "I'm not intending on being here long," she says.

"What about a drink?" I ask. "I could make some coffee, or I could open a bottle of wine. It's no probl–"

Catherine holds up her hand. "Sean, just stop. I haven't come here to get drunk with you. I've come here to hear what you have to say. Just sit down and get on with it please."

I nod and quietly say, "Yes, of course. It's quite a story, though. Do you mind if I have a drink?"

Catherine shrugs and shakes her head again. "Whatever. Just get on with it. This is not where I was planning on spending my Saturday afternoon."

With my back to her, I pour a large slug of Jameson and knock it back, before refilling the tumbler almost three-quarters of the way to the top. When I sit down, Cath frowns when she sees the glass, but she doesn't say anything. Before starting to speak, I take a sip from the glass and take another deep breath.

"Okay, Cath, I'm going to tell you what's been going on, but I need you to listen without interrupting me. You're not going to believe what I'm saying and there is a very real chance that you're going to think that I've lost my marbles, but I need you to listen until I've finished. Is that okay?"

"You're not exactly filling me with confidence," Cath replies drily. "Why don't you just start, and we'll see how it goes."

■ ■ ■ ■ ■ ■ ■

With hindsight, it was naïve to expect that Cath wouldn't interrupt me. Who in their right mind would believe a cock-and-bull story about a dream-traveling detective? Five minutes into my story Cath has already had a gutful and angrily gets to her feet.

"You seriously need help, Sean. I mean it, you're a bloody head case. And if you're not, then you're more of a bastard than I thought you were. You seriously expect me to believe this nonsense?"

Rather unwisely I stand up to block her from leaving and Cath reaches into her handbag for her taser.

"Get out of my way, Sean. I mean it. We are done and I'm leaving."

Knowing full well that she would happily tase me, I move aside to let her pass. Desperate for her not to leave, I rack my brains for something to convince her to stay and hear me out. She is almost at the door when I shout, "Kevin Morgan was right."

This is enough to get Cath's attention and she turns around, "What are you talking about? What was he right about?"

"About my meeting Rosemary Pinois and Patrick Newman before the start of the case."

"All that proves is that you're a liar. It doesn't mean that you're a bloody time traveler, or whatever you called it."

"I know that, Cath. But think about it. In Ashdown Forest, Rosemary said, When you came to my home the first time, you reminded me of someone from my past. And not just me either. Paddy also thought he recognized you. The name was the same, but it's not possible. Morgan thought she hesitated to continue because she was worried about dropping me in it. He was wrong about that, but he was right about my meeting them before. And Rosemary was right about it being a lifetime ago. The first time I met Rosemary and Paddy was in December of 1983."

Catherine shakes her head with frustration. "Just listen to yourself. You weren't even born in 1983. For God's sake, get some help, Sean."

She turns to leave again, and, with no other option, I grab for her arm to stop her. "You were right about Benson and Lane."

Losing patience, Catherine pushes me away and screams for me to stop, "That's enough, Sean. Touch me again and I'll break your bloody hand. I don't care about anything you have to sa–"

"I was there. I was there on the day of the robbery. Benson and Lane were executed by Rosemary with a shot to the back of the head. I bet you've seen the pathologist's report. I'm right, aren't I?"

"That proves nothing," Catherine replies. "DI Gray told you about Benson and Lane yesterday morning."

"She told me that their remains had been identified, not how they died."

"Then it was an educated guess. It still proves nothing, Sean."

Knowing that I only have seconds before she leaves, I desperately scramble for a response. "Wait, what about my warrant card? You saw the state of it. After the robbery, I was pushed into the pit on top of Benson and Lane. Those bastards buried me alive. Cath, you saw my wallet. It was buried underground for thirty-five years before you found it. You saw the state of it. You have to believe–"

Looking completely drained, Cath interrupts me again. "This is madness, Sean. You really don't know how badly I want to believe you. But this doesn't make any sense."

"You're right," I say. "It doesn't make sense. But why would I try and make you believe something so unbelievable if it wasn't true? You're the smartest person I know. Please come back inside, Cath. There is so much more that I need to tell you."

Caught between her own grasp on logic and my desperation for her to believe in an impossible reality, Catherine slowly shakes her head, before reluctantly taking off her coat and hanging it up in the hallway.

"I'm probably going to regret this, but what the hell? In for a penny, in for a pound. I've changed my mind, though. I will have that drink. Make it a large one and pour yourself another while you're at it. This is crunch time, Sean!"

■　■　■　■　■　■　■

Back in the living room, I open a bottle of red and with Cath's assurance that she will listen without interrupting, I start to recount as much as I can remember about the events of the last few months. I also tell her as much as I know about the parameters of my ability to dream travel.

True to her word and despite her obvious urge at times to interrupt or to dismissively laugh off my claims, Catherine continues to listen intently while making notes in her personal diary. After more than an hour, I finish my tale by describing the robbery at the Heathrow Trading Estate and my subsequent burial in the same hole as George Benson and Peter Lane.

"The rest you know, Cath. That's how my wallet and warrant card ended up in that hole and why it was in such bad condition. After that you were there with me for pretty much everything else up to now."

"Apart from the escort detail and the escape," Cath corrects me.

"Well, yes. Apart from that," I agree. "But that's my story. That's it, mate. What do you think?"

I know the answer to my question already, but what I don't know is exactly how Catherine will respond, or whether she will stay long enough for me to move to the next part of my plan. For a moment she says nothing, then to my great relief she picks up the wine bottle and pours herself another glass. She takes a sip and then places the glass back down on the table.

I'm expecting her to speak now, but for the next thirty seconds she just stares intently at me and remains silent.

When she does finally react, it is to shake her head, but she still doesn't say anything. Unable to bear the suspense any longer, I cautiously break the silence.

"I've just told you something that I've never told another living soul, Cath. And believe me, I know how crazy it sounds, but that's exactly why you must believe me. Why on earth would I make up something so unbelievable? Please, Cath. Say something. I need to know what you think."

Catherine looks down to her notes and shakes her head again. "I've already told you what I think, Sean. I want to believe you as much as you believe yourself, but I think you need help. If you genuinely believe what you've just told me, then come with me now and I'll get you the help you need."

"I believe it because it's true," I snap at her. "I believe it because what is unimaginable to you is my daily reality. None of it was my choice, but it's who I–"

"So, you really believe that you first met Maria Pinto in 1994?" Catherine angrily interrupts. "And that Benjamin Pinto is your son?"

I nod. "Yes, Cath. Because it's true."

Catherine looks down to her notes again and then says, "Okay, let's suppose for a moment that what you're saying is true. Tell me, do Maria or Ben know about your superpowers?"

"It's not a superpower," I reply. "It's an ability. And Maria doesn't know about it, but Ben does."

Catherine puts a tick next to Ben's name in her notebook. "Okay, so you were lying again when you just told me that you had never told another soul about any of this."

I try to explain, but Catherine cuts me dead. "It's okay. It doesn't matter. I'm more interested to hear your thoughts on why you thought it would be a good idea to tell him about your ability and why you thought it would be a good idea to involve a kid in our investigations? And don't give me any shit about him being your son."

"Cath, he is my son," I assert. "It's completely crazy, but it's tru–"

"For God's sake," Catherine screams, "just listen to yourself. You're barely older than Ben is. Or are you telling me you were six or seven years old when you shagged Maria in 1994? Is that it?"

I shake my head. "No, of course not. In your reality 1994 was twenty-four years ago. But for me it was just a few months ago and until the Anthony Glennister murder case Ben didn't even exist. Ben was a result of my first encounter with Maria in 1994 and I–"

"You mean he was the result of you dipping your wick without a thought for the consequences," Catherine interrupts.

"I wouldn't quite put it like that. But yes," I reply.

"Okay, but why get him involved in our investigations? If he is your son, then why would you put your own flesh and blood in harm's way?"

Before I have a chance to reply, Catherine holds up her hand. "Wait. Don't tell me. I think I've got it. It's because Ben is a chip off the old block. He's also some kind of time traveler. Is that it? Is Ben also a timelord?"

No words are needed for Catherine to interpret my expression and her previously sarcastic demeanor quickly changes to a look of incredulous disbelief. "You have got to be bloody kidding, Sean. You'll be telling me next that this is Dr. Who's Tardis and not an apartment in London."

Her Tardis comment provides a moment of light relief and I take advantage of it to offer a smile. "No, this was definitely still an apartment last time I checked."

In response, Catherine also allows herself a small smile, and then asks more sympathetically, "But you do believe that Ben is also a time traveler?"

"I don't just believe it, Cath. I know it, and I can prove it."

"And Ben will back you up?" Catherine asks.

I nod confidently. "Yes, he will." Then, more hesitantly, I add, "Now, I need you to promise not to fly off the handle, Cath … but Ben is here. He's in my bedroom."

Asking Cath not to fly off the handle when I've just dropped a bombshell like this is like asking a tom cat not to lick its own balls. Her reaction is exactly the opposite of what I was hoping for. Before I can stop her, she is on her feet and heading for the bedroom. I barely have time to shout a warning to Ben before she is through the door. Ben is usually as cocky as they come, but the sight of Cath in full-on terminator mode is enough to leave him visibly concerned for his safety.

When Catherine orders him into the living room, he wisely keeps his mouth shut and does as he is told.

We take a seat and I watch as Cath finishes the last of her wine. Her hands are shaking and I'm still wondering whether it is through anger or frustration, when I get my answer in no uncertain terms.

"I should bloody arrest you pair of charlatans right now." Then just to Ben, "But if you're as barking mad as he is, what would be the point? Tell me, Ben, is Sean your father?"

Still looking terrified, he looks to me for guidance and I tell him it's okay. Looking decidedly unsure of himself and still hesitating to answer, I remind him of last night's discussion. "It's okay, just tell the truth and do what we agreed, Ben."

With hindsight, I realize my comment is like a red rag to a bull and Cath explodes with rage. "You bloody planned this with him, Sean? Are you seriously trying to make me look like an idiot?"

I shake my head. "All I'm trying to do is make you understand and believe what's been happening." Then, turning to Ben, I add, "For fuck's sake tell her before she leaves."

Given Cath's outburst, Ben is understandably more reluctant than ever to say anything. Cath seizes on the opportunity to launch a new tirade.

"What's wrong, Sean? Is your son not playing ball? Is this not how it was meant to go?"

Ben tries to stand up and I pull him back down. "Don't you bloody dare. I've spilled my guts today and I need you to do the same. For God's sake, just tell her."

Cath turns to him with expectation. "Go on then. Tell me. Is this man, who is hardly any older than you are, your father?"

While Catherine waits for his answer, an unseen jab to his ribs leaves Ben wondering who he has the most to fear from. A further hesitation forces me to jab with more force and he finally splutters out that I am his father.

Her anger long since passed, there is nothing else for Catherine to do but snort in disbelief. "You two are the biggest pair of clowns since Laurel and Hardy. Seriously, you're a pair of bloody comedians, and more fool me for sitting here listening to you both."

She shakes her head again in frustration and then asks, "So that must mean you're also a time traveler, Ben?"

Scared to say more, Ben simply nods and Catherine smirks. "And how is that working out for you? More interesting than your journalism studies, I guess. No need to answer that question. I'm done here, and I'm done with you pair."

She gets up to leave and I follow her to the front door. "Cath, I said I can prove all of this, and I can. Just come back inside and give me a couple of hours more to show you what I mean."

With one arm already in her coat, Catherine stops what she is doing and snaps, "You want a couple of hours more? I've listened to your nonsense for more than two hours already. And as far as I'm concerned that's two hours more than you deserved. Now, get out of my way, I'm leaving."

Out of options and resigned to the fact that part two of my plan will have to wait or will need a rethink, I unlock the door and step aside. I'm surprised, though, to see Catherine hesitate for a moment. I'm even more surprised when she turns around and walks back into the apartment. Unsure of what is going on, I ask her if she has changed her mind. Her answer is unequivocal but presents me with a make-or-break opportunity that is too good to miss.

"That wine has gone right through me. I'm using your bathroom before I leave."

Knowing that I have just minutes to act before she finishes in the bathroom, I drag Ben up off the sofa. "Listen carefully, numb nuts, and keep your bloody mouth shut. If this goes tits up, we are both going to be spending the rest of the weekend in jail."

Ben listens wide-eyed as I explain what we're going to do. When I finish, he shakes his head. "No way. No bloody way, Sean. Catherine is right, you are a bloody head case. I'm not doing it. If this does go wrong, we won't even make it to jail. Catherine will string us up by our balls."

Before he can say more, we both turn towards the bathroom and the sound of the toilet flushing. Ben looks back to me with obvious panic in his eyes and I thrust a roll of duct tape into his hands. "You don't have a bloody choice, son. Help me or don't help me, but she already knows that we set this thing up together, and if this does go tits up, I'll drag you down with me. Now, man the fuck up and wait here until I call you."

■ ■ ■ ■ ■ ■ ■

Catherine's handbag is on the hallway table. As she approaches, I innocently pick it up and comment how nice it looks. "Real leather? It smells like real leather."

Cath looks up from tying the belt on her coat and dismissively replies, "It had better be. It's a Bottega Veneta." She then holds out her hand for the bag, but my heart is beating out of my chest and I play for time to find the right moment.

"What now, Cath? What are you going to tell Morgan and Gray about today?"

Her response is preceded with a look that is tinged with both disbelief at my question and sadness at my situation. "Listen, Sean. As far as I'm concerned, today never happened. I'm not intending to say anything about what has happened here, but equally you need to understand that we are finished. We are finished as partners and I'm sorry to say it, but we are finished as friends."

Hearing this is like a knife in my chest, but my protests are swiftly and brutally cut off.

"Sean, I can't be around you and I can't be associated with you. You're a liability to yourself and others and if you truly believe all the BS you've told me today, then you need the kind of help that I can't give. My advice, for what it's worth, is to tender your resignation and see a psychiatrist. If you don't, you are going to end up back in prison and this time you won't be getting out anytime soon. Get help, Sean. If not for you, do it for that deluded boy in there. You owe him that much at least."

Ready to make my move, I slowly nod and take a deep breath. "Thanks, Cath. You're right and I truly appreciate everything you've done for me. I'll give some serious thought to what you've just said."

Happy that I am finally seeming to see sense, Catherine allows herself a smile. Then, completely unaware of my intentions, she gestures toward her bag and makes a small joke. "That suits you, Sean. I think it suits me better, though. Can I have it, please?"

I return her smile and laugh slightly, before offering the handbag with my left hand. She reaches over to take it, and I carelessly let it fall from my hand. Believing it to be an accident, Catherine innocently bends over to pick it up and I use the distraction to snap a pair of handcuffs onto her wrists before she can fully comprehend what is happening.

For a split second as she stands back up, we stare at each other in shock. Cath is in shock at what has just happened and I'm in shock at how easy it was. Any sense of relief I might be feeling, though, is short-lived as Cath screams for me to remove the cuffs, "What the fuck, Sean! Are you absolutely bloody crazy? Get these off me right now!"

Knowing that I'm at the point of no return, I shake my head and simply say, "I'm sorry, Cath. You didn't give me any other option." Before she can scream again or try to get past me, I clamp my right hand across her mouth and sweep her legs from under her. We hit the ground harder than I would have liked, but despite being winded, Cath has no intention of giving up without a fight.

Using every dirty trick in the self-defense play book, she bites down on my hand with enough force to make a crocodile proud, then quickly follows up by grabbing for my testicles. With one hand across her mouth and the other desperately fending off her attempts to remove my crown jewels, I scream for Ben to get his ass in gear. When he finally gets to me, I gesture to the duct tape. "Don't just bloody stand there. Get some of that over her mouth and then wrap it around her ankles."

He tears a piece of tape off the roll but hesitates when he sees the bite marks and flecks of blood smeared across the fleshy part of my hand. Sensing an opportunity, Catherine pulls her mouth away from my hand and screams, "Ben, don't listen to him. Help me and I'll–"

The rest of her words are cut off as I clasp my hand back across her mouth. "Just get the bloody tape across her mouth. If you don't, we're both going to prison for sure."

The fear of prison is obviously greater than Ben's fear of Catherine. Without my needing to ask again, he kneels down and places the tape firmly across her mouth.

Finally able to release my right hand, I pull away and flip Catherine over onto her stomach. With my weight on her back, I do my best to keep her legs still while Ben winds the roll of tape around her ankles.

Satisfied that she's no longer a threat to us, I roll her back over and stand up. Ben looks like he is about to burst into tears, and it takes a firm slap on the back to bring him back to reality.

"Come on, I need your help getting her back into the living room. I'll get the top half. You grab her legs."

I place my arms around her torso, but Ben doesn't move. When I ask him again for help, he shakes his head and mutters to himself, "What the fuck have we done? This is kidnapping. We're kidnapping a police officer." Then to me, "I'm going to prison, aren't I? Sean, we have to let her go."

I stand up and, as calmly as I can under the circumstances, I tell Ben that if we don't go through with this, we will both be going to prison even if we do let Catherine go.

"You have to trust me, Ben. We've come this far, and you know this can work. Now, pull yourself together and help me carry her into the living room. The sooner we start, the sooner we can get this over with."

With no other option, Ben lifts Catherine's legs and we carry her back into the living room and carefully place her down into one of the armchairs. I tell Ben to sit down and I kneel in front of Catherine, who despite being gagged continues to threaten me with all manner of retribution.

I allow her to vent for another few minutes; then, satisfied she has run out of steam, I quietly say to her, "I really am sorry that we had to do this, but we didn't have any choice. I told you that I can prove what I've been saying, and I can. Now, if you'll promise to stay quiet and hear me out, I'll take the tape off your mouth. Can you do that?"

Although she's now quiet, her eyes tell me all I need to know and I ask again, "I need you to promise not to scream, Cath. Just nod your head and I'll take this off."

Her eyes remain defiant, but she nods, and I reach forward and pull at the edge of the tape. It's barely halfway across her mouth when she starts to read me my rights, "Sean McMillan, I am arresting you for assault and for kidn–"

I quickly replace the tape and tear off another strip from the roll and push it firmly in place across her mouth. For good measure, and because I know now that Catherine is unlikely to play ball, I wind the remainder of the roll around the chair and her upper body.

With her arms firmly held in place and zero chance of her being able to get up from the chair, I take the seat opposite and shake my head.

"Do you realize how ridiculous you sounded just then? We've got you trussed up like a suckling pig and you're trying to arrest me. I admire your spirit, Cath, but you know me well enough to know that I wouldn't do something like this without a bloody good reason.

"Now, I'm hoping we can do this with your cooperation, but if we can't … well, if we can't, then you'll just have to stay gagged until we're done. What's it to be? Are you going to stay quiet?"

From under the tape, she mumbles that she doesn't have a bloody choice and I nod my agreement. "At this point, Cath, no, you don't."

I carefully remove the tape and, apart from calling me an arsehole and threatening Ben with castration, Catherine remains as calm as could be expected under the circumstances. She then asks, "What now, Dr. Who? Is this the part where you get pissed and fall asleep?"

"Actually, yes," I reply. "I told you, though, I don't need to drink as much as I used to previously. Another large one should do it."

"But you are expecting me to sit here and watch you have a nap?" Cath asks. "That's your big plan for making everything right, is it?"

"It's a bit more than just a nap," I say. "It's important for you to see what happens. I know none of this makes sense now, but I promise you it will."

Cath shakes her head in exasperation, then turns to Ben. "You're both absolute bloody fruit cakes. Do you really believe all this rubbish?"

Unsure of how to respond, Ben stays silent and Catherine turns back to face me. "Well, you'd better get on with it then. Whatever 'it' is. I don't suppose you can take my cuffs off and take this bloody tape off my arms?"

I smile and reply, "You suppose right, Cath. Unless, of course, you're intending to sit there quietly?" In response, Cath screws up her face and I laugh. "Yeh, I didn't think so."

I reach under the coffee table for a writing pad and tell Catherine that I am going to write something that I am going to ask her to sign. She's confused of course, but no more confused than she is about any of this. With a shrug of her shoulders, she tells me just to get on with it, then she watches in silence as I compose the note. After two failed drafts, I'm finally happy with the third. I tear the sheet of paper from the pad and slide it across the table for Catherine to read.

"What is it?" Cath asks.

"Easier if you read it yourself," I suggest.

She looks down at the note and reads first in silence and then sarcastically out loud.

"Dear Catherine, this is a note to yourself. By the time you read this again, you will most likely have been tied into a chair for a good few hours. You will probably be feeling tired and confused, but you must understand that this was the only way to make you understand that your friend Sean was telling the truth.

"I'm hoping that by now you remember meeting him in your past and this could only be possible if he was telling the truth about his ability to travel back in time through his dreams. Think back, Catherine. Think hard and the truth will be there for you to see. From me to you.

Catherine to Catherine x

4.10 pm May 5th, 2018."

She finishes reading and looks up. "That's a sweet note, Sean. I particularly like the kiss at the end — but calling us friends is a bit of a stretch. And you're expecting me to sign this, yes?"

"I am," I reply. "Again, I know it doesn't make any sense to you now, but It will. It's important that you sign the note."

The pen is closest to Ben and I tell him to give it to her. "Put the piece of paper onto the pad and hold it so that she can sign it."

Ben is understandably nervous about getting so close to her, but he does as he is told and places the pen in her hands.

Catherine awkwardly scribbles her signature at the bottom of the page and then quietly says, "Thank you, Ben. I know that none of this was your idea."

Lulled into a false sense of security, Ben looks up and smiles. I've seen the look too many times before not to know what is coming, but Ben doesn't. Catherine returns his smile and then jerks her head forward into the side of his face. It's not the best headbutt I've ever seen, but it's enough to leave Ben stunned and Catherine laughing.

"Pussy! That's what you get for playing with the big boys and girls."

I lunge for the tape, but before I can fully get it back across her mouth, Catherine spits at me and screams, "Yours is coming, McMillan. Mark my words, Sean. You're a bloody dead man."

Muffled again, but still calling me every name under the sun, I turn away from Cath to check on Ben. The force of the blow has left an angry red welt on his cheek, but the only other damage appears to be a huge dent in his pride. He gladly accepts the offer of a shot of whiskey to steady his nerves and downs it in one. I nod appreciatively and pour myself another large glass.

"Right, let's get on with this. Hand me the camera and move onto the other armchair, so that I can lie down on the sofa."

Ben obliges without question and I reach under the coffee table to retrieve the picture of Catherine that I had printed the previous evening. Unsure of what she is seeing, Cath takes a break from threatening me and lifts her head for a better view.

To help, I hold the picture up and turn it towards her. The image was taken in 2003, when Catherine would have been in her mid-teens. She recognizes herself instantly and shakes her head in disgust, but surprisingly remains quiet. I take a last look at the image and, satisfied that my destination is clear in my head, I place the photograph down and pick up my glass.

"Okay, I'm ready, Ben. Do not fall asleep." Then, gesturing to the lump on his cheek, I caution him, "You know already what she is capable of. Do not take your eyes off her and do not trust her. Understood?"

When Ben nods, I say, "Good. Now if she is still behaving after a couple of hours, you can try taking the tape off her mouth again. I'm hoping not to take much longer than that."

I gulp back the last of the whiskey and, in a now familiar routine, lie back on the sofa and close my eyes to begin my chant.

"12th June 2003, 12th June 2003, 12th June 200 ..."

The last thing I remember before the light engulfs me is a parting burst of muffled insults from Catherine: "Stalker! Wanker! Pervert!"

The Past – Thursday, 12ᵗʰ June, 2003

The warmth of the sun on my back is an encouraging sign that, if nothing else, I've at least arrived at the right time of the year.

The sun is high in the sky, though. Still slightly disorientated, I foolishly look up without covering my eyes. The intensity of the sun's rays causes me to wince painfully and I quickly look away and curse my own stupidity.

"I don't know about stalker, wanker and pervert, Cath. But you would be right if you called me a dumbass. Fuck me, that hurt."

I rub my eyes and take a deep breath to clear my head. The time is just before two and the hustle and bustle around me has a comfortable familiarity that gives a confidence that I have arrived on or close to the date that I was aiming for.

All around, people are going about their business blissfully unaware that a stranger from the future has just landed in their midst. An elderly couple wish me a polite good afternoon as they pass, and I return the pleasantry with a smile and a muttered, "If only you knew who you've just said hello to."

It wasn't my intention to be heard, but the elderly couple stop and ask if I said something. Taking the opportunity, I smile and say, "I was just wondering what today's date is."

The old man checks his watch.

"It's the 12ᵗʰ of June, young man."

"2003?"

The old man laughs. "It was the last time I checked. Are you okay, son?"

"I am now," I reply. "You've been very helpful."

I'm about to ask another question when I notice a sign on the other side of the road. Thanking them again, I wish the old couple a good day and cross the road to the entrance of the shopping center. Although parts of the sign have been daubed in graffiti, the original message is still clear enough for me to read: "Welcome to the Broadway Shopping Center, Bexleyheath."

With this final confirmation of my accuracy, I quietly congratulate myself and walk into the center to kill some time.

When I pass through the sliding doors, I'm instantly taken back to my own teenage years by the sight of the now defunct brands that once dominated the UK retail scene.

To my left, Woolworths department store conjures up wonderful memories of the gloriously opulent pick and mix confectionary display and to my right the Gateways supermarket transports me back to my first summer job.

For the princely sum of one pound seventy-five an hour I had spent the best part of six mind-numbing weeks robotically stacking shelves with baked beans and canned vegetables for eight hours a day.

One pound seventy-five was shit money even back then and it was years before I could face a can of baked beans without remembering how much I hated the sight of them. The shops, though, are not the only familiar thing today. Beautiful by Christina Aguilera finishes playing over the PA and is replaced by Justin Timberlake singing his cover of Cry Me a River.

This particular JT song reminds me of an awkwardly timed fumble with my first girlfriend at an under-sixteen school disco. I recall nearly dying of embarrassment and praying for the floor to swallow me up. Now, though, it just makes me smile.

For the next hour, I wander from store to store soaking in the memories of my youth. Although only fifteen years in the past, I'm still staggered by the advances in technology we've seen in that time. In the electrical stores, the games consoles that were once considered cutting edge now appear primitive, but the biggest change I can see is the way in which we communicate.

In 2003, Nokia was the dominant player in the telecom market, and the Nokia 1100 was the best-selling mobile phone of all time. But ask a kid today about Nokia and they would likely dismiss it as being behind the times.

Today's big players of course are Apple and Samsung, but in a world ever hungry for new technology, who's to say who the big players of tomorrow might be? Nokia once considered itself unbeatable. And they were. Right up until 2007 when Apple introduced the world to the iPhone. The rest, as they say, is history.

With that final thought, I check the time and say to myself, "Okay, just after three. Time to get going."

A security guard points me in the direction of the taxi rank and after a short wait in the queue, I board a black cab and give directions to my destination. Looking unsure of what I've just said, the driver looks over his shoulder and I repeat the destination.

"Bexleyheath Secondary School for Girls."

"Yeh, I thought that's what you said," the driver grunts accusingly. Then under his breath, "Lazy bastard, it's only a bloody five-minute walk."

∎ ∎ ∎ ∎ ∎ ∎ ∎ ∎

We arrive at the school gates and I smile sarcastically and hand the taxi driver two one-pound coins to pay for the one-pound eighty-pence fare. "Keep the change. Get something nice for the wife and kids."

Unimpressed with my show of generosity, the driver tuts his disapproval and then calls me a prick as I get out and close the cab door. Arsehole cab drivers are not my concern today, though.

I brush off his comment and idly watch for a few minutes as a steady flow of teenage girls start streaming through the gates at the end of the school day.

When the flow slows down to a trickle, I stop a nerdy-looking girl who is the image of Moaning Myrtle from Harry Potter and ask her directions to the sports field.

"There's a hockey match on today, right?"

"That's right," the girl replies. "Bexleyheath are playing St. Margaret's College. Are you here to support one of the teams? If you are, you need to sign in at reception."

"I'm actually here to support my little sister, Catherine Swain," I reply. "Do you know her?"

The girl nods but looks confused. "She's in the year above me. But if it's the same Catherine Swain … well, she's black and you're whi–"

"Different fathers," I interrupt with a smirk. "We've got a Chinese brother as well. Mum was well travelled, if you know what I mean."

Unsure of whether I'm joking or not, the Myrtle lookalike starts to blush. To spare her further embarrassment, I say, "Thanks for your help anyway. Which way was it again?"

She points the way to the sports fields and reminds me again to register at reception, but I'm already walking with no intention of going anywhere near reception to register.

■ ■ ■ ■ ■ ■ ■

When I reach the field, the match is well underway. By my estimation, apart from the players and match officials, there are close to two hundred other spectators scattered along the sides of the pitch. The bulk of these appear to be school friends of the players, but there also seems to be a good representation of parents and siblings enthusiastically cheering the girls on.

Finding a gap halfway down one side of the pitch, I push through and turn towards the scoreboard.

With eight minutes remaining of the second half, the scores are tied at 3-3, but I knew this already. Today's hockey match is the reason why I knew where Catherine would be today, and I now turn my attention towards the field to find her.

Although I've memorized the picture from her Facebook page and she's well known to me, I struggle to positively identify her because the pace of play is frenetic and there are four other young black players on the pitch. Then an opponent hacks at her ankles from behind and she crashes down just a few feet from where I'm standing.

When she gets back to her feet, our eyes meet for just a fleeting moment, but the eyes are always a dead giveaway and a moment is all I need to be certain that it is her. She turns away and in typical Catherine style brushes herself down and rejoins the action none the worse for her fall. I smile and say to myself, "Yep, that's my Catherine alright."

To my right, a short, balding guy in his mid to late fifties has overheard my comment and asks, "Are you a friend of Catherine's?"

His stereotypical tweed jacket with leather elbow patches is an obvious indication that he's a teacher, but I ask the question anyway.

"Sorry, who are you?"

My questioner offers his hand. "Eric Richards. I'm the deputy headmaster of Bexleyheath Secondary. And you are?"

"Mark Travis," I reply with a smile and an easy lie.

Richards smiles back. "I haven't seen you at any of the matches before. You're a friend or a parent of one of the girls?"

"Christ, I hope I don't look old enough to be a parent," I reply with a laugh. "No. I'm a talent scout for the UK Ladies' Field

Hockey Federation. I had a tip-off that there might be some promising young players here today."

My explanation elicits a bigger smile and a nod of approval. Then Richards tells me that usually they are informed in advance if a talent scout is intending to attend a match.

"That's normally the case," I agree. "But I also like to see how the players perform when they don't know they are being watched."

Seemingly satisfied with my explanation, Richards nods again before saying, "Well, you weren't wrong, she is one of our better players and it would be a great achievement for one of our girls to make the national team. That is what you meant, wasn't it?"

With one eye watching Catherine, I'm slightly distracted and only half-listening.

"Sorry. Meant what?"

"Catherine Swain," Richards replies. He then points to where Cath is making a rush towards the halfway line. "You were referring to Catherine Swain when you said that is my Catherine alright? You meant for the UK team. Am I right?"

I turn away from the match action in the hope that if I give a full answer, my interrogator will get bored and leave me alone.

"Um yes. That's right. I've heard good things about her and from what I've seen today, she's very talented. She's a definite candidate for the national trials, but let's keep that between ourselves for now. I'd hate to get her hopes up."

Richards gives me a knowing wink and leans in closer to say quietly, "Mum's the word, Mr. Travis. Your secret is safe with me." He then straightens and points to another girl on the field. "I suspect you've had your eye on her as well. That's Bella Maltby. She's been our number-one offensive striker for the last three seasons. She's a real talent and had trials for the UK ladies under eighteen team last year. Oh, but I expect you knew that already?"

Hoping that Richards is not testing me I decide to bluff it out. "Yes, of course. She did well but didn't quite make the grade last season."

"But in with a chance again this year?" Richards asks hopefully.

I could, of course, leave him with something positive, but he's annoying me now and I'm done talking. So, instead, I grimace and shake my head. "No, not this year, Eric. This year, I've only got my eye on Catherine. Keep encouraging Bella, though. She's still young enough to be in with a chance next year."

Clearly disappointed at the news, Eric offers me his hand again. "Well, if you will excuse me, Mr. Travis, I have homework to mark. Enjoy the rest of the match."

Pleased to see the back of him, I turn my attention back to the game and to Catherine. With less than ninety seconds remaining on the clock and the score still tied, the St. Margaret's players push hard towards the opposing goal. Less than ten feet out, their offensive striker sends in a belter of a shot, which to the obvious relief of the home crowd miraculously goes wide of the net by literally just a few inches.

Catherine, who just a few seconds earlier had been at the complete opposite end of the field, is now screaming for the ball.

"Quick, Libby. To me. This is the last chance we've got. Come on, to me, Libby."

The keeper taps the ball towards Catherine. With the seconds counting down fast, and my heart beating even faster, Catherine turns and makes a run down the left wing.

When she reaches the halfway line unmolested, panic sets in amongst St. Margaret's defense. They rush back to protect their goal, but one by one Cath effortlessly weaves past each of the defenders until there is only one remaining between her and the opposing goalkeeper.

Keen to settle the score, Catherine charges headlong at the player who, minutes earlier, had swept her legs from under her. Although taller and much heavier than Catherine, her opponent is no match for Cath's momentum and determination.

With neither player seemingly prepared to give ground, the St. Margaret's player is effortlessly bowled aside and, with all defense gone, Catherine almost casually chips the ball over the keeper's head and into the back of the net.

With just five seconds remaining of the match, the Bexleyheath supporters erupt in triumph and the sound of the final whistle is lost amongst the ensuing cacophony of boisterous celebration. Catherine herself disappears under an avalanche of teammates keen to embrace and congratulate her. Moments later she resurfaces and is hoisted onto their shoulders, to be carried triumphantly towards the changing rooms.

I watch her out of sight, then walk back towards the school gates to wait for her, until my progress is halted by a rapidly approaching, red-in-the-face deputy headmaster accompanied by a baby-faced young police constable.

"That's him. That's the man," Richards shouts with an accusing finger. "He said that he was a talent scout for the UK Hockey Association. But I checked, and they've never heard of him. And he didn't register at rec–"

The young constable cuts off Richards' rant and calls for me to stay where I am.

"Sir, I'd like a word with you please."

Keen not to make things any more complicated than they need to be I turn around and smile. "Yes, of course. How can I help you, officer?"

"Well, you can start by identifying yourself please, sir."

"Mark Travis. He said his name was Mark Travis," Richards offers. "He's lying, though. There is no Mark Travis at the UK Hock–"

Annoyed at the interruption, the constable cuts Richards off for a second time and says, "Thank you, Mr. Richards. But if you don't mind, I'd like to hear it from this gentleman. Is that correct, sir? Is your name Mark Jarvis?"

I shake my head. "No, it's not. It's Martin Jervis. Then turning to Richards, who looks puzzled, I say, "You must have misheard me. It's an easy enough mistake and understandable for a man of your age."

Richards now looks ready to explode, and he angrily blurts out, "I know exactly what I heard, thank you. And you'll be telling us next that I misheard you when you said you were a talent scout."

"No. That was right," I reply.

"So, you do work for the UK Ladies' Hockey Federation?" the constable asks me.

I nod and say, "That's right. I'm scouting for this year's UK trials."

The constable makes a note in his pocketbook and then asks, "Do you have any ID or credentials to confirm this, sir?"

I make a pretense of checking my pockets before saying, "Oh, I must have left them in my car. If you can give a me a minute, I'll be right back with them."

I turn to leave but the constable asks me to wait. "Probably best if I go with you, sir. The quicker we clear this up, the quicker we can all be on our way."

We casually walk back towards the school gates. The constable stays by my side and Eric Richards awkwardly lurks just a few paces behind us. For the sake of normalcy, I make some small talk about the weather, the state of the economy, and the start of the upcoming football season.

Ten feet from the gates, I stop and ask the constable if he was much of an athlete or a footballer himself in his school days.

"No, not really," he replies. "I was on the tennis and badminton teams as a teen, but I haven't really had the time for much sport since leaving school."

"Really?" I ask, doing my best to sound surprised. "I had you down as a bit of a track star. Or cross-country maybe?"

"No, God, no," he replies with a laugh. "I bloody hate running."

"Good," I say with a smile. "I was hoping you were going to say that."

Before he can ask what I mean, I'm already through the gate and running as fast as my legs will carry me. Behind me, Eric Richards frantically urges the young copper to give chase.

But I'm already too far ahead for him to have any chance of catching up with me. To be safe, though, I run until I'm absolutely certain that I'm not being pursued. Then, conscious that I may miss Catherine leaving school, I double back on myself and find a position in an alleyway with a partial view of the school gates.

Although I'm taking a risk coming back, it's highly unlikely that the boys in blue are going to send out a task force to hunt me down any time soon. At the end of the day, bullshit is hardly the crime of the century. And with only the word of the deputy headmaster to go on, what would they even arrest me for?

Confident that nobody is going to waste time or energy looking for me, I observe for the next ten minutes as a steady stream of spectators and players exit the school in cars and on foot to make their way home. Just when I'm starting to think that Catherine may have already left, she finally appears at the gate, but my heart sinks when I see that she is not alone.

For a full twenty minutes she stands chatting with two of her friends. Then, to my great relief, they finally hug, and her friends leave her alone at the gate.

Another few minutes pass, and it's beginning to look like Catherine might be waiting for someone else, until she checks the time on her watch and puts a set of headphones over her ears. Checking that the traffic is clear, she crosses the street. I ready myself to follow when, to my dismay, she suddenly turns and walks towards the very same alley that I'm waiting in.

My plan had been to follow until we were somewhere quiet. But all I can do now is look the other way and hope she keeps walking. Thankfully, she passes me without looking back and I fall in about twenty feet behind her.

Other than changing her hockey boots for a comfortable pair of Nikes, she's still dressed in her full hockey kit comprising knee-length turquoise socks, a matching skirt, and a long-sleeved white polo shirt. Her hair is scraped back in a tight ponytail and she is wearing a pink backpack adorned with a handful of fluffy animal mascots hanging from the zipper.

In her left hand she is holding an iPod and in her right hand she has her hockey stick. Knowing what I know about Catherine Swain, I make a mental note to steer clear of her right hand, before I call out to her.

"Catherine. It's Catherine, right?"

When she doesn't respond, I look at the iPod and call myself an idiot. Then, taking a huge risk, I tap her on the shoulder, before moving well out of hockey-stick range.

Shocked at my touch, Catherine spins around and pulls off her headphones to confront me. Recognition is instant. Before I can say anything, she drops her iPod and grasps her hockey stick defensively in both hands.

"Woah, there's no need for that," I say. "You've nothing to fear from me. I'm–"

"I know who you are," Cath interrupts, with surprising confidence and attitude for a girl so young. "I saw you looking at me at the game. And Mr. Richards told me that you were asking about me. Is that true?"

"It's true," I say. "But not for any bad reason. Now, is there any chance that you can lower that stick please? It's making me nervous."

Cath shakes her head. "What do you want? I don't even know you. I want to go hom–"

"But I know you," I reply. "And all I want is a picture with you."

I show her the Polaroid camera. "I'm a hockey fan and that was an amazing run today."

Catherine tries to smile, but I can see that she is uncomfortable and much less sure of herself than before.

I try to reassure her by adding, "If it makes you feel safer, you can raise that stick ready to hit me if I try anything."

My comment makes her laugh slightly, but it's a nervous laugh. "Just a picture and then I can go?" she asks, now sounding scared.

"I promise, just a picture and then I'm gone."

Without waiting for her response, I walk slowly forward and move close in against her. Her body is trembling, and I suddenly feel like an absolute bastard for scaring her like this. I'm so close, though, to what I need. Ignoring my feelings of guilt, I awkwardly turn the camera towards us. In a lame attempt to ease the tension, I say, "One, two, three … and … cheese," before pressing firmly down on the shutter button.

The picture starts to emerge from the camera and Catherine takes a step away from me. "There, you've got your picture. I want to go home now please."

"Just a moment," I say. "The picture is actually for you. Here, take it."

"No," she protests. "I don't want it. Please, I just want to go home."

"You can go home," I say. "But take the picture and put it in your purse."

Tears are starting to form, and Catherine asks, "But why? I don't understand. What do you want?"

"Honestly, Cath. I don't want—"

"How do you know my name?" she asks through teary eyes. "Please, what do you want from me?"

I shake my head and give what I hope is a reassuring smile. "I honestly don't want anything from you. Other than for you to take the picture and to promise to keep it safe in your purse. I know things are not making sense now, but they will in the future. Please, Catherine, take the photograph?"

She cautiously extends her arm towards me and I hand her the photograph. "Before you go, you need to promise that you will keep that safe in your purse?"

At this point she would probably say anything to be rid of me, but I know Cath well enough to know that she will keep the picture anyway. Even if only to hunt me down in the future or simply to satisfy her curiosity. Predictably, she nods and promises to keep the picture safe. "Now, can I go please?"

"Yes, of course," I reply. "And I'm sorry again if I scared you. It wasn't intentional, but it will make sense ... eventually."

Catherine wipes her eyes with her sleeves and then turns to leave. I notice that her iPod is still on the floor and I bend over to pick it up, "Wait, you forgot your iP—"

My words are abruptly cut off by the full weight of the hockey stick crashing down onto my left shoulder.

"You picked the wrong bloody girl to mess with, mister. I'm a police cadet and I know how to defend myself."

Unable to react in time, I'm powerless as Catherine raises the stick again and slams it into the side of my left arm. Although stunned, I grab for the stick with my right arm to stop her from hitting me again.

Upright, she has the advantage and easily wrenches the stick away from my grasp. She turns to run and for no other reason than instinct, I lunge for her backpack.

"Cath, no. You were never in any danger," I manage to get out.

Pulling herself free and spinning almost one hundred and eighty degrees, the hockey stick in Catherine's hand is moving at such speed that the result is almost a foregone conclusion.

It strikes the side of my head with a sickening crack and my eyes almost explode out of their sockets.

For a moment, I remain on my knees stunned. I'm frozen to the spot staring at Catherine who has turned as white as a sheet and is near hysterical. "I'm sorry. I'm sorry. I didn't mean for that to happen. Please, I'm sorry. I'm so sorry …"

Although rapidly losing consciousness, I'm aware of something wet wending its way down the side of my face and of the metallic smell of fresh blood in my nostrils. Forcing myself to look up, I try to smile. "It's okay. It wasn't your fault, but maybe you should go for help now."

Hesitating to move and knowing that I don't have long left, I urge her to leave. "Go on, Cath. Go. I'll be fine until you get back."

Reluctantly accepting my assurance, she nods and then rushes past me back towards the school shouting for help. I have no idea whether she has gone far enough for me to be out of sight, but the decision is already out of my hands. With any remaining strength gone I lurch forward and land face-first on the paved surface of the road with another sickening thud.

In the distance I think I hear voices and the sound of approaching footsteps. But if anyone is coming to help, they are already too late. I close my eyes; darkness comes, and I am gone.

Present Day – Early Morning
Sunday, May 6th, 2018

Ben is preoccupied with his phone and only realizes I am awake when I clear my throat and ask him the time.

"It's dark—how long was I out for?"

"Oh, thank God for that," Ben replies. "You were gone for just over eight hours. It's nearly one in the morning." Then, pointing to Catherine, "I take it you found her? She started crying fifteen minutes ago."

I pull myself upright and turn towards Catherine. Her mouth is still covered with the duct tape, and although not crying now, it's clear from her puffy eyes that she has been.

"Why is she still gagged?" I ask.

"I tried taking it off, but she kept threatening me. I was worried that she would wake you."

I move closer to Catherine and quietly say, "I'm going to take this off now. Is that okay?"

With all earlier defiance gone, she meekly nods.

While I carefully remove the tape I tell Ben to make himself useful. "Make some tea and a pot of strong coffee. Oh, and get me a glass of water as well. My mouth is drier than a badger's chuff."

While Ben is busy in the kitchen, I cautiously cut away the tape holding Catherine to the chair and remove the handcuffs.

Just a few hours earlier, this would have been the cue for her to punch me in the face, but the Catherine sitting in front of me now looks both mentally and physically drained.

Twice she tries to speak, but the words fail to come and instead she sobs uncontrollably. Unsure of whether it is appropriate to hug her, I do what I think is the next best thing and hand her a box of tissues.

"Take whatever time you need, Cath. It's a lot to take in, I know. Why don't you use the bathroom and wash your face? The coffee should be ready in a minute and then we can talk."

Wiping the corner of her eyes with a tissue, Catherine stands up and quietly says, "Yes. I will. Thank you."

She leaves and I join Ben in the kitchen. He hands me a glass of water and asks, "How was it? I'm guessing pretty traumatic judging by the tears."

"Yeh, you could say that," I reply. "She caved my skull in with a hockey stick. Obviously, not the ending I was looking for."

Ben grimaces at my comment and says, "Fuck, that can't have been good. Has she said anything yet?"

"Nothing yet. She's in the bathroom freshening up. How long for that tea and coffee?"

Ben points to the coffee pot and two cups, "It's done. Grab hold of that and I'll bring your tea. Just one sugar, right?"

■　■　■　■　■　■　■

When we get back to the living room, Catherine is already there and is reading the note that she signed earlier. She looks up and I ask her if she would like some coffee.

"Thank you, that would be nice," she replies softly.

She places the note back down on the table and Ben puts a steaming cup of black coffee down in front of her. The welt on his cheek has started to mottle with the early indications of bruising and as Cath picks up her drink, she screws up her face slightly. "Thanks for the coffee, Ben … and well, I'm sorry about your face."

Laughing it off, Ben says, "It's okay. I had it coming."

Catherine also laughs slightly and agrees. "Yes you did." Then, turning to me with a small spark of her old self in her eyes, adds, "You both bloody did."

Her words, though, start to break up. To head off any more tears, I point to the note. "Does that make sense now?"

Catherine shakes her head. "It makes a damn sight more sense than it did earlier, but what do you expect me to say, Sean? I've just had my world turned on its head and I really don't know if I'm coming or going."

"You remember me, though?" I ask.

"I remember a stranger asking me for a picture when I was a kid and I remember …"

Her words break again with the emotion and she takes a moment to wipe her eyes before continuing, "I remember being bloody terrified and of a guy on his knees with blood all over his face. And I remember coming back with help only to find you gone and not a single trace of blood on the ground. Just my iPod and a bloody Polaroid camera."

"And that's exactly how it happens, Cath. Remember what I told you earlier about how we travel."

"But it's not possible," Catherine pleads.

"Not in your world, Cath. But it is possible in mine." Then, pointing to Ben, I add, "and it is possible in his. You know it was me. You've just said as much yourself. You just said, I remember coming back with help only to find you gone. You said, you gone, not him gone. You know it was me, Cath. Read the note again."

Catherine shakes her head. "I don't need to read the note again. I know what it says, and it's not proof that I'm not mad. It's a note written by you that I signed under duress. Nothing more."

"So, you still don't believe any of this?"

"It's not a case of not believing, Sean. I'm just … I'm just struggling to take all of this in. For years I convinced myself that I'd either imagined it all, or there was some other logical explanation for what happened to me that day. But, it …"

107

I finish her sentence and say, "But it never made sense until twenty minutes ago when you remembered and recognized the guy you met in the alley across from your school in 2003?"

Catherine rubs her eyes and then says, "Yes, I mean no … I mean maybe. No, I don't know what I mean. This makes no sense. None of this is possible."

"It is possible, and it was me, Catherine. I went to sleep in front of you and I travelled back to 2003, to the day that you scored the winning goal in the hockey match against St. Margaret's College. Everything happened in exactly the way that I told you it does. Did you keep the photograph?"

"The what?"

"The Polaroid photograph—I gave it to you in the alley." I point to her purse. "Is it in there?"

Catherine shakes her head and pulls her bag closer to her.

"No, you don't still have it, or no, you never had it, or no, you don't want to admit you have it?" I ask.

When she remains silent, I point again to the bag. "The answer to all your questions, Cath, is in there. I know you well enough to know that your curiosity wouldn't have allowed you to get rid of it. Open the bag, Cath, and look at the picture."

As she is still hesitant to face the truth, I gently ask her to give me the bag. "Let me help you with that. Is the picture in your purse?"

Reluctant to hand over the bag, Catherine shakes her head. "It's okay. I'll do it myself."

She takes out a wallet-sized photograph album from her handbag and reluctantly hands it to me. "It's tucked inside the back cover."

I remove the small photograph and place it on the table. Ben leans forward for a better look and, without thinking, he smiles and says, "Wow, you were a bit of a cutie, Catherine."

Straightaway, he receives two disapproving looks and tries hard to backtrack. "I mean, what I meant to say is, that it's a pretty good picture for a Polaroid. Good quality, I mean."

After fifteen years, the picture is in fact creased and dog-eared and the colors have faded. But it clearly shows me as I look now with Catherine as she looked fifteen years ago, and I say to her, "This is your proof that you didn't imagine what happened and that you're not mad, Cath. You've been carrying this photograph around for fifteen years wondering what the truth was. Well, now you have it."

Deep down, I'm sure that she knows I'm right, but her strong sense of logic won't allow her to admit it yet. To divert the subject, she points to the coffee pot and Ben tops her up.

I allow her a moment to think, then I try again.

"You know it was me, don't you? You know there is no other possible explanation why you've been carrying a picture of me in your purse for fifteen years. Look at the picture, Catherine, and tell me that it's not me standing next to you."

She reluctantly looks down at the photograph and starts to tear up again. "It certainly looks like you, and I can't explain how ... but it can't be—it's just not possible. These things are not possible."

I nod my head sympathetically. "Believe me, Cath, ten years ago I would have said the same. Then one night I woke up and I wasn't in my bed anymore. I was ten years in the past, scared and alone, with no idea how I'd got there. It took me years to fully understand what was happening to me, so I'm not expecting you to be suddenly relaxed about this. I am asking you, though, to open your mind to the idea that this is real and that dream travel is possible. Can you do that for me?"

Catherine looks up from her coffee cup and shakes her head again. "Sean, you don't know how badly I want for all of this to be real. Accepting it is real would make sense of everything that happened on that day fifteen years ago. More importantly, it would make sense of everything that has happened in the past few months."

She looks at me and half smiles. "It would mean that I could trust you again. But ... I need time and I need more to convince myself that I'm not going mad."

I laugh with relief at this sign of progress. "You're not going mad," I assure her. "And what if I said I had something else that might help convince you?"

Both Catherine and Ben look questioningly at me, and I reach into my trouser pocket for the small item I had placed there just after waking up. I extend my arm towards Catherine and with my palm face up, I slowly open my hand to reveal what I'm holding.

Catherine gasps and reaches for another tissue. Ben looks more confused than ever. "A fluffy pink elephant. What's that got to do with anything?" he asks.

I nod to Catherine, who tells him, "It's mine. I had a few of them on a backpack when I was a teenager." Then, turning to me, "I just thought I had lost that one. But it must have ..."

I nod. "Yeh, it must have come off when I tried to grab your stick so that you wouldn't hit me again." I hand the mascot to Catherine and she smiles sadly and says, "I'm so sorry, Sean."

"Sorry about what?" I ask. "You have nothing to be sorry about."

"About what happened in the alley. I didn't mean to hurt you that badly. It was just instinct. Did it really hurt?"

I laugh. "Only until I died."

In response, Catherine gives me a disapproving frown. "Arsehole! I'm trying to be serious, and I'm trying to apologize for hurting you."

"It's fine, Catherine, honestly. If it wasn't for you smashing my head in with your hockey stick, it would have been some equally horrific ending for me. Remember what I told you about how I get back from the dreams?"

She nods and then says, "So, what now? Where do we go from here?"

"We put things right," I reply.

"You can stop the escape?"

I nod. "Yes. But if I travel back to stop the escape, I will also still need to make things right with you and that's where things get messy."

"In what way?"

"Because if I go back to before the escape, I've no idea if you will remember meeting me in 2003, or indeed if it ever even happened. Dream travel has an inevitable impact on timelines and events that even I still don't fully understand."

I remind her about our investigations into the murder of Anthony Glennister by Paul Donovan. "You remember how I told you about being my own prime suspect at one point. Well, that's what I'm talking about. It can get bloody messy."

"Yes, I can see that. So, what are you suggesting?" Catherine asks.

Although I'm not yet sure of the full details, I do have the outline of a plan, which I share with Catherine and Ben. The climax to the plan is not what either of them were expecting.

Shocked and unconvinced, Catherine shakes her head and rejects the plan out of hand. "No. No, I can't do that."

Ben looks at me for confirmation and when I return his look steadily, he says, "Holy fuck, you're serious, aren't you?"

"I've never been more serious, Ben. That bastard has been plaguing me for far too long. It's the only way."

Ben thinks for a second and then nods. "Yeh, I suppose so. I just wasn't expecting that. So, where do I come into this? You promised that I co–"

"I know what I promised," I interrupt. "But this is about as dangerous as it gets. So, for now, you're out of it. If I think of anything you can help with, I'll let you know."

Cutting off his protest before it's begun, I raise a hand and turn to Catherine. "If we want this to end, it's the only way I can think of right now. What do you say?"

In response to my question, Catherine stands up and picks up her handbag. "I'm a police officer, Sean, and so are you. We both took an oath to uphold and enforce the law. What you are suggesting goes against every principle I hold dear. I can't do it."

She starts to leave, and I call after her, "But, it's the only way, Cath. It's all I have for now."

"Then find another way," she replies curtly. "Until then I'm going to cancel my leave and go back to work on Monday, and I'll do things my way. And that means following the letter of the law."

I follow her into the hallway and plead for her to reconsider my plan. "You'll never find Douglas, Cath. He'll be long gone by now."

"Maybe so," Catherine replies. "But at least I won't have betrayed my principles to stop him, Sean."

As she opens the door, I plead, "Just promise me you'll think about it."

Ignoring my plea, she wishes me a good night. "It's nearly two in the morning, Sean. I'm going home to bed and I suggest you go to bed too."

"Okay, but you'll be in touch?"

Catherine looks at me sadly and slowly shakes her head. "I don't know. Just please don't call me again."

With that, the door shuts and I'm left pondering whether tonight has gone better or worse than expected. On balance—and given the fact that neither Ben nor I have been arrested for kidnap—I decide that it has gone about as well as could be expected.

I rejoin Ben in the living room, and he points to the photograph, which is still on the table. "She forgot to take it with her."

I pick up the photograph and shake my head. "She didn't forget it, Ben. Catherine doesn't forget anything, and she only held onto this in the hope of someday finding the answers to make sense of it. Like it or not she found those answers tonight.

"Anyway, I'm knackered. I'm going to bed. You can flop on the sofa if you want. If you wake up before me, just let yourself out. I'll call you in a couple of days."

Before turning off the living room light, I hand him a woolen blanket. "Thanks for your help tonight, Ben. Goodnight."

He takes the blanket and smiles mischievously. "What, no bedtime story, Daddy?"

My glare says it all and Ben says, "Right, yeh, it's late. Goodnight, Sean."

Present Day – Sunday, May 6th, 2018

Annoyed to see Ben still asleep, I kick the side of the sofa and shout, "Oy, dipshit, what the fuck are you still doing here?"

Instead of answering, he grunts something unintelligible, rolls over to face the wall, and pulls the blanket over his head. In no mood for exercising patience this morning, I roughly pull away the blanket and then piss myself laughing at the sight of his skinny white body clad only in a pair of Looney Tunes boxer shorts.

"Jesus Christ, Ben, I've seen more meat on a butcher's pencil. And would it hurt you to go out in the sun once in a while?"

Unimpressed, he sulkily sits up and pulls on his jeans and a t-shirt. "Fuck you, Dad. It was hot during the night. What time is it?"

"It's already gone twelve," I reply. "So, get your ass in gear and piss off. There is a pint and a pub lunch somewhere with my name on it and I'm not leaving you here to eat me out of house and home. You're like a bloody human locust."

At the mention of food, Ben's eyes light up and he laughs. "Yeh, I can't argue with that. I could just eat a nice Sunday roast washed down with a couple of cold bevvies right now."

"Really? Well, good luck with that because you're not coming with me. I've got a lot of thinking to do and I don't need you hanging around making a nuisance of yourself. Now get a bloody move on."

"Yeh, yeh," Ben says as he pulls on his sneakers. "I know when I'm not wanted. Make sure you call me, though. I want to help if I can."

I walk with him to the front door and assure him that I will call if he's needed. "Just sit tight and I'll be in touch. And no funny business, okay?"

"Funny business?" Ben asks with feigned innocence.

"I mean, no suddenly turning up in one of my dreams, arsehole. This shit is already fucked up enough without you making it more complicated."

With a parting curt nod, I close the door on Ben's smirking face and go back into the living room. For a moment I think about calling Catherine to see how she is but decide against it and put my phone back down on the coffee table.

"Nope, probably not a good idea, Sean. Better to give her some more time to get her head around things. Relax and enjoy the rest of the day. You have all the time in the world."

■ ■ ■ ■ ■ ■ ■

My chosen venue for lunch is The Swan Pub in Walton on Thames. Dating back to 1770, the pub has that charming olde-worlde feel that I like. With tables in the garden overlooking the river and the sun shining, it could hardly be more idyllic.

But I'm not just here for the beer, the food, and the ambience. Ten minutes after taking a seat at my table, my eyes light up when I see Maria coming into the garden.

Although casually dressed in comparison to when I last saw her, I am still taken aback at how effortlessly beautiful she is. I stand up to meet her and, with early-stage-relationship butterflies going crazy in my stomach, I nervously kiss her on both cheeks and whisper in her ear, "You look amazing, Maria. As always."

Blushing slightly, Maria modestly brushes off the compliment and looks down to her shoes. "Thanks, but hardly amazing. These flats make me look like a munchkin. I couldn't face heels today, though. I hope that's okay?"

"Of course it's okay," I reply. "And thanks for accepting the offer of lunch at such short notice. I hate to eat alone."

I pull out one of the chairs for her to sit down; but, before taking a seat, Maria looks over her shoulder towards the entrance, and then back to me.

"Actually, and speaking of eating alone, I hope you don't mind, but I brought ..."bit

The rest of her words are lost to me as I spot Ben striding towards us grinning more broadly than the Cheshire Cat. Nonplussed, I turn back to Maria, who is smiling sweetly.

"You don't mind, do you, Sean? Ben worked a double shift last night in the petrol station and he only got home just over an hour ago. I was going to cook for us both, but your invitation was too good to turn down."

Knowing that I'm in no position to object if I want to keep Maria sweet, Ben confidently takes a seat and picks up the menu. Hiding my irritation, I smile at Maria and lie through my teeth. "I don't mind at all. The more the merrier, in fact."

Then to Ben, I comment, "Good to see you again, mate. You must be starving after working all night."

"Yeh, just a bit," Ben replies with a smirk. "The bloke I work with is a right lazy bastard. He spent half the night asleep while I was working, so I barely had time for a cup of coffee."

I raise my eyebrows and say, "Hmm, he sounds like a bit of a tit. Perhaps you should find yourself a new line of work?"

Ben looks up from the menu and shakes his head. "Nah. He is a tit, but he'd struggle without me."

Picking up on the vibes, Maria asks, "What are you two talking about? Come on, what's the joke?"

Ben shakes his head. "Nothing, Mum. Just a bit of banter." Then to change the subject, he points to the faded bruising left over from my run-in with Paddy Newman and Rosemary Pinois. "What happened there, Sean? Have you been scrapping again?"

Maria looks to me for an answer and surprises me by saying, "We saw something in the news on Friday about a prisoner escape. Was that anything to do with you and Clive Douglas? Do we have anything to worry about?"

With a swift 'you'll keep' look cast at Ben, I smile reassuringly at Maria. "The only thing you need to worry about is whether or not you're going to have room for dessert. The roasts in here are big enough to choke a goat. Now come on, I'm starving. Let's order."

"Amen to that," says Ben. "My stomach feels like my throat's been cut. Get the drinks in, Sean."

■ ■ ■ ■ ■ ■ ■ ■

Six pints, three glasses of wine, three roast dinners and three desserts later, we are all fit to burst. In a moment of silence, Ben loudly burps and then laughs, much to the annoyance of Maria.

"Oh, Ben. That's disgusting. Where are your manners?"

"They do say, better out then in, Mum."

Maria looks to me for support, but I'm warming to Ben. Much as I hate to admit it, we share more than just blood and our ability to dream travel. We also share a twisted sense of humor.

Rather than offering support, I say, "Actually, Maria. In some countries it's considered polite to burp after eating. It lets your host know how much you enjoyed the meal."

Ben nods his agreement. "Yeh, I heard that too. Go on, Sean, I think you should burp as well."

"Don't you bloody dare, Sean McMillan," Maria says with a laugh. "If you do, I'll leave you both here to burp all over each other."

The extra emphasis Maria uses with my name makes me smile and for a moment our eyes meet across the table. The moment is quickly lost, though, when Ben exclaims, "Oh God, give it a break, you pair. Any more of that and I'm going to be bringing up my lunch. And trust me, that won't be pleasant."

In response, I wink at Ben and blow him a kiss. "Ah, you're just jealous. Don't be, though. I'm sure there's a desperate girl out there somewhere for you."

To Ben's obvious annoyance, Maria, who is a little bit tipsy, chuckles at my comment. Ben shakes his head at her and then says to me, "Yeh. Good one, schmuck. How about a last drink before we split?"

I'm already on my feet and say, "Sure. I need to use the bathroom anyway. Hang tight here and I'll order on my way."

. . . .

When I get back to the bar, the drinks are ready, but they are not the only thing waiting for me. Catherine casually looks up from her glass of wine and gestures towards the beer garden.

"I never really had you down as the family type, Sean. Well, not until recently anyway."

Shocked to see her, I stumble over my reply, "Cath, what … why … I mean what are you doing here? How did you know where to find me?"

She holds up her cell phone and smiles. "An idea I got from you. The Apple 'Find my iPhone' app. I called Darren Phillips to get your iCloud address and password."

"Fair enough," I say. "But why are you here? Have you had a change of heart? Let me finish with Maria and Ben and we can ta–"

"Sean, I haven't had a change of heart," Catherine interrupts. "There is something I want you to do, though."

She hands me a small plastic bag marked with the branding of Boots the Chemist.

Puzzled, I ask, "What is it?"

"It's the final piece of confirmation I need, Sean. There are two home DNA paternity kits in the bag. I want you and Ben to use one each. You just need to take a swab from inside your cheek and then seal them up in the airtight bags."

"And then?" I ask.

"Then, just leave it to me. I've a couple of friends in the lab that owe me a favor. I can get the results back in less than twenty-four hours. One way or another, by tomorrow, I'll know for sure if you've been telling me the truth."

I'm about to ask another question but pause when Maria appears on her way to the bathroom. When she sees us together, she stops and says with a smile, "Catherine, how lovely to see you." Then, frowning at me, "Sean didn't say that you were coming. You could have joined us for lunch."

Tactfully taking the bag from me, Catherine returns the smile and says to Maria, "Actually it was a spur of the moment thing. Sean mentioned this morning that he was having lunch here. I was passing and just dropped in to update him on a couple of things we are working on."

"But you'll stay for a drink?" Maria asks.

"I think Catherine is in a hurry," I reply looking to her for agreement.

"No, no hurry," Catherine says. "That would be lovely, thank you."

Smiling at us both, Maria nods. "Great. That's settled then. I'll see you both in the garden."

While Maria goes to the ladies, I ask Catherine what she is playing at. "Just leave me the kits. I'll get the swabs to you later today."

Catherine rips the top off one of the boxes and hands me the other. "No time like the present, Sean. Come on, let's get this done before she gets back."

119

I follow Cath out to the garden and Ben gets to his feet when he sees us both coming. "What the fuck? What's she doing here, Sean?"

Catherine thrusts a long cotton-tipped swab into Ben's hand. "She, Ben, has come to find out once and for all if you really are the result of an encounter between your mum and DS McMillan in 1994. Now take a good swab from inside your cheek and then drop it into this bag."

"What? What are you on about?" Ben blurts.

I've already completed my swab and hand Catherine the sealed bag. 'It's a home paternity test," I explain, "Just get on with it before your mother gets back."

When he still hesitates, Catherine holds out her hand for the swab. "Unless you prefer for me to do it for you?"

Ben shakes his head. "No, that's okay. I'd like to keep my face in one piece, if that's alright with you?" He puts the swab into his mouth and wipes the tip against the inside of his cheek until Catherine is satisfied.

"Okay, that's enough. Drop it in here."

Just before Maria gets back to the table, Catherine takes a third swab from her pocket and unwraps it. She picks up Maria's empty wine glass and we watch as she swabs the sides of the glass. She closes the bag and I ask if that was necessary.

She shakes her head. "No. Not strictly speaking necessary, but while I'm here it would be a shame to miss the opportunity. Right—put a smile on your face. She's coming back."

As Maria sits down, there is an uneasy silence and she asks jokingly, "What's going on. Did somebody die?"

I start to reply, but Catherine stops me, "Actually, it was my fault, Maria. I think I embarrassed your two boys here."

"Really?" Maria asks with a questioning frown and a small laugh. "I haven't been able to get much of a word in for the last couple of hours. What was it you said that managed to make them so quiet?"

Catherine shrugs. "Oh, nothing much. I just asked Sean if he was planning to pop the question anytime soon, and I asked Ben if he would be okay having Sean as a stepfather."

While Maria looks questioningly at me and Ben, I half-scowl at Catherine and say, "Cheers for that, mate. Way to put a guy well and truly on the spot."

Maria smiles at me and then turns to Catherine. "I'm not sure I would say yes, anyway. I still haven't quite worked him out yet."

To regain control of the conversation, I raise my glass and toast the group, "Here's to good friends and always having each other's back."

Catherine nods at Maria. "I hear you there, Maria. Our Sean McMillan is quite the mystery man," and then she looks directly at me with her own glass raised, "Anyway, here's to good friends and always having each other's back."

Present Day – Monday, May 7th, 2018

Thankful for the rest of the afternoon passing off without further sly comment or incident, I finally part company with the others just over an hour after Catherine's arrival. We are all in high spirits.

Before leaving, Cath promises to get in touch with me as soon as the results are in. So, with nothing else to do but wait, I polish off half a bottle of red and a couple of whiskeys that night in front of the TV before going to bed.

Today is another day, and I'm like a cat on a hot tin roof waiting for news. When at 2 pm I still haven't heard anything from Cath, I put on my running kit and smash out a 10k along the banks of the Thames to kill some time.

When I still haven't heard anything by seven, I risk her wrath and call her. The call goes straight to answerphone, but a few minutes later she calls back and angrily chastises me. "I bloody told you to wait for my call, Sean."

"Yeh, I know. I'm sorry, I was just wonde–"

"I know what you're wondering, but I was busy all day, and I was on another call just now. And may I remind you that I'm going out on a limb for you, Sean. So how about you do as you're told and don't make things harder for me?"

I hastily apologize. "Sorry, yes, you're right, Cath. I really appreciate everything you're doing for me. I didn't mean to–"

Cutting me off again, Catherine says, "Forget it. I guess I'd probably do the same if I was in your shoes. Anyway, we need to talk again. Put the coffee on, I'll be up in a few minutes."

"Sorry?" I ask. "Where are you?"

"I'm just parking outside your building. A sandwich or some beans on toast would be nice as well. I'm bloody starving."

■ ■ ■ ■ ■ ■ ■

Not wishing to annoy her or to appear like I'm only looking out for myself, I let Catherine finish her sandwich with nothing more than a few general pleasantries to break the silence.

When she finally puts the empty plate down on the kitchen counter, I venture to ask a question, "Any progress today with tracking down Clive Douglas?"

Catherine takes a sip of her coffee and then opens her purse. Shaking her head, she hands me an envelope, "The samples match to a 99.8% probability. Maria is Ben's mother, as we knew all along. And you, Sean—and God help the boy—are indeed his father."

Not needing to see the test results myself, I place the envelope on the counter. "So, you believe me now about everything else?"

Rubbing her forehead, Cath slowly nods. "This certainly goes a long way to explaining everything that has happened, but I'm still going to need some time to fully get my head around it."

"Of course. Take as much time as you need."

"And don't expect me to apologize for anything, Sean. Nobody else would have believed you either."

I shake my head. "Understood. I do want to apologize to you again, though."

"For what?" Catherine asks with a smirk. "For lying to me constantly, for making me think I was delusional, or for assaulting and kidnapping me?"

I think about if for a second and then say, "I think all of the above. I really am sorry, Cath. At least now, though, you understand why all of that was necessary. Am I forgiven?"

Cath tuts to herself before saying slowly, "I accept your apology, but I'll reserve judgment on the forgiveness. You've still got work to do to earn that."

It's not quite what I was looking for but having her accept my apology is a good start. I smile and ask, "Friends again?"

Putting down her coffee cup, Catherine holds open her arms, "We were always friends, Sean. Come here, arsehole."

We embrace and I kiss her on the cheek and whisper in her ear, "Thank you, Cath. This means a lot." Then I cheekily add, "It also means that I'm your boss again, DC Swain."

Pushing me away, Cath laughs and shakes her head. "You had to have the final word, didn't you, Sean? Bloody hell, you're infuriating at times. I might just put in for a transfer to spite you."

I shake my head. "Nah, you don't want to do that. You would soon miss me. I am looking forward to working with you again, Cath."

She nods and smiles politely. "Me too, Sean. But let's take one thing at a time, yes?"

I nod. "Sure. So, what now? Any progress with Douglas today?"

"Not much," Cath admits. "We're confident that we know where he landed, but after that the trail goes cold. Our counterparts over the water are following up for us, but I'm not hopeful of getting anything soon."

I shake my head. "Yeh, the Garda Síochána are not the fastest to respond to a request from the UK police—particularly when there might be a republican connection."

"No, Sean," Cath corrects me. "I'm not talking about the Garda. Our boy landed north of the border. I'm talking about the Police Service of Northern Ireland, the PSNI."

"Oh, wow!" I exclaim. "That probably means that there is a republican connection then. Where exactly did they land?"

Catherine takes a UK and Ireland roadmap from her handbag and points to a spot just over the border separating the north from the southern part of Ireland.

"Just here, three miles north-west of Newry in South Armagh, at a place called Bessbrook Mill. Until June 2007, it was a British military barracks and heliport. It was decommissioned as part of the Good Friday Agreement. Apparently, it's still mothballed."

"So, a bloody perfect place to land."

"What are you thinking?" Catherine asks.

I point to the main road and rail arteries running through Newry. "That's the A1, Dublin to Belfast Road, and this is the main rail network. With the border controls gone, Dublin and Belfast are both easy options by car and train. And from either place—"

Catherine finishes my sentence by saying, "From either place, it would be easy for them to disappear or take another flight to somewhere else."

"Exactly, Cath. You can be sure that Douglas would have had money and documents stashed away or available to him for an eventuality such as this. You're not hopeful that the PSNI are going to be much help?"

Catherine shakes her head. "It's not that. I'm sure they are doing everything they can. I just think that by the time they do make any progress, Douglas will be long gone. It's already been three days since the escape. For all we know, he could be in Australia by now."

I nod my agreement. "Just say the word, Cath, and we can do what we spoke about yesterday. Just say the word and all of this can be over."

"No, Sean. I've already told you that I won't do that. I won't compromise my own principles or stoop to the level of Clive Douglas."

"Then what?" I ask. "Because you are rapidly running out of time, Cath. You've just said it, Douglas and his buddies already have a three-day head start and the trail is getting colder by the minute."

Shaking her head in frustration, Catherine agrees.

"Yes, I know that, Sean. That's really why I'm here."

"Meaning?"

"Meaning, I could have texted you the paternity results, or told you over the phone. I didn't need to come here specifically just for that."

"So why are you here?" I ask. "You've already said that you don't want my help."

"That's not what I said," Catherine quickly corrects me. "I said I wasn't willing to go ahead with the plan we discussed yesterday. We do need your help, though. Well, what I mean to say is, I need your help. I need you to do your thing and find out where they went after landing at Bessbrook Mill."

"You want me to travel, Cath?"

She nods slowly. "Yes, I do. If we can at least find out where they were heading, then we may have a fighting chance of catching up with them." Pointing to my bedroom, she adds, "I need you to do it now, though."

I smile and point to my laptop at the end of the kitchen counter. "Okay, get on there and find out as much as you can about Bessbrook Mill. And find some recent pictures of it. I need a clear image as a stimulus to travel."

"Yes, you told me that. Go get yourself ready and I'll see what I can find."

Leaving her tapping away on the keyboard, I change into a pair of jeans, a black polo shirt, and dark blue running shoes. I empty my wallet of anything that could identify me and before rejoining Cath in the kitchen, I pick up a black leather jacket and reach inside a tear in my mattress to retrieve the unlicensed automatic last used to frighten Stuart Goldsmith.

When Catherine sees me return holding the gun, she simply shakes her head and turns back to the laptop. "I don't even want to know where you got that from."

"That's probably for the best," I say. "I've no idea what I'm heading into, though. The Troubles may be over, but South Armagh was bandit country back then, and there are still a lot of bad people around. Better to have something to fall back on if needed. We don't want my trip to be over before I've had a chance to find out where they went."

Without taking her eyes off the laptop screen, Catherine replies, "Like I said, Sean, I don't want to know. My priority is finding out where they went. So, just do whatever you need to do."

She then clicks the mouse on the laptop and my printer whirrs to life. "I've found a really good aerial shot of the mill and a nice fact sheet."

Catherine hands me the two sheets of paper and I commit as much detail to memory as I can. The fact sheet is mainly historical and describes the Mill's origins in textile production and its use by the British Military during The Troubles, but the aerial photograph is the clincher. It not only gives me useful insights into the Mill layout, but it also shows the surrounding area and topography. Confident that the image is clear in my mind, I tell Cath that I'm ready to go.

She follows me into the living room and watches as I pour myself a large glass of Jameson Whiskey.

"Given where you're going, I suppose that's more appropriate than a glass of Scotch. But is it really necessary?"

"Not so necessary recently," I admit. "But it does help me to travel. And it helps to steady the nerves."

I down the whiskey in one large gulp and lick my lips with a satisfied sigh. "And it's bloody delicious. Feel free to help yourself while I'm gone."

Catherine dismissively shakes her head. "I'm good, thanks."

"Suit yourself." Getting myself comfortable on the sofa, I say, "Right, Cath. Same drill as before. I've no idea how long this is going to take."

"That's okay," Cath says. "I'm not going anywhere. Before you go, though, I have a request to make. I want you to bring something back to prove that you were there."

"Really? You still don't believe that this is real?"

"No, I do believe you. But it's surreal and messing with my head. Just humor me please."

"Sure, no problem. Anything in particular you want?"

"No. I'll leave that to you, Sean. Just anything to say you were in Newry, or to prove you caught up with Clive Douglas."

I chuckle slightly and say, "Consider it done, Cath. Now, anymore requests before I go?"

"Not a request, but I do have one question," Cath replies. "When are you going to tell Maria that you're Ben's dad?"

The unexpected question makes me sit back up.

"Seriously, Cath? It was bloody traumatic enough telling you. I think it's going to be quite some time before I'm ready to have that conversation with Maria."

Catherine says drily, "Fair enough. But make sure I'm there when you do finally decide to tell her. I'll bring the popcorn and nachos—because that shit will be better than anything the movies have to offer."

I shake my head and raise my eyebrows. "Thanks, Cath. I knew you were a bloody sadist. Can I go now?"

She smirks and gestures for me to lie back down.

"Sure, be my guest. Safe travels and sleep tight, Sean."

The Past – Friday, 4th May, 2018

The sound of tires screeching on the tarmac and the smell of burning rubber filling my nostrils is unmistakable. I force open my eyes—but too late to move. I brace myself for impact as the driver of the oncoming car desperately wrestles with the wheel to avoid a collision. But we are so close that hitting me is inevitable. At the last second, I instinctively jump. The front bumper shatters my kneecaps and flips me forward onto the hood of the Mercedes and face-first through the windscreen.

Through a mist of blood and shattered glass, I can barely make out the young woman in the driving seat. Horrified at the sight of my terribly lacerated face protruding through the hole in her windscreen, she recoils and starts to scream hysterically.

Not wishing to die in front of her, I push desperately against the remnants of the windscreen to free myself. Sliding backwards down the hood towards the front of the car, I grab for the Mercedes Benz hood ornament to stop myself falling. Looking back towards the young woman, I force a smile and say, "This never happened, I wasn't here, it was all just a dream."

A split second later the ornament snaps off in my hand and I drop heavily onto the road. Although terribly hurt, I am still conscious and in danger of some do-gooder helping me out if I don't die quickly.

Desperate to leave, I drag myself almost twenty yards to the side of the road and painfully pull myself up to look down over the wall. Although I have right royally messed up by landing in the middle of the A1, fate has also handed me an opportunity for redemption by placing me on an overpass looking down onto the main Dublin to Belfast railway line.

With several cars stopping to help already, I pull myself up onto the wall with the last of my strength. Completely drained, I lie back and wait for my moment. I watch as two middle-aged men help the young woman to get out of the Mercedes.

She points in my direction and while one of them stays with her the other runs towards me clutching a small first-aid kit. It's going to take more than a couple of Band-Aids and a Panadol to help me, though. Turning away, I roll to the side and plummet from the bridge into the path of the oncoming Dublin to Belfast Express. By the time my rescuer gets to the wall and looks over, the train is gone, I'm gone, and there is no trace that I was ever there.

■ ■ ■ ■ ■ ■ ■

I wake up to find Catherine standing over me shaking my shoulders.

"Sean, what happened? You screamed. Are you hurt?"

I blink to adjust to the light and then take a deep breath.

"Cath, I'm fine. I told you, getting hurt in a dream doesn't affect me in the real world."

"Okay, so what happened? Why are you back? You were only out for a few minutes."

I show her the Mercedes hood ornament. "I fucked up, Cath. I landed in the middle of the bloody A1."

"You got run over?" Catherine exclaims. "You were killed by a car?"

I laugh and say, "Actually, I was killed by a train. But that's another story."

Incredulous, Catherine takes the ornament and then cringes when she realizes there's blood on it. "Cripes, this is so messed up."

"Yeh, tell me about it, Cath." Then, pointing to the ornament, I ask her, "Is that enough proof for you, or do you still need another souvenir from Ireland?"

"That will do for now," she replies. "What now?"

"You pass me that bottle of whiskey and photograph, and I try again."

Catherine obligingly pours me another large slug of Jameson while I memorize again the layout of Bessbrook Mill.

Confident that I now know every inch of the mill and surrounding area, I finish the whiskey, lie back down, and close my eyes.

"Okay, here we go again. Sean's trip to Bessbrook Mill, take two." Then after another deep breath, "4th May 2018, 4th May 2018, 4th May 20 …"

The Past – Friday, 4th May, 2018

This time, I don't need to open my eyes to know that I'm not in imminent danger of being mown down by a silver Mercedes or any other vehicle. The quiet serenity of the countryside is a stark contrast to the traffic of the A1 and in the far distance I can see the peaks of the Mourne Mountains.

Just ahead I can see the village of Bessbrook and behind that the familiar shape of the mill. I start to walk. As I pass through the village, I can't help but admire the chocolate-box granite cottages built for the original mill workers and now providing an air of peaceful tranquility that belies the recent turbulent past of this province.

Today, Ireland's recent past is not my main concern. Although walking as casually as I can to keep a low profile, my sudden presence in the village elicits a barrage of unsuppressed looks of suspicion from the locals as I pass on the street.

With hindsight I should have known that the presence of a stranger in such a close-knit, yet religiously divided, community was bound to raise a few eyebrows. Regretting not choosing to skirt around the village instead of walking right through the middle, I pick up the pace and focus on the mill ahead.

Behind me, three teenage boys on mountain bikes fall in behind and keep pace with me until we reach the edge of the village when one of them suddenly shouts, "Oy, mister, where are you going?"

Without looking back, I reply, "Just out for a walk, lads."

Hearing my accent, the boys ride past and then skid to a halt in front of me. The bigger of the three boys points accusingly at me. "You're a fucking Brit?"

There's no point in denying it, not with my accent, so I smile and say, "That's right. Is there a problem with that?"

"That all depends on you, mister," the boy replies. "There's a toll for Brits to pass through Bessbrook."

I look slowly at each of the three boys and then ask, "Is that right?"

The ringleader nods his head, "My da says it's to make up for what youse all did to us during the war. Reparations, he said."

"That's a big fancy word and The Troubles were a long time ago," I reply.

"Maybe to you, fella, but it's recent history to us," pipes up one of the other boys.

"That's right," the ringleader adds. Then, with a smirk at his mates, "So, if you want to pass through here, it's twenty quid … for each of us."

I raise my eyebrows. "And what If I don't pay and tell you all to fuck off?"

Looking at each other the boys all laugh, and their leader says to me, "Look over there. You can either pay up, or I can tell my da and his mates that you're a Brit. They'd be happy to tear you a new arsehole, mister."

To my left, a group of middle-aged and older men drinking outside a pub are starting to take an unhealthy interest in what is happening. Not wishing to hang around any longer than I need to, or to get involved in an unnecessary altercation, I reluctantly take out my wallet and remove two twenties and a ten.

"This is all I have. Take it or leave it."

The money is eagerly snatched from my hand and the ringleader moves his bike to one side to let me pass. When I get level with him, he holds out his hand for me to stop and asks, "So, why are you going to the mill? It's all closed up."

Feigning confusion, I shake my head. "I didn't say I was going to the mill. I'm just out for a walk."

Obviously not fooled, my questioner nods and says, "Yeh, sure you are mister." Lowering his hand, he lets me go.

The boys watch until I almost reach the top of the street. Just before turning the corner and moving out of sight, I casually look back over my shoulder to where the boys have now joined the older men outside the pub. It's clear from the body language and the gestures that fleecing the Brit is the hot topic of conversation.

Whatever they're plotting next, I'm in no mood to find out. I turn the corner and break into a run until I reach the barbed-wire-topped fence that marks the boundaries of Bessbrook Mill.

Two hundred yards further on I come to the entrance. The gate itself and the barbed wire on top are rusted, but the chain and padlock securing the gate look conspicuously new.

Worried that somebody may be watching the entrance, I casually turn away to find another way in. Luckily for me, most of the fence line is shielded by trees or heavy foliage. Teens or thieves have also cut the fence in numerous places, so I don't have to search for long to find a suitable entry point.

Deciding on a shielded vantage point overlooking the front of the mill and the landing pads, I pull aside a cut section of fence and settle down just inside the wire to observe.

Although long since abandoned, close up Bessbrook Mill is far more imposing than the photographs would have you believe. With its formidable granite walls rising four and five stories high, it looks more to me like a former Victorian prison than it does a former textile mill. In its military heyday with hundreds of flights coming and going every week it must have been quite a sight. Now it is deserted and overgrown. But not entirely.

Two brand-new Black Mercedes Sprinter panel vans are parked next to one of the landing spots and half a dozen middle-aged men are busy with stiff brooms and an electric strimmer readying the site for an imminent landing. One of the men is holding a radio and every now and then he looks upwards to scan the horizon.

The time is approaching 1.25 pm. The ambush was sprung at Gallows Corner at 11.25 am and Clive made his escape in the chopper around ten minutes later at 11.35. The flight-tracking information then confirmed an approximate landing time in Bessbrook of 1.28 pm. Realizing too late that I have no ready means of following them when they leave the mill, I quietly curse myself, "Fuck. I need a car."

In the distance, the very faint thump of rotor-blades becomes audible and the guy holding the radio lifts it to his ear and turns to face eastwards.

Knowing I probably only have five or ten minutes to blag myself a ride before they leave the mill, I pull up the cut section of fence and bend over to push my way back through. When I stand back up on the other side of the fence, four men and a teenager waiting in the shadows of the trees step out to meet me.

The same boy from earlier grins and confirms who I am. "Yep, that's him, Da. That's the fella."

Three of the men are holding various blunt objects to pummel me with, but the man referred to as 'Da' is armed with a sawn-off shotgun, which is pointed menacingly close to my chest.

Smiling, he moves closer and asks, "What's your business here, fella?" Then, turning his ear towards the sound of the rapidly approaching chopper, he adds, "As if I didn't fooking know already."

Gesturing for me to get down onto my knees, he orders his men to search me. My handgun is quickly found and is handed over to Da along with my wallet, which now contains just a five-pound note and a couple of crumpled old family photographs.

Tossing the empty wallet onto the ground, Da hands the shotgun to one of his friends. Pointing my own handgun in my face, he gestures upwards to the chopper that's making its landing approach. "So, mystery man, how about you tell me who you are and what business you have with our friends up there? Because I'm guessing you're not a cop and you're not undercover army."

In response, I shake my head. "I don't know what you're talking about. I was just snooping around to see if there was anything worth stealing in there. I panicked when I saw the vans and heard the helicopter coming. If you let me go, I'll be on my way and we'll say no more abo—"

The butt of the shotgun shatters my right cheekbone and, groggy, I'm pulled back up onto my knees. Da kneels down and grabs a fistful of my hair to wrench back my head. "You'd be wise not to play the smartarse with me, boy. I know ways of inflicting pain that you can only imagine in your worst nightmares. Now, how about you start by telling me your name?"

Reasoning with myself that it's better for me to die now and to start the dream again, I lift my head and spit in Da's face. "Fuck you, Paddy!"

Completely unemotional, Da stands up and wipes his face with the back of his sleeve. "That's okay, boy. We've plenty of time to get to the bottom of this. Conor, pass me your phone, son."

Da takes the phone from his son but is forced to wait for the sound of the helicopter engines to die down before he can make himself heard. "Yes, it's Pádraig," he confirms into the phone. "Pádraig Clancy, from Bessbrook. I'm Liam's brother. We have a small problem."

He tells whoever he's talking to about my unwelcome presence. There is a short pause and then he says, "Yes, that's what I said. He's a Brit. He was snooping around inside the mill, but tried to bolt when he heard the chopper coming in."

Then after another pause, "No. No ID on him, but he was carrying an automatic … No, he's definitely not security services.

The serial numbers on the piece have been wiped and he's too stupid to be MI5 or SAS."

The person he is talking to must have asked what I look like because Da looks me over and pulls a face. "I don't know. Five eleven to six feet, I guess. Dark hair, stubble, and a pasty complexion. Should we bring him to you?"

The call continues for another couple of minutes and all Da contributes to the mostly one-sided exchange before the call ends is, "Okay, sure, got it and understood."

Da hands back the phone to Conor and then tells his men to stand me up. Taking back his shotgun he pushes the barrel under my chin and says, "The good news, fella, is that our friends in the mill have no interest in you. The bad news, however, is that you're mine now and it's been a long time since I had a Brit to play with."

Before I can say anything or ask what he means, the wooden stock of the shotgun strikes me directly on the bridge of my nose. I fall forward with the taste of warm blood filling my mouth. Plasticuffs are forced onto my wrists and a black hood is roughly pulled over my head.

"Take the bastard to the farmhouse. I'll be along shortly with my tools."

∎ ∎ ∎ ∎ ∎ ∎ ∎

The ride to the farmhouse takes just a few minutes and it's clear as soon as my hood is removed that I'm not the first visitor to arrive here under such circumstances. The chair I'm in is bolted to the floor in a dingy outhouse and the shackles now constraining me are firmly attached to the chair. I couldn't get away now even if I wanted to. Resigned to a slow and painful death, I wait silently for Pádraig Clancy to arrive with his tool bag.

When he finally arrives after more than forty minutes, it is with another hard-looking man who takes half a dozen pictures of me on a cell phone before both men leave again.

I foolishly ask one of my captors what is happening. By way of a response I receive a vicious backhander across my already badly swollen right cheek and am told to shut my fucking Brit mouth. A moment later, Pádraig returns and hearing my moans asks what is going on.

Nodding towards me, my assailant grins and says, "Nothing, just this fucker trying to be a smartarse again. What's the craic anyway? Are we going to get on with it?"

To my obvious relief, Pádraig shakes his head. "Sorry Owen, not today. We sent his mugshot and it turns out that the boys want to see this fucker after all. Unlock him."

My shackles are removed and Owen, along with a second man, drags me out towards a waiting BMW. The guy who had earlier taken my picture is waiting next to it with two very intense-looking young men.

Holding up his cell phone for me to see one of the pictures, he says, "We've no idea how you got here so fast, Sean. But you're a long way from home and mark my words, son, you're going to bloody regret coming here."

Then to his lads, "Get him in the trunk, but put his hood back on and secure his hands first."

■ ■ ■ ■ ■ ■ ■ ■

After nearly two and a half hours of breakneck driving, we finally start to slow down. I carefully lift my head and press my ear against one of the side panels. For another ten minutes, all I can hear is the sound of the engine and other cars passing in the opposite direction. Then I hear a new sound. At first it is faint, and I think I might be mistaken. But then I hear it again and this time there is no mistake. I've heard squawking seagulls a hundred times before and this lot are squawking with the best of them. The smell of the sea confirms my suspicion and I surmise that we are probably somewhere on the west coast—possibly Mayo or Galway. But it could just as easily be another of the many ports on the Irish coast.

Shortly after this, we stop completely. There is a brief discussion, which I can't properly hear, before a metal gate creaks open and we move forward again and pick up speed. Within a few minutes we slow down once again, and I'm thrown to the back of the trunk as the front of the car abruptly inclines upwards. The sound of tires on a steel gangway reminds me of driving my own car onto a cross-channel ferry and I say to myself, "We're going on to a container ship or a freighter. Fuck, these cocky arseholes are not even in a hurry to get away."

■　■　■　■　■　■　■　■

Three hours later and I am still locked in the trunk of the BMW. I'm now badly dehydrated and much more concerned that my captors also don't appear to be in any particular hurry to deal with me.

Ordinarily, of course, dying unseen in the back of a car would have suited me down to the ground, but on this occasion, I've still no idea as to Clive's final destination. In fact, other than knowing that I am on a ship, I'm no further forward than I was before I started this trip. In an effort to remain conscious, I focus on the luminous dial on my watch and count as the second hand silently sweeps through three hundred and sixty degrees.

Another two hours pass, and I'm jolted back to reality by the soft rumble and vibration of the ship's turbine engines far below me. I feel the car move slightly as the ship slowly inches away from its berth and steers a course towards the open sea.

Hopeful that they will come for me soon, I focus again on the hands of my watch to stay awake.

In the end it's another thirty minutes before I hear voices and the sound of approaching footsteps.

Thirty seconds later, a remote-control key fob beeps and the boot springs open. Rough hands drag me upwards and the hood is yanked off my head. Overhead, a powerful halogen light blinds me, but the cold fresh air is welcoming. I hungrily gulp it in, before a fist in my stomach doubles me over.

"Enough of that, you fucker. That's the taste and smell of freedom, boy. Grab his arm, Ciaran."

Unable to stand properly, the two intense young men from earlier today drag me unceremoniously across what looks like a cargo deck and up three flights of narrow steel stairs. We emerge into the moonlight Illuminating the main deck and a scene that can best be described as surreal.

Half a dozen picnic benches are laid out on the rusting deck and a Mediterranean-looking chef in grubby whites is toiling over a pair of shiny new BBQ grills. Traditional Irish music is playing from a pair of small speakers and a dozen or so men are gathered around chatting and swigging from bottles of ice-cold beer.

When they see us coming, Clive Douglas puts down his beer bottle and tells one of the men to turn the music off. Then, indicating to the lads holding me up, he orders, "Take those off his wrists and sit him down over here."

The plasticuffs are cut away and I'm roughly pushed down into a cheap green plastic chair. Douglas sits down in a chair directly opposite and a third chair is taken by a stocky guy in his mid to late forties with a thick black moustache.

The balaclava concealing his face earlier today is gone, but I recognize the clothes and know it's the Irishman.

Noticing my spark of recognition, he smiles and says, "No hard feelings, McMillan. It was a job that's all."

"Executing a police officer was the job?" I ask.

"No, he was collateral damage. You can blame your boss for that. If she hadn't tried to play the hero, then I wou–"

"Enough," Douglas snaps impatiently. "Save your love story for later." Then, looking at me, he demands, "I want to know how the fuck you managed to get to Bessbrook before we did? And how did you know to come here?"

Playing for time, I slowly look around to see what clues I can find that could help us to locate them in the real world. Disappointingly, all I see is the rusting grey bridge of this hulk rising up in front of me and piles of nondescript shipping containers lining either side of the deck.

With no ship name or number visible anywhere, I ask, "So, where are we going, Clive? With these boys on board, my guess is the US. Am I right? Are the sympathizers stateside helping you out?"

Douglas laughs and takes a swig from his bottle. "This is a party, Sean. You really need to lighten up. In fact, have a beer and a burger. You look like you could use one."

He lifts the lid on a cooler and flips off the cap from a bottle of Budweiser before offering it to me. "It's not Stella, but beggars can't be choosers."

I take the bottle and Douglas calls over to the chef, "How about a burger for this man?"

"Don't go to any trouble on my behalf," I say sarcastically.

Douglas chuckles and then says, "Trust me, Sean, providing you with your last meal is no trouble. But suit yourself. Hold the burger, Franco. Now, how about you answer my question and tell me how you managed to get to Bessbrook before us and how you knew to come here?"

I take a drink from my bottle and ask a question of my own, "You really want to know, Clive?"

Douglas nods his head. "Yes, I do. And I'm rapidly running out of patience. So, I suggest you start talking."

All eyes are focused on me in anticipation of my answer. I lean forward and look first to the paddy executioner before quietly saying to Clive, "Don't tell anyone, but I'm a time traveler."

Smiling, I lean back and lift the bottle to my lips. Douglas shakes his head and the paddy effortlessly swats the bottle out of my hand and it shatters against the side of a shipping container. He gets to his feet and Douglas says, "You were never formally introduced, but this gentleman is Liam Clancy. I believe you met his brother earlier today?"

I nod my head. "The fella with the tools I'm guessing?"

"That's right," Douglas replies. "The Clancy brothers are quite famous in South Armagh for their interview skills."

I laugh slightly and say, "And there was me thinking that the Clancy brothers were entertainers."

"You're not completely wrong," Douglas says. "This is going to be very entertaining for me and the boys. Get him up on his feet."

I'm pulled out of the chair and turned so that I am facing away from the party. The two younger guys hold tightly to my arms and Liam Clancy positions himself behind me.

Clive stands up and joins us. "Now, Sean, these boys would be quite happy to go to work on you in the way that they know best, but we're both civilized men. So, why don't you tell me how you got to Bessbrook and I promise I'll make it quick for you."

I look over my shoulder at him. "Don't make me laugh, Clive. You're running out of time and you know it. You've been pegged right from the start. It's only a matter of time before the rest of the team get here."

Douglas turns his ear towards the sky and then shrugs. "Really, Sean? Because I don't hear any rescue choppers or warships out there. No, unless the navy seals are clinging to the side of this tub, I think you're all on your own. In fact, I bet Morgan and Gray don't even know that you're here."

"The navy seals are American," I say. "In the UK, it's the SAS and the SBS."

Losing patience, Douglas nods to Clancy. "Take one of his kneecaps off."

Without question or hesitation, Liam Clancy pushes the muzzle of his automatic against the back of my left knee and pulls the trigger. The pain is instant and blinding, but my captors don't let me fall. Pointing to the rapidly growing pool of blood on the deck, Douglas calmly says, "It's up to you, Sean. We can do this piece by piece or we can do it quickly."

Barely able to focus through the pain, I say, "Uh, I'll tell you. I'll tell you … but I want to know the name of this ship and where you're going."

Douglas yanks back my head and shakes his own. "You're really not in any position to be issuing demands, Sean. Now unless you tell me what I want to know, your other knee is next."

Summoning up all my remaining strength, I snap back, "I know that I'm going to die, you fuckling arsehole. So, what harm is there in telling me the name of the ship and where you're going?"

Liam Clancy turns to Clive and laughs. "Christ almighty, he's a feisty wee fucker, isn't he?" Then, turning back to me, "You're on the MV Dalia. Happy now, McMillan?"

"US bound?" I croak.

Liam is about to answer, but Douglas cuts him off, "Shut it, Clancy. Enough of the games. Take his other kneecap."

Clancy shrugs and says, "You're the boss, boss."

I'm in so much pain already that the loss of my second kneecap barely registers. This time, however, my captors let me fall to the ground. Douglas kneels down next to me and whispers in my ear, "Last chance, Sean. How the hell did you get to Bessbrook ahead of us when I left you behind at Gallows Corner roundabout? And how did you know to come here?"

I can now barely speak, and Douglas needs to move closer to hear me. "What was that you said? I couldn't hear you. Say it again."

"I said … I said, I'm a time traveler, Clive. And you're fucked!"

Douglas shakes his head in disgust and stands up. "Turn this piece of shit over and hand me your gun, Liam. I want the last thing he sees to be me firing the bullet that kills him."

The two young guys flip me over and Clancy obligingly hands over his automatic. Douglas stands over me and points the weapon at my forehead. "Any last words before we say goodbye, Sean? Perhaps a nice message for Catherine, Maria, or Ben that I can pass on the next time I see them?"

I shake my head and force a smile. "No need, Clive. I have every intention of seeing them again. I'll also be seeing you again and quite soon in fact. Enjoy the rest of the party. Try not to choke on one of those burgers, you fat fuck."

Douglas raises his eyebrows. "That's what I like about you, Sean. Even in the face of your own imminent death, you manage to remain optimistic." Then, just a split second before he pulls the trigger, "It's a misguided optimism, though. And I'm bored with you now. Goodbye, Sergeant McMillan. It was nice knowing you."

Present Day – Tuesday, May 8th, 2018

Exhausted from the previous night's efforts and fascinated with the soft hum of Cath's breathing nearby, I'm reluctant to open my eyes. But it's already starting to get light and I know that Catherine will be angry if I don't wake her up soon. I force open my eyes to check the time and then quietly say to myself, "Wow, it's nearly five-thirty already."

As quietly as I can, I go to the kitchen to make some coffee. When I get back, Cath is starting to stir, and I gently touch her on the shoulder. "Hey, I made you some coffee. Come on, it's time to wake up. We've got work to do."

For a moment she doesn't react, then remembering where she is, she sits up with a jolt and stares at me with wide-eyed suspicion. "What? What happened? When did you get back?"

I reassure her that it's only been a few minutes. Then I point to the coffee cup on the table next to her. "Go on, drink some of that and I'll fill you in."

Eager to hear what I have to say, she takes a single sip of the coffee and then reaches for her pocketbook and pen. "Okay, I'm ready. Please tell me that you found them."

I nod my head and smile. "Yep, the flight data information was bang on. The chopper landed in Bessbrook Mill."

For the next twenty minutes I describe, in as much detail as I can remember, everything that happened from the moment I arrived in Bessbrook until the moment Clive Douglas finished me off with a bullet to the head.

Once or twice during my story, Catherine winces and I stop to reassure her that I'm unharmed. When I finish speaking, Catherine refers to her notes and asks, "And you're sure it was the MV Dalia?"

I nod and answer, "I'm sure Cath. I was already as good as dead. There was no reason for Clancy to lie to me."

"But they didn't confirm one way or another whether it was going to the US?"

"No, sorry. But, if we did sail from the west coast of Ireland, then the US is the obvious destination."

"But that's assuming you did leave from the west coast," Catherine points out with a frown. She reaches into her handbag and spreads her map out onto the table. "You say you drove for approximately two hours from Bessbrook?"

"That's right. And I'm guessing that we were doing at least eighty to ninety for most of that time. So, you can assume that we could have covered anywhere between one hundred and fifty and two hundred miles."

Catherine points to various spots on the map and says, "They could just have easily reached any of the ports on the east coast in two hours."

"Yes, they could," I agree. "But that would take them out into the Irish sea and back towards Britain."

"Or into the Irish Sea and south towards the English Channel and Europe?" Catherine offers.

I shake my head. "No, that makes no sense. If Europe was the final destination, then why waste time heading west to Ireland? That chopper could just as easily have turned east and crossed the channel in the same amount of time."

Catherine frowns and scratches her head. "Yes, I guess so. I'm just checking the possibilities." She then folds the map and puts it back into her handbag.

"So, apart from Liam and Pádraig Clancy, the only other names you heard were Conor, Ciaran, and Owen?"

"That's right, Cath. Conor was Padraig's son and Owen was one of his heavies. Ciaran was the young guy that punched me in the stomach. Oh, and there was Franco the chef, but I'm not sure he's going to be of any help."

Catherine smiles and touches my hand. "That's okay, this has been a big help, Sean. We have the name of the ship and that's the most important thing. With that, it should be easy enough to find out its port of departure and destination. Plus, if we can get a fix on the transponder, we can either arrange for them to be intercepted at sea or we can ask our international counterparts to have a welcoming party waiting for them dockside."

Catherine stands up and smiles again. "You know what, Sean? I think today is going to be a good day."

I walk with her to the front door and ask, "What about me, Cath? If you do locate and apprehend Douglas and crew, that still leaves me out in the dark with DCI Morgan and DI Gray."

Unsure of how to respond, Cath sympathetically touches my arm. "I'm sorry, Sean. We can figure that out once we have Clive Douglas back in custody. Please don't think that I'm not grateful for your help, but for now my number-one priority is catching up with Douglas and getting him back behind bars."

"Great! So, I'm just expected to wait here like a spare prick at a wedding, am I?" I snap at her unfairly.

Disappointed at my outburst, Catherine shakes her head. "What do you want me to say, Sean? You're currently suspended, and you might want to take a close look in the mirror and ask yourself why. After that, do yourself a favor and make an appointment to see Jean Monroe again. If things don't work out in the way we hope, you might be needing her again."

Without another word, Catherine leaves and I check the time. Although I'm annoyed that I still can't take an active part in the hunt for Douglas, Catherine's advice makes sense. We don't know how things are going to play out, so I probably should meet with Jean Monroe again. But it's not yet six-thirty in the morning.

With nothing else to do for now, I set an alarm for nine and go back to bed.

■ ■ ■ ■ ■ ■ ■

When she is not acting as a legal aid and duty solicitor for the Metropolitan Police, Jean Monroe practices law from a suite of offices in Hounslow that she jointly occupies with three other solicitors. Today is the first time I have met her in her regular place of work and, compared to our previous meetings in some altogether less salubrious locations, our meeting today should be a pleasant first for me.

Although sparse, the reception area decor exudes an air of comfortable professionalism that you would expect from a legal practice. The neutrality of the cream-colored walls is cleverly broken up by carefully placed prints; two small, but tasteful sculptures adorn a glass-topped coffee table and the reception desk. The only other visible decoration is a crystal vase of seasonal flowers on the coffee table.

I step from the elevator, and the pretty young woman at the shared reception desk looks up from her keyboard and politely smiles at me. "Good afternoon, sir. You have an appointment with us today?"

"Sean McMillan for Jean Monroe," I reply. "She should be expecting me."

The young woman smiles again and says, "Ah yes, Detective Sergeant McMillan. Ms. Monroe is waiting for you in office number three. It's the second door on the left. Can I get you something to drink?"

I decline the offer and make my way to Jean's office where she is already waiting with the door open.

"Please, come in, Sean. Make yourself comfortable," she greets me.

I take a seat and while Jean powers up her laptop, I look around the room and comment on how organized everything looks. "This room is so *you*, Jean. Not a single item out of place."

Raising her eyebrows, she says, "Would you expect any less of me, Sergeant McMillan? Organization is one of the cornerstones of being a good legal practitioner."

"Yes, of course. Believe me, though, I've dealt with quite a few solicitors in my time who turned out to be anything but organized."

"Well, luckily for you, I'm not one of them. Because two hours ago, I received a formal notification that you are to be interviewed again. I've already—"

Impatient, I cut her off and ask, "Morgan and Gray?"

Jean frowns and shakes her head. "No, they've handed over the case to the Serious Crimes Squad. You have seventy-two—"

Without thinking, and much to Jean's annoyance, I interrupt her again and curse, "Fuck, that's all I bloody need right now! What can we do to delay the interview?"

Jean waits for a moment and then says, "Well, the first thing we are *not* going to do, Sean, is panic. Then you are going to allow me to finish what I was saying—if that's okay with you?"

"Yes. Yes, of course. Sorry, Jean. Please continue."

Pushing her spectacles further back onto the bridge of her nose, Jean looks down to the open file in front of her. "As I was saying, your case has been passed to the Serious Crimes Squad and they have requested that you present yourself for interview within seventy-two hours from 9 am this morning."

I shake my head. "That can't happen. We need to find a way to delay it. I need you to—"

Jean holds up her hand. "Sean, I have in fact already lodged an application to delay the interview." Then, subtly putting me in my place, she asks, "I hope I wasn't taking a liberty in assuming that you would be looking for a postponement?"

"No, of course not. Sorry for interrupting you. What grounds have you cited for the postponement?"

Frowning, Jean replies, "The only reasonable grounds that we have. By the way, how was your PTSD over the weekend?"

The reference to my fictitious psychological issues makes me chuckle. "Oh yeh, that's right. My PTSD. I'd forgotten about that. But that's a smart move. Thank you."

If I thought for a moment that my compliment was going to be taken well, I'm quickly proven wrong as Jean once again puts me in my place.

"I'm glad you find this funny, DS McMillan. Believe me, this is no laughing matter. You are in trouble up to your neck and right now your *post-traumatic stress disorder* is the only thing standing between you and an extremely lengthy jail term. So, the next time somebody asks you about your PTSD, '*I'd forgotten about that*' is not the answer that you should be giving. Am I making myself clear?"

I don't answer, but my look tells Jean that the point is well made. After a suitable pause, I ask, "So, what do you suggest now? A written application will only buy us a few extra days at most. After that, the SCS boys will want something a bit more substantial."

Jean pushes a yellow Post-it Note across the desk. 'Yes, I'm well aware of that. This is the address of a clinical psychologist in–"

"You want me to see a bloody shrink?" I interrupt with a look of astonishment.

Jean nods. "Yes, I do. And quite frankly, you don't have any choice—not if you want to delay the interview by more than a few days."

Frustrated, I shake my head. "Okay, I understand that. But what will I say?"

"How about the truth?" Jean suggests. "Let's face it, Sean. After what you've been through in the past few months, there is a very real chance that you actually are suffering from PTSD."

150

"Okay," I say. "But who is this guy? How do I know we can trust him?"

Handing me the note, Jean smiles. "I trust him, Sean. Which means that you can trust him. He's completely independent from the police and he does a lot of work with Iraq and Afghanistan veterans. Even just registering for PTSD counselling will be enough in itself to keep the wolves at bay for now. I've made you an appointment for this afternoon." Trying unsuccessfully to suppress a grin, she adds for good measure, "And who knows, it might even do you some good to talk about what's going on in that head of yours, Sergeant McMillan."

This instantly lightens the mood and I shrug and put the post-it into my top pocket. "Thanks, Jean. I'm sure you're right, but I'm not sure that I really want to know."

I take the note back out of my pocket and ask, "So, what time is my appointment with this … Doctor Wiz ... nee .. ew …"

Jean helps me out. "It's Wiśniewski. It's Polish and Doctor Wiśniewski is expecting you at four this afternoon."

It's just after three, so I thank Jean and she walks me out. At reception, I turn to thank her but stop when my cell phone rings. Catherine's number flashes up on the screen.

"Sorry, Jean. Do you mind if I take this? It could be important."

Ever polite, Jean gestures for me to carry on. "Of course, be my guest."

Turning away I shield the phone with my left hand and quietly say, "Cath what's going on?"

"Not over the phone," Catherine replies. "I need to see you again urgently."

"Okay, but I've something I need to do this afternoon. Why don't you meet me at my place around six? I'll order in some pizza or Chinese food."

With more insistence this time, Catherine raises her voice and says loudly, "No, Sean, I need to see you right now."

Conscious that Jean may have overheard her, I turn, and her frown confirms it. I raise my hands and quietly whisper sorry to her before turning away again.

"Okay, I'm at Jean Monroe's office. I'll jump in a cab and will meet you at my place at 3.30–"

"Forget the cab," Cath interrupts. "I'm outside."

"What? How the fu … oh right, don't tell me, you tracked my phone again?"

Catherine laughs and says, "Yep, it's a neat trick. Now, get your ass down here. We're running out of time."

I hang up the call and sheepishly turn around to face Jean. She shakes her head and asks, "None of my business really, but was that DC Swain?"

I confirm that it was and then add, "She needs my help to clear up a few details around the escape."

"I'm sure she does," Jean says with a frown. "And will clearing up these details help your own case?"

Not knowing how to answer that, I hesitate before saying, "I'm sorry, Jean. I need to go. I'll call you later."

"Really? Is that before or after your appointment with Doctor Wiśniewski?"

Again, I'm lost for words, and I'm also now more than a little embarrassed, "Um, yeh, sorry. Perhaps we can take a raincheck on that. Maybe reschedule for tomorrow?"

Clearly annoyed, Jean shakes her head again. "Just go and do whatever is so important to you. I'll do what I can to keep Serious Crimes off your back for as long as I can. You need to start helping yourself, though, Sean. There is only so much I can do for you."

Grateful for her support and understanding, however grudging, I thank her. "I promise. As soon as I'm done today, I'll call you and we can make a new appointment with Doctor Woz … Doctor Wiz …"

Jean raises her eyebrows. "It's Doctor Wiśniewski."

"Right, yes. Doctor Wiśniewski," I repeat.

I stride to the elevator and turn to say one last time, "Thanks again for all your help. You're an absolute angel." Feeling mischievous, I blow her a kiss and wink at her before the elevator door closes. "Truly, Jean, you're one in a million."

■ ■ ■ ■ ■ ■ ■

I barely have time to close the passenger side door before Cath pulls away from the curb and noses her way into the traffic on Hanworth Road. Taking her eyes off the road for a moment, she turns and asks if I'm okay.

I laugh. "Yep, apart from a couple of minor charges hanging over my head, that is." Then knowingly raising my eyebrows, "Oh and remind me to change my iCloud password. I'm not sure I like you knowing where I am all the time."

"Yes, sorry about that," says Cath without sounding sorry at all. "I needed to see you, though."

"I gathered that. What's going on? What's the big panic?"

Shaking her head, Catherine says, "I'm sorry, but I need you to travel again. The MV Dalia was a dead end. It was–"

"A dead end? What do you mean? That was solid information. Did you find–"

Catherine interrupts my own interruption and firmly cuts me off, "Sean, not now please. I need time to think. We'll be at your place in fifteen minutes. Just sit there quietly. I'll explain everything when we get there."

"Cath, you're worrying me. What's happened?"

"Nothing's happened," Cath replies. "And that's the bloody problem. Now please, just give me some time to think."

■ ■ ■ ■ ■ ■ ■ ■

Ignoring my offer of tea or coffee, Catherine strides into the living room. Spotting my bar-cart, she picks up a half-full bottle of Jameson and proceeds to fill a tumbler almost to the top.

"This is what you normally use, right?"

Bewildered, I nod. "Yes, it is, but how about you tell me what's going on first, so that I can properly prepare myself?"

Catherine hands me the tumbler of whiskey and says, "Sorry, yes. What was I thinking? You can drink while we talk."

We sit down and I lift my hands expectantly. "Okay, so what happened today? You obviously checked into the MV Dalia."

"You were right," Catherine says after taking a deep breath. "It departed from Galway docks at 10.02 pm on Friday."

"Westbound?" I ask.

"Westbound to Miami," Catherine confirms. "Or that's what the port departure log says anyway. But whether Miami is or isn't the destination, it has to be somewhere in the US."

"Exactly," I say. "And in an old tub like the Dalia, that's at least a two-week crossing time. That's plenty of time to track them and set up an intercept—or to get the Yanks lined up to arrest Douglas in the US. You need to start working on an international arrest warra–"

"Stop. There's not going to be any arrest warrant for any of them, because we have no idea where they are."

"What are you talking about, Cath? You know the name of the ship and where it departed from. What about the transponder? Ships of that size all have an automatic tracking system."

"And so does the MV Dalia." Then, shaking her head, Cath adds, "But it stopped broadcasting at just after one on Saturday morning. That would be a couple of hours after–"

I nod and finish her sentence, "A couple of hours after I was shot in the head by Clive Douglas. Fuck! My showing up there obviously panicked them into disabling the ATS. So, we have no idea where they could be?"

"None at all."

"What about helicopters or search planes? We know the direction they were heading. Is DCI Morgan talking to the home office? They have the power to authorize the coast guard or RAF to start a search."

Catherine's look says it all.

"You haven't told anyone else about this have you?"

Cath shakes her head. "I hadn't figured out yet how to explain where I got my information from. I was hoping to have a firm fix on Douglas' location before needing to cross that bridge."

I shake my head and Cath says, "What? You think this is easy for me? I can hardly tell Morgan and Gray that I was tipped off by my currently suspended time-traveling partner, can I?"

"It's dream traveling, not time traveling," I correct her.

Catherine scowls. "Sorry, what?"

"I said, it's dream traveling. Not ti–"

"I heard what you bloody said, Sean. And it hardly bloody matters right now, does it? We need to figure out what to do next. If they were spooked enough to disable the ATS, then it's probably reasonable to assume that they also changed course and destination. That's what I would do."

"Yeh, you're probably right," I say. "But without an active transponder, the only way we are going to find them is from the air. What about telling Morgan that you received an anonymous tip off about the Dalia?"

"That's a little unlikely, don't you think?"

I give a short laugh. "It's always worked for me in the past."

"Yes, and how's that working out for you now?" Cath replies. "Not too good the last time I looked. And besides, even if we could get approval for an aerial search, which is highly unlikely, they have a five-day head start on us in forty-one million square miles of ocean. The proverbial needle in a haystack doesn't even come close."

"Okay, fair point. What about the republican link and the Clancy brothers? If they have connections in the US, that could give us a clue to a possible destination."

Frustrated, Cath laughs and opens her pocketbook. "We were barking up the wrong tree with an IRA or republican link. The Clancy brothers were both enforcers during The Troubles. But not for the provos. They were both hardcore Ulster Volunteer Force. Protestant hardliners through and through. And guess what?"

"Go on, surprise me."

"Oh, you'll love this one. Both brothers were suspected of being informers and of colluding with the Ulster Constabulary, Special Branch, and the British Army during The Troubles."

"Colluding?"

"Working with them to supply information on the provos and to carry out hits on Catholics."

"And do you think Special Branch could be the connection to Douglas?"

"It's the only thing that makes sense, Sean. Douglas was never assigned to Northern Ireland to my knowledge, but as head of Serious Crimes, he would almost certainly have had dealings with Special Branch. Either way, the republican connection is dead. I'm not aware of the UVF or any of the other loyalist paramilitary groups having any connection or support network in the US."

"Fuck! I would have put money on those bastards being IRA. Particularly after what Pádraig's son said about what the Brits had done to them during the war. So, basically, my trip was a complete waste of bloody time."

Cath slowly nods her head. "Yes, that's why I need you to go back."

"Yes of course." I say. "This time though, I'll–"

Catherine cuts me off and says, "I was thinking that you should go straight to the port this time. Just watch the Dalia leave and then do your thing ... well, you know what I mean."

"Kill myself?"

Slightly embarrassed, Cath replies, "Yes. Well, what I meant to say is, there is no need to go on board this time. I mean there is no point spooking them again. If they think that they have got away scot-free, then it's possible that they will leave the transponder on."

"And if you can get a fix on the location, you'll tell Morgan you were tipped off?"

"Yes. If I get a confirmed location and a real shot at catching up with Clive Douglas, then telling Morgan and Gray will be worth all the questions."

I take a large gulp of whiskey. "Yes, that would be worth it."

Interested to know what else has been happening, I ask, "What have Morgan and Gray managed to dig up? What angles are they working on?"

Her earlier sheepish expression returns, and I look questioningly at her, "What? What is it?"

"We've been shut down," Cath replies. "After your interview on Friday, the Chief Superintendent called Morgan and ordered him to hand everything over to regional SCS."

"I guess that was to be expected. Morgan said as much during my interview and this doesn't really fall within the parameters of a cold case investigation. So, Morgan and Gray are not even looking into the escape?"

Catherine shakes her head. "No, the order was for a full cease and desist. I had to make all my calls on the quiet today. I didn't even go into the office this morning. DI Gray thinks that I've taken a day for personal time."

I slowly nod and then ask, "If this happened on Friday, then how come you didn't tell me about this before?"

"Because Saturday and Sunday were a bit messed up," Cath subtly reminds me. "And yesterday I had other more pressing issues to deal with. Is that okay?"

Suitably reprimanded, I stifle a smirk and ask, "Sure. Any other revelations I need to know about?"

Cath nods. "Yes, the SCS also have your file now, so you can expect a call." Then a little more sympathetically, "Sorry about that, mate. I was going to tell you, but I only found out about it myself this morning."

"That's okay. I already knew about that one. Jean Monroe gave me that nugget of good news earlier. They want to interview me sometime within the next seventy-two hours."

Unlike me, Catherine rarely uses bad language and when she does it is usually under considerable duress. This time she is obviously more concerned than I am about being interviewed by the SCS, "Fuck, Sean, how did things get so fucking messed up?" Then, pointing to my glass, "Finish that while I get you another. You need to get going now if we're to have any hope of sorting this bloody mess out."

As she stands up, her phone rings. She looks down at the screen and then lifts a finger to her mouth. "It's Sarah Gray. Don't say anything please."

Catherine picks up her phone and turns away, "Hi, ma'am. Is everything alright?"

For thirty seconds Catherine listens without saying anything; then she suddenly blurts out, "No. No, that can't be right."

The emotion in her words is telling and I stand up.

Catherine turns and holds out her left hand to stop me from coming any closer. Tears are welling in the corners of her eyes and her whole body is trembling as she speaks, "Yes, ma'am. I understand. I appreciate your calling personally to give me the news. Yes, ma'am, I will. Thank you."

The call ends and an ashen-faced Catherine returns to the sofa. Her cell phone falls from her hand and, unable to hold back any longer, the sobs come in a tidal wave of emotion.

I join her on the sofa, but at first am unsure what to do. I nervously wrap my arms around her and pull her towards me. Cath responds by turning her face into my chest and burrowing in deeper. I softly kiss her on the top of the head and quietly ask, "What's happened, mate? Tell me what's happened, so that I can help you."

I wait for another minute until Catherine's breathing and tears slow down and then I ask again, "Tell me what's happened, Cath. What did DI Gray tell you to get you so upset?"

Lifting her head, Catherine pulls away and takes a tissue from the box on my coffee table. Wiping away her tears, she shakes her head and says, "DI Mike Thurgood passed away thirty minutes ago. The medical team couldn't see any hope for his recovery, and his father gave permission to switch off his life support."

She's barely finished speaking before the tears come again. I leave her for a few moments to cry it out before I speak again, "The death of Mike Thurgood is just one more reason for me to travel again, Cath. One way or another, I can make all this right."

Catherine nods. Then she rubs her eyes and takes a deep breath to clear her head. The time for tears and emotion has passed and her demeanor is suddenly once more alert and focused on what needs to be done.

"You can make it right, Sean. But not by following those bastards to Galway. I want this to end and I want it to end now. Tell me again what you told me on Sunday."

"I'll tell you," I say, somewhat surprised. "But you have to be sure this is what you want. If we go ahead with this, then we will be crossing a line that there is no coming back from."

As an answer, Cath picks up my glass and swallows the remainder of my whisky. Then, looking defiant, she stands up. "I've never been surer of anything in my life. I'll get us some fresh drinks and then I want to know every detail of your plan."

I nod sympathetically and Cath adds, "I mean it, Sean. That bastard has crossed the line one too many times. This ends here."

. . . .

Apart from asking one or two questions, Catherine listens in complete silence while I take her through the details of my plan. When I've finished, I ask her again if this is what she really wants. Shaking her head and frowning, she drains the last drops of whiskey in her glass and then says, "It's not what I want, but I don't see that we have a choice."

She then looks to me questioningly and I nod. "No, you're right, we don't have a choice. This is the only way I can see of ending this and putting things right. It's a big ask, though, Cath, so if you're still not comfortable, then say so now and I'll try to figure something else out."

Catherine shakes her head again. "No. I've made up my mind. And besides, we don't know how much time you have before Serious Crimes get their claws into you. Once that happens, I assume it would be harder for you to travel."

"Harder, but not impossible," I say.

"Whatever, I just want this over and done with now, Sean. So, what next?"

I reach for the pad on my coffee table and start writing.

"What's that for?" Catherine asks.

Smiling, I say, "It's a reminder that I'm one of the good guys. If all goes to plan, then the next time we meet will be just after the escape. None of the last few days will have happened. I'm not even sure that you will fully remember our encounter in 2003."

Laughing, Catherine says, "I'm sure I will, mate. It's not every day that I bash someone's skull in with a hockey stick."

"Yeh, okay. You will probably remember that. But without this, it still won't make any sense."

I check the sports pages from Sunday's newspaper and add a couple of more lines to the letter. When I finish writing, I sign the bottom of the note and double underline today's date. I hand it to her and say, "Here, you sign as well, Cath."

She reads the letter and nods approvingly at the last entries as she adds her signature. Then, handing me the note, "That's very smart, boss. I'm impressed."

Smiling, I say, "Thanks, Cath. That means a lot."

Looking unsure at what I mean, she points to the letter and clarifies, "I mean it. It's a good idea and the last part is a master str–"

I shake my head and smile again, "I wasn't talking about the letter, Cath. You called me *boss*. A few days ago, it was inconceivable that you would ever call me that again. It really does mean the world to me to have your confidence back."

Blushing slightly, Catherine shrugs off my praise and stands up. "We're on the home straight, mate. That's all that matters."

We walk together to the door and I hand Catherine her coat.

"Are you sure there is nothing I can do to help?" she asks.

"No, you just need to leave everything to me now," I reply. "Go back into work tomorrow and carry on as if everything is normal."

Cath laughs. "Normal? That's bloody easy for you to say, Mr. Time Traveler."

I start to correct her, but Cath shakes her head and puts one of her hands across my mouth. "Yes, I know. You're a bloody dream traveler, not a time traveler. It's fun winding you up, though, DS McMillan."

She pulls me close and, as we hug, she whispers softly into my ear, "You have my confidence back, but it will mean the world to me to have my partner back."

We break our embrace and Catherine opens the door. Turning back, but in a hurry to leave before the tear drops forming in her eyes get any bigger, Cath forces a smile.

"Sleep well, Sean, and please go safe."

The door closes behind her and I nod to myself.

"Go safe indeed. You were right when you said it was crunch time, Cath."

■ ■ ■ ■ ■ ■ ■

It's only just after 4.00 pm. By my reckoning and barring any foul ups, and if I get my skates on, I can get my life and career back on track by midday tomorrow. I open my laptop and punch in a few different search terms. Within five minutes I find what I'm looking for and read the headline out loud: *Firearms fanatic caught with largest arsenal of weapons ever seized in Leicestershire*. "That's perfect," I say to myself, "and I'm sure you won't mind my borrowing one or two items, Mr. Stephen McConnell. You're gonna lose the lot anyway."

The reporter from the *Daily Star* has helpfully included a picture of McConnell's house along with the article. I click on the photo and thirty seconds later the image of a red-brick terrace with one boarded-up window and a faded green door drops into the printer tray. In my bedroom, I rummage through my drawers looking for anything that might give me some much-needed credibility.

The last drawer in the bedside table contains a disorganized pile of old bills, letters, and personal papers. It also contains a shoe box full of my old police bits and bobs. I lift the lid and take out a small black wallet. The fresh-faced young cadet bobby staring back at me from the ID card is a stark contrast to how I look now, and I ask myself, "Christ, was I really ever that young?"

A Hendon Police College ID card wouldn't fool most criminals, but in the absence of my warrant card and official police ID, it will have to do. Besides, the article mentioned that prior to his arrest for the firearms seizure, McConnell had a clean record. If I go in hard and confident, the ID shouldn't be that much of an issue. Already tipsy and tired, I close the bedroom curtains and lie down on my bed to start my journey.

The picture of McConnell's house could just as easily be any one of a million other terraced houses up and down the country, but the single boarded-up window and the faded green door are what make this house stand out from the rest.

I concentrate in particular on the door and the tarnished brass numbers.

"74, Gaskell Lane, Coalville, Leicestershire. Get ready, Stephen. I'm coming to ruin your day. February 2nd, 2018, February 2nd, 2018, February 2nd …"

The Past – Saturday, 2nd February, 2018

It's just my luck for it to be raining, but a passing young couple helpfully point me in the direction of Gaskell Lane, which turns out to be less than a two-minute walk away. At the top of the lane, a group of hoodies are drinking and smoking in a bus shelter. When I draw level, they all stop whatever they are doing and turn to face me. Nothing is said, but one of them smirks and flicks the still burning butt of his cigarette towards me.

The butt bounces off my arm in a small shower of sparks and ash. Keen to avoid a confrontation for now, I don't react and instead maintain my stride. Behind me, someone sneers, "Yeh keep walking, you old fuck." This first insult is followed by a general chorus of laughter and further verbal abuse from the other boys, emboldened by my lack of response.

"Yeh, fuck off, you old wanker." And, "Go on, fuck off, you old shit."

Completely unconcerned, I continue walking until I catch sight of number seventy-four. The paint on the door is even more faded then the picture portrays. I'm more interested, though, in the boarded-up window on the second floor. "Why just that window, Stephen? What are you hiding in there?" I muse to myself.

I already know the answer of course. I check the time, which is just after 2 pm, before confidently walking up the driveway and pushing the doorbell. Inside, I can clearly hear movement, but the door remains firmly closed.

I press the bell a second time. This time the brass letter flap at waist height slowly creaks opens, and a gruff Midlands-accented voice asks, "Who is it? What do you want?"

Bending over, I peer through the flap, which abruptly snaps shut.

"Mr. McConnell, I'm DS McMillan from East Midlands Constabulary. I'm here to do a routine follow-up on your mother's death. Can I come in please?"

Behind the door it is silent. I tap on the woodwork and call again, "Mr. McConnell, can you hear me? Your mother passed away recently. Is that correct?"

The letter flap slowly opens again, and the same voice says, "My mother died naturally in her sleep. What's that got to do with the police?"

"It's just a routine follow-up," I reply. "It's really nothing to worry about. If you can let me in, I just have a few questions for my report and then I'll be on my way."

The flap closes and twenty seconds pass before I hear the bolt on the back of the door sliding across. At 47 years old, with a sizeable paunch and badly receding unkempt gray hair, McConnell is an unremarkable looking man.

His demeanor and general bearing mark him out, however, as a typical recluse. Not necessarily dangerous, but it is understandable how he was able to amass such a large collection of weapons undetected for so long.

In a classic disarming move, I smile and offer my hand. "Stephen, it's very nice to meet you. It's okay if I call you Stephen, right?"

Although clearly suspicious, he nods and shakes my hand. Without waiting for an invitation, I push past and walk into his living room. A football match is just about to start on the television, and a half-eaten, roast-chicken dinner is on a side table next to a moth-eaten old armchair.

"Oh, I'm sorry. Have I disturbed your lunch?"

Ignoring the question, McConnell pushes past and picks up the remote control to turn off the TV. I stop him and say, "Hang on. Who's playing today?"

Although clearly irritated at my presence, he replies politely enough, "It's West Brom. They're up against Manchester City today."

I smile as I look at the TV and back at Stephen and comment cheerfully, "And I'm guessing that you're probably rooting for the local side?"

Confused and suspicious again, McConnell asks, "Sorry, who did you say you were again?"

"DS McMillan, East Midlands Constabulary. You're a big West Brom fan, right?"

He nods and I knowingly raise my eyebrows. "Yeh, I thought so. I wouldn't bother watching the match then if I were you. City are going to win by three goals to nil. Bony and Fernando will score for City in the first half and DaSilva is going to seal the deal with number three in the seventy-seventh minute."

With McConnell now lost for words, I reach forward and take the remote from his hands. "Let me do that for you," I offer.

I switch off the TV and gesture towards his lunch. "Those potatoes look good. May I?"

Unsure of himself, McConnell slowly nods. I smile and reach forward to skewer a crisp-looking roast potato with his fork.

Taking a small bite, I slowly chew. Then looking him squarely in the eyes, I spit the piece of potato back onto the plate and screw up my face.

"Christ, Stephen, are you trying to bloody poison me? Is that it? Are you trying to murder a police officer?"

The color instantly drains from his face, and he desperately tries to protest his innocence. "No, no. Of course not. I've been doing my potatoes like that for–"

Knowing that he is now well and truly on the backfoot, I laugh and touch his arm. "Stephen, chill, mate. I'm just messing with you. That's actually a bloody good roastie. Your mother's recipe?"

He nods and I walk towards the fireplace. In the center of the mantelpiece there is a brass-framed photograph of a middle-aged couple and a young boy. "You and your parents, Stephen? How old were you in that picture?"

"I was eleven or twelve," McConnell replies quietly. Then he says, "You said that you were here about my mum. Can we get on with it please?"

In response, I stare without speaking for a few seconds. Then I smile again and say, "Yes of course, Stephen. It was on the 9th of January, wasn't it?"

"What was?" McConnell asks.

"Your mother. She passed away on January 9th. And you say it was from natural causes. Is that right?"

"Yes," McConnell says nodding. "My mother was nearly ninety years old. She died peacefully in her sleep. But … but I'm not sure what this has to do with the police."

"Just routine," I reassure him. "I'd like to see her bedroom please."

Nervous, Stephen shakes his head. "Why do you need to see her bedroom? That's private."

Ignoring him, I walk towards the stairs. He hurries after me and instinctively grabs one of my wrists. "Wait. You can't go up there. Don't you need my permission or a warrant or something?"

I look back and down towards his hand. "Now, if I was a real hard-ass I could arrest you for assault and for obstructing a police officer in the execution of his lawful duty."

He carefully releases his grip and I nod appreciatively. "But I understand that this is a difficult time for you. So, this time, I'm going to look the other way. Is that okay?"

Relieved, McConnell nods and he follows me to the top of the stairs. To my right an open door leads into a large bedroom. Ignoring it completely, I turn to my left and point to a door firmly secured with a stainless-steel hasp and staple and a heavy-duty Chubb lock.

"That's interesting. What's in that room, Stephen?"

"That's nothing," he replies nervously. "It was my father's study. It's just full of books and old papers." Then, pointing to the bedroom, he adds, "This was my mother's bedroom. It's my bedroom now, but it was hers before she died. Go in, if–"

"No, that's okay," I interrupt. "I'd rather see what's in this room, actually. You have the key?"

McConnell shakes his head. "No. It was my father's study. I haven't been in there since he died three years ago."

"Really? You haven't been in there all this time? And you've never wondered why he needed such a big lock? Don't you think it's a bit over the top for just a few old books and some papers?"

A bead of perspiration is running down the side of Stephen's face and I stare at him as he desperately searches for an answer to satisfy my curiosity. I wait a few more seconds before I break the silence, "Is there something you want to tell me about what I'm going to find in there?"

Stephen shakes his head. "It's just old papers and books." Then, with a little more confidence, he says, "You can't go in anyway. Not without my permission or a warrant."

"Oh, right," I say. "So, now you know the law better than I do. Is that what you're telling me?"

"I didn't say that. I just know that you're not allowed to search my property without my permission, or … justif …" For a moment he struggles to find the right words, then he blurts out, "justifiable cause. You have to have justifiable cause. Yes, that's it. I read about it."

To humor him, I nod and acknowledge the accuracy of his statement. "Wow, I wasn't expecting that. You're absolutely right. I do need to have justifiable cause to search that room."

Relaxing slightly and thinking that I've given up on the locked room, McConnell half smiles and points to the open bedroom.

I shake my head. "No. I'm not here for your mother. I just said that so that you'd let me in."

Any previously returned color drains from his face and McConnell starts to tremble. "You ... you're not a policeman, are you? What do you want?"

I take out my wallet and hold up my police college credentials at arm's length for his inspection. "I can assure you, Stephen, that I am a police officer and unless you start cooperating, things are not going to go well for you today."

He leans forward but before he can properly focus, I snap the wallet shut and tuck it back inside my jacket pocket.

"Hang on," he protests, "I didn't see that clearly. And what about a warrant?"

"A warrant? A fucking warrant?" I shout. "Wake up to yourself, man. Either you can open that door for me right now or you can wait another two days for an armed response team to smash the door down and drag your sorry ass off to jail."

As I can see that he is still not fully comprehending what is happening to him, I point to the door and spell it out for him, "You'll get at least ten years for what they will find in there."

Through teary eyes, he continues to deny any wrongdoing. "It's just books. Books and old papers. I swear it."

"So, open the door," I say. "If it really is just books and papers, then you have nothing to worry about."

I sense a willingness to cooperate but still a hesitation. So, I quietly nudge him along. "But it's not just books and papers, is it?"

McConnell stares for a moment and then says, "Well, there might be a bit of my father's old military reenactment stuff and one or two old BB guns."

"Nothing else?" I ask with a raise of my eyebrows.

When he shakes his head again, I finally lose all patience. "Listen, you fucking muppet, I know what you have inside that room. Now open that door before I put your thick head through it."

My threat of violence shocks him into backing away and his head drops. Keen to move on, I change to more subtle tactics.

"Stephen, listen to me. I can see that you're not a bad guy and I know that you've never been in trouble with the police before. And that's why I'm here."

Lifting his head, he eyes me with suspicion. "I don't understand. What do you mean?"

"I mean that I'm here to help you. I was tipped off by a confidential source that you've been collecting weapons and that you keep them in that room. Was that information correct?"

He slowly nods his head and then says, "It's just a collection. I wasn't going to do anything with them."

I nod sympathetically. "I know that, Stephen. I know you're a good guy. But not everybody thinks like me. So, now you have a choice. Open that door and let me inspect your collection or wait for the armed response team."

McConnell looks at me questioningly, and I say, "That's right. At 8 am on Monday morning an armed response team are going to batter down your front door. But what they find on Monday … well, that's entirely up to you."

Caught between a rock and a hard place, McConnell walks towards the locked door and retrieves a key from the pocket of his grubby jeans. Turning the key, he unhooks the heavy padlock and lifts the steel hasp before stepping aside.

Preferring to keep him where I can see him, I gesture to the door and say, "After you, and no sudden movements please."

What greets me inside the room is a veritable Aladdin's cave of legal and illegal weaponry. A pair of oak tables and a row of shelves are heavily laden with handguns, rifles, shotguns and all manner of edged weapons. On the floor, a wooden crate contains, amongst other things, stun guns, vicious-looking knuckle dusters, ninja throwing stars, and plastic tubs of live and blank ammunition of various caliber. A second crate is filled to the brim with firearms manuals and what looks suspiciously like a German stick grenade. I carefully lift it out of the crate and ask, "Is this what I think it is?"

McConnell confirms it is. Then he helpfully adds, "But it's not live. It's been deactivated. I can show you the certificate."

I hold up my hand. "That's not necessary." Then, looking again around the room in wonderment, I exclaim, "Christ on a bike, Stephen, where in God's name did you get all of this?"

Shrugging, he starts to point proudly at various items around the room. "Some I got off the internet, some from antique and junk shops, and some from friends."

"Friends?" I ask.

"Well, not really friends. People I meet on the internet. Lorry drivers mainly. They bring me stuff."

"Go on," I urge. "You mean these lorry drivers are smuggling weapons in from the Continent for you?"

He's hesitant at first but then says, "I don't want to get anyone into trouble."

"That's okay," I respond soothingly. "I don't need names, but that is what they do, yes?"

"Yes, they advertise on the dark web and whatever you want gets smuggled in through one of the UK ports."

Seemingly pleased at his confirmation, I smile and nod. "Good, we thought that was how they were doing it. And because of your cooperation, I'm going to let you get rid of all of this before my colleagues can get their hands on it. I will, though, be taking a few pieces as insurance, if that's okay?"

"Insurance?" Stephen asks quizzically.

"You're a good guy," I say. "And I'm here unofficially to do you a favor. But how do I know that you won't tell my colleagues that I was here tipping you off about the raid?"

"I wouldn't. I wouldn't say anything," McConnell assures me, vehemently shaking his head.

"I'm sure you wouldn't. Because you're a good guy. But a little bit of insurance will make me sleep a whole lot better at night."

With no real choice anyway, McDonnel nods. "Okay, I understand."

Then, eager to help and for me to be gone, he points to a pump-action shotgun leaning against the far wall. "That's a Mossberg 500 series assault shotgun. The SAS and US special forces use them. Oh, and what about this?"

He hands me a Smith & Wesson .38 special snub-nose revolver. "This one is great if you want it for concealed carry. It packs a real punch for its size."

My look of disapproval at his comment elicits a swift back scuttle and clarification. "Well, that's what I heard anyway. I've never used it myself, you understand."

Hardly interested anyway but remembering that I lost my last clandestine weapon to the Clancy brothers, I stuff the revolver inside my jacket pocket and ask, "You have ammunition for it?"

McConnell rummages around in the wooden crates and then hands me a cardboard sleeve containing fifty rounds of .38 caliber ammunition. "These are hollow points. You could stop a rhino with these babies. You need shells for the Mossberg?"

I shake my head. "Forget the Mossberg. I'm looking for something a little more specialist."

McConnell's expression is blank as he asks, "Specialist? This is everything I have."

I lift a finger and knowingly wag it in his face. "No, no, no. That's not completely true now, is it? Where's the Dragunov?"

His expression changes in an instant and, now defensive, his eyes flick around the room as he decides whether to reach for a weapon. With his brain working overtime and his heart beating out of his chest, he quietly asks, "How could you possibly know about that?

When his eyes settle on an unsheathed machete just a few feet away from him, I raise my finger again.

"No, no, no. I wouldn't recommend that. You need to quickly decide whether I can load this snub nose and pull the trigger faster than you can get to that blade. Your choice, Stephen."

While he makes his decision, my eyes wander to a tall wardrobe in the corner of the room. "I bet it's in there, isn't it?"

He reluctantly nods and I tell him to open the door. "Same as before. Just hand me the rifle and no sudden movements."

The Dragunov is clearly Stephen's prize possession. The barrel and other metal parts have barely a scratch on them and the woodwork is smooth and highly polished. I raise the butt to my shoulder and peer through the telescopic sights before placing the weapon down onto the table.

"This is a beautiful weapon. Where did you get it?"

"A Polish guy sold it to me."

"And where did he get it?"

"I don't know for certain. He said he got it from a Bosnian chap when he was making a delivery in Germany, but he could be lying I suppose."

"No, it makes sense," I say. "The Dragunov was the sniper rifle of choice for all sides in the Balkan wars. What about a case and ammunition?"

McConnell hands me a canvas rifle cover and a magazine for the Dragunov containing just three rounds of ammunition.

I inspect each of the rounds and then ask, "That's all you have?"

He confirms it is and I point to the black-painted tip of one of the rounds. "Why is this one different from the others?"

Clearly proud of himself, he smiles and says, "A black tip means it's armor piercing. Very expensive, though, and hard to come by."

I nod my approval and push each of the rounds back into the magazine with the armor-piercing round on the bottom.

"That's perfect, Stephen. I've no idea what you thought you needed armor-piercing rounds for. But no matter. It might come in handy."

I zip up the canvas cover and pick up one of the stun guns. "I'll take this as well. Oh, and this pair of binoculars. The rest is yours, but if I were you, I'd get rid of everything as fast as you can."

I sling the rifle case over my shoulder and am already at the door when Stephen says, "You're not a real policeman, are you?"

I turn back to face him, "I am. But whether I am or not makes no difference now. I'm going to leave and if you've got any sense, you'll take this lot out in the woods and dump it all in a lake. I mean it, Stephen. At 8 am on Monday morning, the boys in blue are going to be on your doorstep."

Still unsure, he nods and says, "Okay, well, thanks for the advice. I'll have a think about what to do."

"You should do more than just think," I suggest.

"You're really telling me the truth?" Stephen asks.

I smirk. "I'm a man in the know. And I've no reason to lie to you." Then I add, "Check the football results later. Manchester City 3, West Bromwich Albion 0. If I'm wrong, ignore everything I've said and hang on to your collection." Then, shaking my head, I add as a parting shot, "I wouldn't recommend that, though. Trust me, you won't survive a ten stretch in prison."

■　■　■　■　■　■　■

The hoodies are still making a nuisance of themselves in the bus shelter and look surprised when I walk up to them smiling. The guy who had flicked the cigarette butt earlier stands up and is obviously spoiling for a fight.

"What the fuck are you looking at, Grandad?"

I look beyond him and through the glass of the bus shelter to where a pimped-up black Ford Fiesta is parked. "Nice car. Whose is it?"

Another boy stands up defensively and says, "It's mine. What of it?"

I hold out my hand and smile. "Hand over the keys, dipshit."

While the rest of the group get to their feet, the first two boys look at each other and laugh. The butt flicker then squares up to me and confidently says, "Look around you, old man. There are eight of us and one of you. Are you really that desperate for a kicking?"

The last words are barely out of his mouth before the prongs of the stun gun pierce the flesh of his neck and the electrical arc drops him convulsing to the floor.

Shocked to silence, the rest of the crew press as far to the back of the shelter as they can. Smiling I step forward and extend my hand to the car owner. "Now, give me the keys or you're next."

"But it was a present from my dad," the boy protests. "He'll bloody kill me."

I take the unloaded Smith & Wesson from my pocket and feed a single round into one of the chambers. I spin the cylinder and then point it at the boy's face. "You've heard of Russian roulette, right?" Then, channeling my best Clint Eastwood, Dirty Harry, "Do you feel lucky? Well, do ya … punk?"

With his hands shaking, the boy fumbles in his pockets and hands over the keys. "Here take them. Please, just take them and go."

I take the keys and in a final act of revenge for the earlier abuse, I move the gun slowly from left to right, pointing towards each boy in turn. My delight in watching them squirm is matched only by my delight at the sight of the quivering young thug at my feet.

I lower the revolver and kick one of his feet. "Don't even think about bloody reporting this to the police. I know where you and all your girlfriends live. You get me, homeboy?"

With saliva and snot running down his chin, the boy nods his head and I smile. "That's good. Well, carry on then, ladies."

I place the Dragunov and the binoculars on the backseat and buckle up. Before leaving, I U-turn and pull up next to the bus shelter. Rolling down the window I do my best Mr. Chow impression and wave casually from the window as I speed away.

"Toodle-oo, motherfuckers!"

■ ■ ■ ■ ■ ■ ■

A little over two hours later, I'm approaching the Gallows Corner roundabout in search of an appropriate vantage point from which to view Clive's escape. The perfect spot needs to be elevated and far enough away for an observer to remain undetected. But not so far as to require anything more than a basic level of shooting skill.

I reject the first two possibilities and pull off the A1 towards a narrow 'B' road that ascends steeply towards a sparse copse of trees overlooking the roundabout. Most importantly, this particular spot looks out to the west.

I park the car out of sight and remove the Dragunov and the binoculars from the case. In the middle of winter, the trees are sparsely covered with foliage and afford very little cover for a sniper. In May this should be less of a problem and I reason with myself that nobody is going to be expecting a sniper attack anyway. And even if they are, hopefully by the time they realize where it's coming from, it will already be too late.

I check a few different positions and finally settle on what I think is a good spot. I lean the rifle against a tree and lift the binoculars up to scan the road below. At this range the clarity is perfect, and I focus on where I think the helicopter landed.

"Yep, that's it," I mutter to myself.

I put down the binoculars and take a prone position with the front stock of the Dragunov resting on a tree stump. I estimate that the landing spot is around 600 yards away and I fiddle with the telescopic lens until the crosshairs are neatly aimed at where I imagine the windscreen canopy of the chopper will be.

"Nice and easy does it," I tell myself. "Just breathe, breathe, breathe. Then slowly pull the trigger and put one through the cockpit glass and into the pilot's shoulder. That should be enough to screw their chances of an easy getaway."

Happy that I'm as prepared as I can be, I return to the car and check for anything that could be of use to me.

Returning to the firing point, I scrape away at the hard earth below the stump with a tire iron until I've made a pit just deep enough to conceal the rifle. Next, I add an additional note to the envelope I'm carrying, before placing it into the canvas cover along with the Dragunov and the binoculars.

Finally, and as some added protection against the elements, I wrap the entire thing in a pair of grubby refuse sacks that previously contained Fiesta boy's filthy soccer kit and secure them tightly with the remains of a roll of red electrical tape.

I finish by replacing the soil scraped from the hole and lightly pack it down.

"Well, that's going to have to do, Sean," I tell myself. "All you can do now is pray that nobody finds it between now and May 4th."

The light is starting to fade, and I check my watch.

"Right. It's time you weren't here, Sean boy. Time to find a way home."

I pin my location on Google maps, then I get back onto the A1 and head back towards Coalville until I reach Markfield Service station at Junction 22 on the M1 motorway. Parking in the furthest and darkest corner of the car park, I get out to stretch my legs and to check my options for getting home. Finding nothing that wouldn't draw attention, I retrieve the tire iron from the back seat and pop the catch to lift the hood.

As expected, the opposite ends of the battery are protected with red and black plastic covers, but they open easily to reveal the positive and negative terminals beneath.

My original intention had been to attach a set of jumper cables to electrocute myself, but Fiesta boy doesn't have any and I can't be bothered walking back to the service station to buy a set. This then is where the tire iron comes in. Positioning myself directly over the battery and holding the tire iron firmly in the center with both hands, I take a deep breath and count to three.

On three, I lunge forward and place the ends of the tire iron across the exposed electrical terminals. I'm expecting to fry, but when nothing happens, I look down confused and realign the ends of the iron. This time, the effect is instantaneous, a huge arc of fire crosses the terminals and I watch transfixed as the skin on my hands melts around the tire iron like a molten candle.

A split second later I'm thrown backwards by a surge of electricity coursing through my body and the back of my skull is sheared wide open by the force of it crashing into the curbstone.

Barely conscience, my last recollection is of the smell of smoke, burning hair, and charred flesh.

Present Day – Wednesday, May 9th, 2018

I wake up bathed in sweat and shudder at the memory of the skin falling away from my hands like burnt caramel.

"Jesus Christ, Sean," I ask myself, "what is it with you and bloody electrocution?"

My bedside lamp is on and it takes a minute or so before I can properly focus on my phone to check the time. It's just after three in the morning and there are two missed calls from Maria and a message asking me to call her. There are also three missed calls from a number that I don't recognize.

Curious, I call the number and hang up immediately when I'm connected to the Serious Crimes Squad switchboard. "Sorry, boys. I've got other more important things to be dealing with right now. And with any luck, by the time I next wake up, you won't be needing to see me."

Focused on what I need to do, I stash the Smith & Wesson and the stun gun inside the hole in the side of my mattress for future use. Next, I shower and change into the same suit I was wearing on May 4th. Finally, I walk into the living room to fetch the rest of the Jameson. I'm about to go back into my bedroom when the light from my laptop screen catches my attention.

The previous headline, *Firearms fanatic caught with largest arsenal of weapons ever seized in Leicestershire,* has changed completely and now says, *East Midlands Constabulary in bungled raid on innocent Coalville resident.*

The picture accompanying the article is of Stephen McConnell standing in front of his damaged front door looking decidedly pissed off. The article itself describes the details of the raid.

The quote from the official police spokesman is particularly satisfying: "I can confirm that a tactical firearms unit from East Midlands Constabulary carried out a planned intervention operation at a private residence in the Coalville area of Leicestershire in the early hours of this morning. This operation was authorized and carried out on the basis of credible information received. This information, however, turned out to be incorrect and so I would like to apologize unreservedly to the householder on behalf of East Midlands Constabulary for any inconvenience or distress caused as a result of this operation. There will, of course, be a full internal inquiry into the events leading up this operation and its subsequent execution."

At the end of the article, there is a short quote from the man himself: "This was a complete surprise to me. I'm a law-abiding citizen and have never been in trouble with the police before. I shall now be speaking to a solicitor and will be seeking substantial damages for emotional distress and the damage caused to my property."

I finish reading the story and smile again. "Good decision Stephen, but don't milk it, eh? Take my advice again and quit while you're ahead."

I close the laptop and go back to my bedroom. Outside it's starting to get light and I figure that I have seven to eight hours at most before SCS start calling again. Worse still, and regardless of my seventy-two-hour window to present myself, they may come looking for me even sooner if I don't answer their calls.

Faced with quite possibly the most serious dilemma of my personal life and career to date, I swallow the remainder of the Jameson and lie back down on my bed.

"This is it, Sean boy. This is make-or-break. This really is crunch time now."

My mind wanders to nearly a week previously and to my meeting with DI Sarah Gray. I focus on her office and our discussion. I picture what she was wearing, and I close my eyes, "May 4th, 2018, May 4th, 2018, …"

The Past – Friday, 4th May, 2018

Sergeant Morris steps from behind the counter and lightly taps me on the shoulder. "Are you sure you're okay, Sean? You look like you're in a world of your own there."

With a strong sense of déjà vu, I shake my head and force a smile.

"Um, no. I'm fine, Ted. Sorry, what did you just ask me?"

Morris points to my battered wallet and laughs. "I was asking if you've been digging spuds up with that?" Then, pointing to the bruises and scrapes on my face, "It looks almost as bad as you do."

I grimace slightly and lift a hand to my injuries. "Yeh, not much I can do about the face, but probably worth ordering a new ID and warrant card. I can't very well be walking around with this is my pocket, can I?"

"Right you are," Morris says. "I'll sort out the paperwork today. "You want me to buzz you in?"

"No need," I reply, confidently placing my station access card against the scanner. To Ted's astonishment there is an accepting buzz and the gate opens to let me through.

"Well, bugger me sideways! I'd have put money on that not working. No matter—I'll order a new set for you anyway."

I thank him for his help, and he smiles. "All in a day's work, Sean. Have a good day, mate. Oh, and good job, by the way, in getting DCI Morgan back."

■ ■ ■ ■ ■ ■ ■ ■

I step out of the lift, but this time I don't immediately go to Gray's office. Conscious of what is at stake today, I wait a few minutes in the corridor to gather my thoughts. I pause again at her open office door and watch for a moment as she reviews the case file in front of her. Ready, I take a deep breath and am about to knock when Gray looks up and smiles.

"Oh wow, sorry, I didn't see you there. Please come in, Sean, and take a seat."

She locks away the case file and grimaces as she turns back to face me. "Those bruises look worse than they were yesterday, Sean. How are you feeling? That was a pretty traumatic couple of days for you both."

As before, I run my hand across the lump on the back of my head and am surprised to find that the previously receded swelling is back in all its former glory. Doing my best to contain my surprise, I mentally add it to my ever-growing list of unexplained dream-travel mysteries and shrug off the extent of my injuries.

"I'm fine, ma'am. This lump has gone right down and the bruises on my face look much worse than they are."

Clearly not convinced, Gray slowly nods. "Maybe so, but no one would blame you if you wanted to take a few days' personal time. There is no shame in it."

I know full well what she means, but in light of recent events and as a backup if my plan goes awry, I feign confusion. "Sorry, ma'am. No shame in what?"

"PTSD, Sean. Post-traumatic stress disorder. It would be perfectly understandable under the circumstances. PTSD is fully recognized these days and counselling is available free of charge to all officers who have suffered any kind of trauma."

"Thank you, ma'am, I really appreciate your concern. But, apart from feeling a little stressed and jumpy, I honestly feel fine. And besides, it's nearly the weekend and my only plan is to put my feet up and relax. I'm sure I'll feel much better by Monday morning."

Although still not entirely convinced, Gray nods again and smiles. "Okay, well, that's good to hear. But if you do start feeling anxious or feel like you need some professional guidance, the Force counselling service is there for that very reason. Just let me know and I can arrange for you to–"

Keen to move on and confident that I have sowed enough of a PTSD seed in case it is needed, I interrupt in the hope of closing down the subject. "Ma'am, I'm fine, honestly. I took a few knocks, that's all. Now if it's okay, can we just leave it please?"

Reluctantly, Gray agrees to my request. "Okay, let's park this for now, but if you change your mind, you only have to say. In the meantime, it wouldn't do you any harm to take some leave. DC Swain has taken off until the 14th. Why don't you do the same?"

I smile and nod my agreement. "Thanks, ma'am. Yes, I think I will. DC Swain called me this morning to say that she was taking some leave. I think it's a good idea."

"It is, Sean. A spell of leave is long overdue for the pair of you. DC Swain was sounding as rough as you look this morning."

"You spoke to her?" I ask.

"Yes, she called me at just after seven this morning to say that she wasn't feeling great and asked to be excused duty today. I offered the leave and suggested some counselling. Like you, she declined the counselling but accepted the offer of leave, as you already know. I'm worried about her, though, Sean. The boss said that she took a nasty fall into that pit yesterday."

I replay the scene in my mind and shudder. "Yes, she did. DC Swain is a fighter, though, ma'am. I'm sure she'll be fine after a decent break. That woman is one tough cookie."

Gray stares directly at me for a few seconds and then says, "I certainly hope so. Keep an eye on her, Sean. It doesn't do any good to keep things bottled up inside."

I nod. "Of course, ma'am. You can rely on me."

To keep the conversation flowing, I ask about DCI Morgan, "You've spoken to the boss, ma'am? How is he?"

"I visited him in hospital last night," Gray replies. "Considering what he's been through, he's doing okay. He'll be off work for at least a couple of weeks, but he did ask me to pass on his thanks for your part in his rescue. He brought me up to speed with the details. Using the Find My iPhone application was a stroke of genius, Sean."

"A stroke of genius that my partner is now stalking me with," I mutter under my breath.

"Sorry, what was that?"

"I said, it was nothing, ma'am. I'm just glad everything worked out and Clive Douglas is back where he belongs."

As before, my comment makes her frown slightly. "Take the praise while you can, Sean. I suspect, once the boss is back on his feet, you might be in for a bit of a bollocking for again involving a civilian in one of your cases. You might want to think very carefully about that during your leave of absence. It's unlikely that the boss will be returning to work before you get back, so use the time wisely."

I thank her for the advice and stand up to leave. As expected, DI Gray gestures for me to retake my seat. "Before you go, I have a couple of case updates that you might be interested in. This won't take long, Sean."

She slides a piece of paper across the desk and gives me the news about the bodies found in the pit being two of the three missing security guards.

Maintaining the charade, I frown in concentration as I scan the sheet, and ask, "Any luck on identifying which of them they are?"

Gray points to the bottom of the sheet. "Actually, yes. Whoever killed and buried them was either supremely confident that they would never be found, or they were just too lazy or too stupid to cover their tracks. The wallets of both men were still in their pockets."

As before, I read the names George John Benson and Peter Edwin Lane aloud. "So, ma'am, this just leaves Stuart Goldsmith unaccounted for?"

DI Gray takes back the sheet of paper. "Correct. Mr. Goldsmith remains as a person of interest in this case. But not as a suspect. Because of this and because of the length of time since his disappearance it's doubtful that the Met are going to dedicate much time or many resources in trying to find him."

Hearing this for a second time is no less disappointing than it was the first time. In fact, with the benefit of repetition, I'm probably more annoyed at the apparent lack of empathy and, as before, I do little to hide my annoyance. "But surely they will at least try, ma'am? They can't just write off a man's life."

Gray nods, and I have to hold back from interrupting her less-than-reassuring response. However, not wishing to alter the chain of events too far, I shake my head in a display of frustration before I once again berate her for her seeming lack of sympathy for the missing man.

Trying my best not to smirk, I watch and wait as DI Gray weighs up an appropriate response to reassert her authority, which of course she does after a pregnant pause. She calmly reminds me that the first priority is to get Clive Douglas back to a high-security Category A facility and the second to make sure Rosemary Pinois is remanded in custody until her trial. She finishes with the sarcastic question, "Is that okay with you, DS McMillan?"

Still stifling a smirk, I nod with fake sincerity and apologize.

Gray stops me mid-sentence to reassure me that she understands my personal interest in the case but that we need to focus on what we can do.

I nod my agreement and the conversation continues much the same as before, until we reach the part about Clive Douglas' transfer to Yarwood. I interrupt her to ask how many vehicles there will be in the convoy and how many armed officers.

Annoyed at my interruption and questioning of the arrangements, Gray holds up her hand and protests, "Sean, enough please. We know exactly who we are dealing with here. Standard protocol is for a three-vehicle convoy. The prisoner will be in the armored transfer vehicle with pairs of armed officers in rapid response vehicles to the front and rear. And I'll be riding shotgun with Clive to keep him company on the trip north. Good enough?"

"So, four armed officers plus yourself and the driver of the armored vehicle?"

"Correct. Now, please go home and take some well-deserved leave, Sean. I'll message you when we get to Yarwood. Okay?"

"Actually, ma'am, I'd like to make a suggestion, if I may?"

"Would it make any difference if I said no?" Gray asks with a sigh. "Go on then, what is it?"

"Swap the rapid response vehicles for armor. They are much sa–"

"What? No. There is no need for that," Gray cuts in. "And besides, the arrangements are already made."

"Ma'am, please," I plead. "You don't know Clive Douglas as well as I do. He's got his fingers in a million pies and is capable of anything."

Gray looks at me with suspicion and asks, "Is there something you want to get off your chest, DS McMillan?"

"No, ma'am. I just think it's a sensible precaution. Please ma'am, make the call now before it's too late."

Unconvinced, Gray looks me up and down, but knowing I won't take no for an answer, she finally relents. "Fine. I can't guarantee anything, but I'll discuss your suggestion with Inspector Thurgood."

She then stands up to show me out. "Now, go and enjoy your leave, Sean. You've earned it."

I nod and turn to leave but wait at the door for a second before turning back around to say, "I want to come with you. I want to be there on the escort."

Gray, who by now has already sat down at her desk, stands back up and angrily points to the door. "You are testing my patience, DS McMillan. Either go home willingly or I will have you escorted home. What's it to be?"

Previously, my main reason for wanting to be on the escort was my own selfish desire to see Clive Douglas returned to Yarwood. This time around my presence is critical. Lives depend on it and I have no intention of taking no for an answer.

"Ma'am, I'm not doubting your arrangements for the escort. I know that Inspector Thurgood and his men are more than capable of handling anything that might happen."

Gray raises her hands in confusion and asks, "So, what is it then? Why is it so important for you to be there? Haven't you had a gutful of Clive Douglas by now?"

Not wishing to sound rehearsed, I hesitate to answer, and Gray asks again, "Well, what is? Either spit it out or go home and let me get on with my job, DS McMillan."

"It's … it's personal," I reply. "With Clive Douglas I mean. I blame myself for him getting out of Yarwood in the first place. I should have ignored him from the very first time he made contact. Maybe then the boss wouldn't have got hurt. Maybe then–"

Sarah Gray cuts me off mid-sentence. "Sean, you followed up on a line of enquiry, as you were meant to. Any other good copper would have done the same. And the boss losing his finger wasn't down to you. We all know that, with or without Clive

Douglas, Rosemary was bound to have figured out the boss's connection to the death of her father eventually."

She's right of course, but I continue to play the sinner in search of redemption. "Maybe, ma'am, but this is something I need to do. I need to look that bastard in the eye one more time. Call it closure. I need closure, ma'am."

Gray shakes her head, but when she speaks again her tone has softened, "Closure? So, that's what this is all about?"

I close my eyes for a moment in what looks like quiet contemplation. In reality I'm actually trying to remember my response to Gray's question. Confident that I have it almost right, I open my eyes and take a deep breath, "Yes, ma'am. I can't just sit at home waiting to find out what has happened. I need to be there. Let me join the escort and as soon as it's done I promise I'll go on leave and you won't hear from me again until the fourteenth."

Reluctantly and probably against her better judgment, DI Gray agrees to my request and tells me to meet her outside Meerholt Prison at 10.45. "The prisoner escort is due to leave at 11 am sharp. You can ride in the armored transport with me and use the time on the way up to say your fond farewells to Douglas. I'm sure he will appreciate your company."

I raise my eyebrows and my words this time have much more significance than they had before, "Thank you, ma'am. I'm not sure how much Douglas will enjoy the trip, but I damn well know I will."

Gray walks me to the door. "Good, that's settled then. Now, if there's nothing else, I have a few things to do before I leave for Meerholt."

"Actually, ma'am. There is one other thing."

"You're pushing your luck, Sergeant McMillan. What is it?"

"Just wondering if I can hitch a lift with you to Meerholt, ma'am? My car is still in the workshop having the windscreen replaced."

DI Gray shakes her head, but she also gives me a grudging smile. "You're a cheeky bastard, McMillan. Meet me at the reception in an hour. Oh, and shut the door on your way out."

■ ■ ■ ■ ■ ■ ■

I take a seat in the quietest part of the canteen to wolf down a bacon and egg sandwich that somehow doesn't taste nearly as good as it did the first time around. I put this latest phenomenon down to nervous apprehension and take out my phone.

As before, my first call goes unanswered and the second goes straight to Catherine's voicemail.

I wait for the message to finish, then I hang up to consider carefully what I want to say. Worried that I might screw up, I open my pocketbook and begin to write. Ten minutes and three rewrites later, I'm finally happy to redial.

With my pulse racing, I listen again to Catherine's message and wait patiently for the beep before beginning to recite my own message.

"Hi, Cath, I know how pissed off you are with me right now, and you have every right to be. I'm calling you, though, because I need your help more than I've ever needed it before. So please listen to the end and take what I'm saying seriously.

"If you don't ... well, what I'm trying to say is, if you don't take this seriously and choose to ignore me, the consequences quite frankly are unimaginable. Lives literally are at stake here.

"Okay, so firstly, you were right about me, Cath. I have been holding back and I have been hiding things from you. But I promise everything I've done has been for the right reasons.

"Second, I fully intend to tell you the truth and come clean about everything when we meet again. I promise that by this time next week you will have the answers to all your questions. More importantly, we will be friends and partners again. For now, though, I need to ask you to trust me one final time. If not for me, do it for DI Gray, DI Thurgood, and for the rest of the officers on the escort detail taking Clive Douglas back to Yarwood today.

"Cath, I can't tell you how I know, but there is going to be an attempt made to spring Douglas during the escort. I'm joining the escort and I'll do what I can to stop it, but I need your help. I know this sounds crazy, and this is a big thing to ask, but I also need you to keep this information to yourself and just do as I ask."

I hesitate for a second and then continue, "I can't say how, but I know things. Like how you killed that guy with your hockey stick when you were fifteen."

Well and truly committed, I go on, "I'm sorry if that shocks you. That wasn't the intention. I just need you to know that I'm serious. I'll explain more about that when all of this is over. For now, please just trust me, Cath. Trust me and help me stop that bastard escaping.

"I'm going to SMS you a location. You need to go there now. Look for a tree stump overlooking the Gallows Corner roundabout. I've left something there for you with instructions what to–"

The second beep to signal the end of the recording cuts off the call and I'm left wondering if I've said enough. On balance, I think I have, but only time will tell.

I SMS the location of the hidden stash and add the rest of the message: When you get there, scrape away the earth underneath the tree stump. There is a letter inside the bag. Most of it won't make sense, but it will when you see what is happening. Only you can stop him, Cath.

I get myself a second cup of tea and then return to the same table and put my phone down with the screen facing towards me. Part of me is hoping that Catherine will call or message, but another part of me doesn't want her to because I have no idea what more I can say to her.

My phone stays silent and I meet DI Gray in the car park as planned.

■ ■ ■ ■ ■ ■ ■ ■

We arrive at Meerholt with twenty minutes to spare before the start of the escort. As before, Senior Officer Bayliss is there to meet us. His smile and the normal exchange of pleasantries alerts me to the fact that Catherine either hasn't yet seen or heard my messages, or she has opted to trust me and follow my instructions.

While I ponder which is the more likely, Gray shakes Bayliss' hand.

"It's good to meet you, Officer Bayliss. I hope your guest hasn't been giving you too much trouble?"

Bayliss smiles and shakes his head. "We haven't heard so much as a peep from him since he arrived yesterday. He really looks broken this time. I don't think he's going to be giving you any trouble. Are you ready for us to bring him out?"

Gray nods and asks if DI Thurgood and his men have arrived.

"Yes, ma'am. The rest of your escort party are assembled in the yard. Officer Tyler will show you the way."

Bayliss leaves us to get Clive Douglas, and PO Tyler leads us towards the prison yard. As soon as Bayliss is out of earshot, Gray asks me, "I take it from our earlier conversation that you don't believe what Bayliss said?"

"About him being a broken man? Not a bloody word of it. Clive Douglas will keep fighting until the last breath leaves his body. You can be sure of that, ma'am."

I then shake my head and smirk. "And given our past history, I think he is going to be more than a little pissed off when he sees me."

"So, definitely not a broken man?" Gray asks with a smirk of her own.

"No. Not a chance of it," I reply. "I think that we are in for an interesting trip, ma'am."

In the prison yard, DI Thurgood is busy briefing his team. While he continues, DI Gray taps my arm and points towards the assembled convoy.

"It looks like they took your advice, Sean."

To my great relief, the rapid response vehicles have been replaced by a pair of armored Land Rovers. Although not as formidable as the main armored escort vehicle, they are a marked improvement on the rapid response vehicles and will certainly offer a vastly improved level of collision protection for Mike Thurgood and his officers.

We wait for DI Thurgood to finish his team briefing before joining him next to the convoy.

"All ready?" Gray asks him.

"Yep, all set, Sarah. PC Mark Jarvis is your driver. Two of my other lads will be up front and I'll take tail end Charlie behind the meat wagon with Bob Wilkins."

Thurgood then looks to me and gestures towards one of the Land Rovers.

"DI Gray passed on your message, Sean. What's your concern? Insider information, or just a hunch?"

I shake my head. "Nothing like that, sir. Just a sensible precaution, that's all."

Thurgood nods. "Okay, no harm in erring on the side of caution, I guess. How are you feeling anyway? After everything that happened yesterday, I was a bit surprised when Sarah told me that you would be joining us on this little shindig."

"Last minute change of plan," Gray responds on my behalf. "Sean wanted to finish what he'd started. He'll be riding in with me to keep Clive company."

Thurgood thinks about it for a second, then he raises his eyebrows and nods. "Fair enough. I can understand that. Good to have you on board anyway, Sean."

He then looks beyond us and smiles. "Right then. I think it's time to get this show on the road."

I turn to see Clive Douglas slowly shuffling towards us surrounded by half a dozen prison officers. The scene plays out as before, with Clive doing his best to portray the broken man but fooling no one. The second he catches sight of us, his back straightens and his demeanor changes from cowed to arrogant.

When DI Gray steps forward to introduce herself, he cuts her off with a snarl and the savage comment, "In person, you're even more underwhelming than I was expecting, DI Gray."

As Sarah struggles to find a fitting response, Douglas gloats at his victory and asks her if he's hit a nerve. The words are barely out of his mouth before Patrick Bayliss uses his nightstick to deliver the painful jab into the small of Clive's back.

Clive doubles over, and Bayliss yanks him back up by the handcuffs and warns him that he will be making this trip Hannibal Lecter style if he doesn't cease the smartass comments. "Do we understand each other?"

Douglas gives a grudging nod and Bayliss releases his grip.

While Sarah Gray signs the transfer papers, I move closer to discretely congratulate Bayliss.

"Nice shot, Patrick. That should keep him quiet for a while. Next time a bit harder, though, please."

Bayliss smiles and says that Douglas had it coming before he turns and takes back the clipboard from DI Gray, and officially hands Douglas over. "He's all yours. Good luck."

Two of Mike Thurgood's officers step forward and take a firm grip of Douglas' arms. We follow as they lead him to the back of the armored truck where PC Jarvis is waiting for us with the door open. With Douglas secured inside the internal cage, we take our seats. Jarvis locks us in and takes his own seat up front.

A few minutes pass and my attention leapfrogs between watching Douglas staring impassively at the windowless side wall of his cage and pondering the odds of whether Cath has received and acted upon my messages.

I'm still weighing up my chances of her intervention when Douglas turns to face me.

Impatient to get going, he starts to speak but is interrupted as Sarah Gray's radio crackles to life.

"All call signs, this is alpha sierra one, confirmed ready to move. Alpha sierra two and three, your status please?"

Thurgood's second team responds, "Sierra two, good to go, boss."

Gray waits for them to finish before she responds, "Alpha sierra three, good to go."

With the escort convoy finally under way, Douglas turns back to face the wall. I'm happy for now to leave him to it. I look away, check the time, and wonder again if Cath will bring home the bacon or leave me floundering.

■ ■ ■ ■ ■ ■ ■

While I'm stressing over the many what ifs, Catherine has arrived on the hill overlooking the A12 and the Gallows Corner roundabout, but she is far from convinced that she has made the right decision.

Muttering to herself about what she's doing there and roundly cursing me, she considers leaving, but then reads back my SMS and asks herself, "Okay, so what's under the tree stump, Sean? And how the hell could you possibly know about what happened to me fifteen years ago? That is just not possible."

Still undecided, she remains in the car for another five minutes desperately searching for answers, until curiosity finally gets the better of her and she switches off the engine. "But what have I got to lose? Apart from my career and freedom that is …"

Catherine walks towards a group of small trees, and quickly locates the tree stump and the black plastic poking out from beneath the lightly packed soil. She cautiously pulls at one corner and, confident that it's not booby trapped, carefully lifts the package from its hiding place. Shaking off the loose soil, she strips away the electrical tape and refuse sacks to reveal the familiar shape of the canvas rifle cover beneath.

"You have got to be bloody kidding me, Sean. What am I now—an assassin?"

Her initial shock turns quickly to panic when she unzips the cover and reveals its contents. "Holy shit! If that is what I think it is, then that is hardcore."

The rifle case falls from Catherine's hands and she backs away. "This is too much. I'm sorry, mate. You're on …"

She stops when she notices the envelope and binoculars spilling out from the case. The envelope is addressed to her and scribbled on the front are the words: You only have three shots, Cath. And go easy, the last one is armor-piercing.

Intrigued enough to want to know what's inside, Cath sits down on the tree stump and tears open the envelope. Inside the outer envelope, there are two smaller envelopes and a handwritten letter.

She starts reading and is surprised to see her name and signature at the bottom of the letter. She is even more surprised to see that the letter is dated May 8th, four days from now.

"What the hell? I didn't sign this. I couldn't have signed this."

Despite common sense telling her to leave, she continues to read my letter.

Dear Cath,

By the time you read this, you will be looking down onto the A12 waiting for our escort convoy to arrive. For reasons that will become clear to you later, I know with 100% certainty that our convoy is going to be ambushed at around 11.25 am. Shortly afterwards a helicopter is going to land to pick up Douglas and his rescuers.

I will do everything I can to prevent this and to protect our escort team, but I can't do this alone.

Use the rifle to wound the pilot. This is the only way we can be sure of stopping them getting away. Just point and shoot, Cath. Aim for his shoulder. It's the only way, if you want to save the lives of your fellow officers. Take the shot and end this once and for all.

Now, I know that this is a big ask and it goes against all your principles, but I promise you, there is no other way.

I don't expect you to believe any of this, of course. So, to help, there are two other envelopes for you to open.

They may not answer your questions, nor indeed will they take away your doubts, but you can't deny that they will make you wonder who I really am.

If you are still unconvinced, then simply just wait around Cath and use the binoculars to watch what is happening. Just wait around, watch, and make your decision. Surely, that's not too much to ask, is it?

Below this is another sentence heavily underlined: <u>Listen to Sean, he is telling the truth. This is the only way to save your colleagues and end this now.</u> Cath's signature next to it is unmistakable.

The letter ends with a random selection of tomorrow's football results.

Premier League Results, Saturday May 5th, 2018.

Leicester City 0, West Ham 2

Watford 2, Newcastle United 1

West Bromwich Albion 1, Tottenham Hotspur 0

Catherine shakes her head in bewilderment. "So what are you telling me now, Sean? That you can predict the future?"

More confused than she was before she started reading, she puts the letter in her pocket and reaches for the two smaller envelopes. The first contains the results of Ben's and Maria's DNA tests along with my own. Understandably shocked, she struggles to comprehend what she is reading.

"Christ, Sean. This just gets better and better. What next?"

She tears open the remaining envelope and almost faints when she sees what is inside.

The small dog-eared Polaroid photograph is of a young girl with a man that she first met in an alleyway opposite her school fifteen years ago. A man she last saw fighting for his life. A man who until now had remained a nameless ghost from the past.

Terrified to be confronted by the truth that has haunted her for so long, Catherine fights for breath and struggles to compose herself. "How? I mean, it can't be. How can it be you?"

Wiping her eyes, Catherine reaches for the binoculars and stands up. "I don't know about anything else, Sean McMillan, but you are right about one thing … I do want to know who the bloody hell you are."

■ ■ ■ ■ ■ ■ ■

Ten minutes into the convoy, I check my watch and ask Douglas, "Happy to be going home, Clive?"

Quite unperturbed by my question, he turns towards me with a grin and says, "Over the moon, Sean, my boy." Then, offering up his cuffed wrists, he adds, "I don't suppose you can remove these cuffs until we get there? They are playing havoc with my wrists."

"You suppose right," Gray replies on my behalf. "Now button it, unless you want us to gag you as well." Then to me she says, "Don't encourage him please, DS McMillan."

Douglas ignores the comment from Gray and turns to me with a smirk. "It's not like you to let the ladies do the talking for you, Sean. What's wrong? Are you getting soft in your old age?"

Before Gray can intervene, I tell her to save her breath. "It's okay, ma'am. You'd be wasting your time with this one. Where he's going, there will be precious little chance for conversation anyway. Let him have his fun while he can. What's on your mind, Clive?"

After staring intently at DI Gray for a moment, he looks back at me. "I wasn't expecting to see you today, Sean. Surely you must be ready for a few days off by now?"

"What, and miss seeing you returned to solitary?" I quip. "No, Clive, I wouldn't have missed this little trip for the world."

Douglas smiles and chuckles slightly. "Well, enjoy it while you can. You know what they say about all good things coming to an end."

"Yes, I do. And so should you," I reply. Then, with far more emphasis than the last time I said it, I add, "This is the end of the line for you, Douglas. No more games, no more chances. Just four walls and a small barred window to remind you of what you are going to be missing for the next forty to fifty years. Think on that, why don't you?"

Douglas sneers and shakes his head. "Wow, you sound very bitter, Sean. But no, I don't think so. If it's all the same with you I'd rather think about somewhere and something altogether more pleasant."

"Sure, knock yourself out, Clive. Positive thinking and pipe dreams like that will do you well in solitary. For the first five or six years at least. I hear that for most people five or six years is the tipping point."

"Yes well, that's the difference between me and most people. And I include you amongst most people, Sean. You're a typical glass half-empty type, whereas my glass is always at least half-full."

DI Gray, who until now has been sitting quietly, leans forward to ask Clive, "So, you think you can make your own little piece of paradise in a nine by six segregation cell just by staying positive?"

"Anywhere can be a paradise with the right attitude, Sarah," Douglas says with a shrug. Then, turning back to address me, "Speaking of which, do I sense trouble in your own little paradise, Sergeant McMillan?"

I know full well what he is referring to, but I play along and ask anyway. "Sorry? I'm not following you."

"No partner today, Sean? I would have thought a trip like this would have been right up Catherine's alley. I do hope she's okay. That was a nasty fall she took yesterday."

I shake my head. "Not that it's any of your concern, but DC Swain is taking a well-earned break. I'm sure she's close by, though, and thinking about you."

Or at least I certainly hope she is. My mind wanders briefly to the possible scenarios if Catherine is a no-show. Taking Douglas and crew down on my own is not an option I relish, but neither is letting them leave without putting up a fight this time.

I'm still lost in thought when Douglas breaks the silence.

"You look troubled, Sean. What is it? More worried about DC Swain than you care to admit, or is domestic bliss with the Pintos not quite as blissful as you were expecting?"

Before DI Gray can react to the domestic bliss comment, I divert the subject back to Catherine.

"DC Swain is fine. In fact, she asked me to pass on her best wishes and to tell you that she will be sure to visit you in solitary the next time she has the urge to feel nauseous."

Douglas chuckles to himself again. "Very good, Sean. Very droll. I'll look forward to that. You didn't answer my other question, though. And what about Maria and Benjamin? How are they?"

DI Gray gives me a sideways glance, but I ignore it and instead remind Douglas to be careful what he says. "Don't push it, Clive. The Pintos are off-limits, as you well know."

He nods to me and then smirks at Sarah Gray. "Such a lovely family. You can understand his concern, can't you?"

Gray turns to me questioningly, "Sean?"

"Ignore him, ma'am. He's just trying to provoke a reaction. He knows that I'm friendly with the Pintos. He likes to play games with veiled threats, don't you, Clive?"

Douglas slowly shakes his head. "You should know by now, Sean, that I don't play games. Think what you want, though. It makes no difference to me. Where are we anyway? How long until we get there?"

Gray looks down at her watch. "Get comfortable, Clive. We've still at least another three and a half hours if the traffic remains clear. We'll be joining the M1 shortly, so why don't you just sit back and keep quiet? Question time is over."

Knowing how close we are to the ambush site, my heart rate quickens, and I feel myself starting to sweat. Still concerned about Catherine, I briefly consider warning DI Gray and ending the escape attempt before it's even begun.

To do so, though, would risk further disruption to the timeline and the associated consequences. I shrug off the thought and turn to face a smiling Clive Douglas.

"I should probably thank you now, Sean. Just in case I don't get the chance later."

Concerned by his comment, Gray first looks to me and then to Clive. "What the hell are you talking about?" she demands.

I tell her to ignore him and Douglas smiles again and shakes his head. "Don't be so modest. I really couldn't have got this far without your help, Sean. We really are a good team."

Alarmed, Gray edges away from me, "Sean, what's going on. What's he talking about?"

"Ma'am, ignore him, he's playing his bloody mind games. It's what he does. Don't listen to him."

Unconvinced, Gray turns back towards Douglas. "What are you–?"

"What am I talking about, DI Gray? I'm saying that DS McMillan–"

With the ambush imminent, I get to my feet and kick the side of the cage. "Shut your bloody lying mouth, Douglas. Nobody wants to hear it." Then, turning to Gray, "Ma'am, something doesn't feel right. Get on the radio and warn DI Thurgood."

Clearly confused, Gray removes her radio from her pocket and asks, "Warn him about what, Sean? You're not making any sense."

"Just bloody do it," I snap. "I can't explain. Just warn him to be on his guard."

Alarmed by my outburst, DI Gray backs away from me and reaches into her jacket for her sidearm. With it pointed squarely at my chest, she lifts her radio with her free hand and calmly sends a message to the other call signs.

"Alpha sierra one, alpha sierra two, this is alpha sierra three. Escort is believed compromised; I repeat escort is compromised. Advise immediate return to safe loca–"

A split second later our vehicle comes to a sudden and dramatic halt and Gray's message is interrupted by the unmistakable and ungodly sound of the stolen buses ramming into the side of the armored Land Rovers. This time, however, I don't hear the sound of breaking glass, which I take to be a good sign.

■ ■ ■ ■ ■ ■ ■

On the hill above, Catherine has spent the last ten minutes observing the free-flowing traffic on the A12 through the binoculars. Still convinced that I've sent her on a fool's errand, she barely reacts when our convoy comes into sight at 11.24 am.

"Okay, Sean. You were right about the timing of the convoy reaching here. Let's see if you were right about everything else."

Unconcerned, she casually follows our progress towards the roundabout, until something unusual catches her eye. Turning the binoculars for a better view, she jumps to her feet.

"Fuck! That's not right."

The two stolen buses are moving at high speed in both lanes of the slip road on a direct collision course with the escort convoy.

Dropping the binoculars, Cath desperately screams a warning and frantically waves her arms. She's too far away, though, and it's already too late. The buses careen into the side of the Land Rovers. Miraculously, the front vehicle stays upright, but Thurgood's vehicle is flipped onto its side and smoke starts to billow out from under the hood.

Angry with herself for not bringing her radio, Cath reaches for her cell phone to call for backup but hesitates when she remembers a line from my letter: <u>Listen to Sean, he is telling the truth. This is the only way to save your colleagues and end this now.</u>

Placing her cell phone onto the tree stump, Catherine picks up the binoculars and focuses on the crash scene.

"I'm trusting you, Sean McMillan. Don't you bloody dare let me down again."

■ ■ ■ ■ ■ ■ ■

As the noise outside subsides, I try to stand up, but Gray orders me to sit back down.

"What the hell just happened?" she shouts.

"Ma'am, I've no idea. Let me go and find out."

Gray points her Glock at my face. "DS McMillan, I'm warning you. Until I know what is going on, everyone needs to stay seated with their hands where I can see them."

Douglas has moved unnoticed to the front of the cage and sarcastically asks, "Does that include me, Sarah?"

Gray swings her weapon towards him. "Especially you. Sit down, Douglas, or I won't be responsible for my actions."

He sits back down with an irritating grin on his face and, keeping her weapon firmly pointed in my direction, DI Gray attempts to contact the other call signs.

"All call signs, this is alpha sierra three, please advise your status. Sierra one, sierra two, please advise your status."

A voice that sounds like DI Thurgood starts to speak, but there are barely two or three words heard before a shot rings out and the transmission ends.

Fearing that Thurgood or one of his men has just been executed, I turn to Gray who appears stunned.

"Ma'am, we need to do something. We can't just sit here and do nothing."

DI Gray gets to her feet. "Okay, but just stay where I can see you." She nervously edges past me to tap on the driver's partition with the muzzle of the Glock. "Jarvis, what's going on? What can you see?"

As before, PC Jarvis at first ignores the question; then he slowly turns. The same bead of sweat is snaking its way down the side of his face and his complexion is as unnaturally sallow as it was before as he mumbles his apology, "I'm sorry, ma'am, I had no choice. I'm sorry."

Ignoring Gray's demands for him to explain what he means he turns away and climbs out of the cab. Moments later we hear the rear door being unlocked and I watch as Gray fruitlessly tries to establish contact with base.

When the door opens, the sight of DI Thurgood and PC Wilkins on their knees at gunpoint with hands cuffed behind their backs is enough to make her put down the radio.

For me, though, seeing them is a huge relief. Other than a few minor cuts and bruises, both men appear to be unhurt. I can only hope the same for the other two officers and pray that the shot we heard was just a warning.

■ ■ ■ ■ ■ ■ ■

From her vantage point amongst the trees, Catherine watches as four heavily armed masked men climb down from the buses and swarm towards the front escort vehicle. Using what looks like a hydraulic ram of some sort, the passenger side door is wrenched from its hinges. Both officers are pulled out and wisely offer no resistance as they are disarmed, thrown to the ground, and bound hand and foot with plasticuffs.

Turning their attention to the burning rear vehicle, two of the attackers climb up onto the driver's side door and one of them taps on the window. A moment later he raises a weapon and fires a shot into the air. There is a pause, then it looks like the shooter is talking to the officers in the Land Rover.

Soon after, the attackers climb down from the vehicle. Faced with a choice of staying and being burnt alive or giving themselves up, the driver's door swings upwards and PC Wilkins awkwardly emerges. His weapons have been left inside the vehicle and his hands are on his head as he steps down.

When DI Thurgood appears, Catherine decides she has seen enough. She puts down the binoculars and reaches for the canvas rifle cover. "Whatever or whoever you are, Sean, in the words of Will Smith in Bad Boys, this shit just got real."

■ ■ ■ ■ ■ ■ ■

One captor orders Sarah to drop her weapon and hand over her cell phone. She immediately complies, and PC Jarvis nervously steps forward, proffering her a key. "They want you to open the cage and take his cuffs off, ma'am."

Gray takes a step back. "I'm sorry. I can't do that, PC Jarvis." Then, shaking her head at him in disapproval, "Can I ask why … Mark? It is Mark, isn't it?"

I watch with justifiable nervousness as Jarvis hesitates to respond. Irritated, another of the masked men pushes him aside and points a shotgun at Gray's chest. "Unlock the cage and take his cuffs off. Do it now please, DI Gray. I won't be asking again so politely."

I hope against hope that Gray will see sense this time, but she dismisses my pleading look to open the cage and once again refuses to cooperate. Knowing what's coming next, I step forward and say, "Jarvis, give me the key."

Gray tries to protest, but I'm quick to cut her off. "Ma'am, these men are serious. And trust me, Clive Douglas is not worth any of us dying for."

The big Irishman takes the keys from Jarvis and hands them to me before saying to Gray, "Listen to your man, Sarah. He's talking sense." Then pointing the shotgun at Bob Wilkins' chest, adds, "We are dangerous. Now get that bloody cage open, McMillan."

Still reluctant, but with no other choice, Gray steps aside to let me pass. The Irishman jabs the shotgun barrel into the small of her back. "You too, Gray. In you get. Just do as you're told, and nobody needs to get hurt. And you, Jarvis. Come on, bloody well move yourselves."

Inside the cage, Douglas is already on his feet and is beaming from ear to ear as I turn the key in the lock. The door is barely open before he pushes past me and holds his wrists out impatiently towards Gray.

"Get these bloody things off me, right now!"

The cuffs fall to the floor and Douglas rubs his wrists, before bending over to pick up DI Gray's sidearm and radio.

"What now?" the Irishman asks him.

Douglas steps down from the wagon and orders PC Jarvis into the cage. He then turns his weapon towards me and Gray. "On your bloody feet. Get in there with Jarvis."

Sarah Gray enters the cage and takes a seat next to PC Jarvis. I make a pretense of following, but, as before, the Irishman stops me and points me towards Clive Douglas, who is smiling and shaking his head. "Not you, Sean," he says. "Not after everything you've done for me. You're coming with us. You can join the lads outside."

I turn back to try to tell Gray that I have nothing to do with this. "Ma'am, you have to believe me, Douglas is setting me up. This is what he does. You have to believe m–"

She cuts me off mid-sentence with a disgusted, "And is this what you meant by closure, Sean?"

"Save it, McMillan. We've a ride to catch and it won't wait," says the Irishman and I brace myself for the vicious prod in the back from his shotgun, which sends me careering towards the end of the wagon.

Douglas watches over me, while the Irishman secures the cage and kicks the key out of reach, under one of the seats.

He then slams shut the rear door and snaps off the key in the lock to further hinder any rescue attempt. Turning to Douglas, he quips, "I hope they bring a locksmith with them … or a little chunk of Semtex."

Douglas rewards the quip with half a smile, but his mind is elsewhere. Behind the crash site, cars have started to backup, and a small group of onlookers are moving cautiously towards us to find out what has happened.

The sight of the armed men and the sound of two shots being fired into the air from the Glock Douglas is holding is enough to halt their progress.

Nervously looking to the sky, Douglas grumbles, "Where the hell is it? It should be here by now."

The big Irishman tells him not to worry. Then he turns to scan the horizon. Right on cue comes the sound of incoming rotor blades. Just thirty seconds later, a sleek black chopper breaks through the low-lying clouds and descends rapidly onto the middle of the roundabout.

■ ■ ■ ■ ■ ■ ■ ■

Although highly proficient with handguns and small assault weapons, Catherine has limited experience with rifles, and has certainly never had the need to fire one in anger.

In comparison to using a close-range police-issue MP5K or the Glock pistol, the thought of hitting a live target in the shoulder at this range with a beast of a weapon like the Dragunov fills her with dread.

Despite having the tree stump to rest the weapon on, she is struggling to focus and control her breathing as she shifts her aim to keep up with the rapidly changing scene unfolding in front of her.

She watches as I climb back into the armored truck with Gray and Jarvis. And she watches as I emerge with just Douglas, and as the paddy locks the rear doors.

"What the hell, Sean? What's going on now?"

When Douglas fires two warning shots into the air, Catherine flinches and then quickly turns her head upwards towards the sound of the incoming chopper. Moments later a black flash thunders so close overhead that the trees sway and the ground trembles beneath her.

Not quite believing what she is seeing, Catherine watches fascinated as the chopper lands. Re-focusing, she feeds a round into the breach of the Dragunov and quietly curses me, "Goddamn you, Sean McMillan. Why is it that the one time I was hoping you were lying, you turn out to be telling the bloody truth?"

∎ ∎ ∎ ∎ ∎ ∎ ∎

The noise from the engine subsides and the Irishman points to Thurgood and Wilkins. "What do you want to do with them?"

Douglas smiles and makes a chopping gesture with the Glock. "Give them a parting gift, lads. Something to remember us by."

Without any hesitation, two of the masked men viciously strike Wilkins and Thurgood across the back of their necks with the butt of their weapons. Wilkins falls to the side, seemingly out cold; Thurgood slumps face-first to the ground with a sickening crunch.

The Irishman orders his men onto the chopper. I rush to help Thurgood but am stopped by a warning from Douglas. "Don't you bloody move, McMillan. Our business is not finished." He then offers me DI Gray's sidearm. "Here, take it."

I refuse it, of course, and Douglas gestures again for me to take the weapon. The Irishman impatiently asks Douglas what he's playing at. "Clive, for fuck's sake, we need to get going. Just get it over with and get yourself on board before one of these gawkers tries to play the bloody hero."

Douglas dismissively waves the Irishman away. "Go on, get on board. I just need a minute. Go on, do as I tell you."

Reluctantly, the Irishman turns towards the chopper, but not before muttering again about all Englishmen being mad.

Alone with Douglas, I tell him that I'm not going to play whatever game he is playing. "I'm done with you, Clive. Just get on with it, whatever it is."

Douglas shakes his head. "No, Sean. You and me, we're never going to be done. I see a long and prosperous future for us on the horizon. I would, of course, love to discuss it further with you, but as I'm sure you can appreciate, time is against me right now. So, take the fucking gun and shake my hand."

"What? Why the hell would I shake your hand and what makes you think I wouldn't shoot you with that?"

"Because, Sean, we're surrounded by witnesses and you're not a cold-blooded murderer. And well … well, I guess I am."

Douglas drops to one knee and lifts DI Thurgood's head. He presses the muzzle of the Glock to Thurgood's temple and says, "And quite frankly if you don't take this weapon and shake my hand, I'll execute this piece of shit without a second thought. It's your choice. What's it to be, McMillan?"

With the timeline more or less intact, we've reached a now or never moment. As casually as I can, I glance up towards the copse for any sign that Catherine might be there.

Impatient, Douglas pulls off Thurgood's ballistic helmet. "I'm warning you, McMillan. Take this weapon or this man is going to die." Then, dropping Thurgood's head with a thump, he points his weapon at Wilkins. "Fuck it! I might just kill them both for the hell of it."

Running out of time and options, I nervously glance back and forth between Douglas and the hill where Cath should be. The Irishman screams at Douglas from the chopper, "Come on, Clive. We need to leave right now!"

The intensity of the engines increases and then I see it. It's brief and barely noticeable, but the sun glinting off the lens of the telescopic sights is enough of a confirmation to know that I am not alone.

With renewed confidence, I stick out my hand to take the gun. "Okay. Just leave them both alone."

Douglas stands up and hands me the weapon. "I knew you would see sense. It's always such a pleasure working with you, Sean. I'm just sorry that you can't come with us." Then, pointing to the chopper, "But it's only a six-seater."

Smiling, he extends his arm, "Now shake my hand."

I shake my head. "No, I don't think so, Clive. We've known about this from the start. You're screwed, mate."

■   ■   ■   ■   ■   ■   ■

A light film of perspiration has formed on her forehead, but her breathing is more or less under control now. The shaking has also stopped enough for Catherine to focus her crosshairs on the pilot's right shoulder. She takes two deep breaths to steady herself further and then shifts her finger from the trigger guard to the trigger itself.

Squeezing gently, she is about to commit to the shot when the assault on Thurgood and Wilkins forces her to switch aim towards the assailants.

"Bastards! There was no bloody need for that."

Despite an overwhelming urge for payback, Catherine uses all her reserves of self-control and training to hold herself back from taking them out, carefully removing her finger from the trigger.

She watches as they board the chopper and as Douglas tries to hand me the Glock. When Douglas puts the muzzle to Mike Thurgood's head her pulse quickens. Sweat is now burning her eyes. Wiping them with her sleeve, she repositions herself and focuses the Dragunov sights on Clive Douglas' chest.

"Don't you dare. Don't you bloody dare."

Then she sees me looking towards her. "Yes, Sean. Against my better judgment, I'm here, putting my ass on the line yet again for you. This had better be worth it."

She sees me looking towards her again and asks herself, "What do you want? For heaven's sake, give me a bloody sign or something. You want me to shoot now?"

It isn't until she sees me look her way a third time that it dawns on her that it is me that needs the sign.

Still focused on the scene below, she very slightly tips the Dragunov right and left until the sun lightly glances off the telescopic lens like a signal mirror. Concerned about giving herself away, she realigns and remains still. "I hope that was enough, mate."

When she sees me turn and take the weapon from Douglas, she allows herself a moment of self-congratulation. "I guess it was then. Good job, DC Swain. Back over to you, DS McMillan. What next?"

■ ■ ■ ■ ■ ■ ■

212

Not overly concerned by my last comment, Douglas shakes his head. "Yes, of course you knew about this from the start, Sean. That must be why DI Gray is now locked in the back of that truck and the rest of your buddies are trussed up like so many joints of beef ready for the oven."

Then with a dollop of added venom, he yells, "You don't know, shit, DS Fucknuts! I've always been one step ahead of you. Anyway, I'm bored with you now. Have a shitty life, McMillan."

He turns towards the chopper, but my next comment stops him dead. "All aboard for Bessbrook Mill. That is where you're going, isn't it?"

Clive Douglas is rarely lost for words, but he is now. With color rapidly draining from his face, he is caught between his obvious desire to leave and the need to know more.

"What … how could you know about Bessbrook? It's not possible."

Gesturing towards the helicopter with the Glock, I single out the big Irishman. "I know a lot of things, Clive. For instance, I know Mr. Liam Clancy there. A buddy from the old days, is he? Just do yourself a favor and give yourself up."

Concerned at the delay and alerted by my gesture, the Irishman alights from the helicopter. "What the hell is going on? And why did you give him a gun?"

"They're on to us," Douglas says. "They know about, Bessbrook and …"

"What? What do they know?" Clancy barks.

Douglas points to me accusingly. "Everything. They know everything. About the escape plan. About Bessbrook. About you."

"He's bluffing," the Irishman snarls. "Come on, we're wasting time."

"He's not fucking bluffing," Douglas screams. "He knows who you are, Liam."

At the mention of his name, the Irishman rips off his balaclava and raises the shotgun. "Well, in that case I've no need for this and I've nothing to lose by killing this bastard then, have I?"

■ ■ ■ ■ ■ ■ ■ ■

From a range of six hundred yards, it takes less than half a second for the 7.62 mm bullet from the Dragunov to find its target. The impact punches a fist-sized exit wound in the back of his throat and Liam Clancy is dead before he even knows he's been hit. Shocked by her own accuracy, Catherine stares dumbstruck through the sights at her handiwork, before nausea forces her to turn away and retch.

■ ■ ■ ■ ■ ■ ■ ■

Clive Douglas is equally dumbstruck and struggles for a moment to understand what has just happened. It takes a screamed warning from the chopper to bring him back to his senses.

"Get on the fooking bird, Douglas, or we're leaving without you!"

Suddenly remarkably calm considering what he has just witnessed, Douglas nods towards where Catherine is concealed. "I should have known that bitch of yours wouldn't be too far away." Then, looking at the body of Liam Clancy, he adds, "Can I thank DC Swain for this?"

"You can," I say. "And you can be sure that she will happily do the same for you if you try to get onto that chopper."

Confident, Douglas shakes his head, "No. Killing Clancy was to protect you, Sean. I'm unarmed. I'm no threat to you."

To illustrate his point, Douglas slowly raises his arms above his head and smiles. "See, no threat at all. She's not going to shoot me, and neither are you."

He's right of course and unsure whether Cath will be confident enough to take a shot at the pilot, I raise my own weapon. "Don't test me, Douglas."

Douglas chuckles and waves his hands in the air comically. "Too many witnesses, Sean. You're not going to pull that trigger."

Behind him the intensity of the engine increases again, and the chopper lifts a few feet off the ground.

"I think that's my cue to go," Douglas says. "It's been nice knowing you. Give my love to Catherine and Maria." He turns to leave, and, out of options, I fire a shot into the ground at his feet.

The shot is enough to stop him, but he doesn't turn back around. He shakes his head and then, urged on by his rescuers, runs to the chopper and climbs aboard.

There is barely time for him to take his seat before the pilot adjusts the pitch of the rotor blades and the chopper starts to rise. Helpless, I turn towards the firing point. "Take the shot, Cath. Take the bloody shot before it's too late."

Unbeknown to me, my pleas are not required.

A bullet from the Dragunov is already slicing its way through the air. The shot is too low, though. Unable to compensate in time for the lift, Cath's second round smashes into the cockpit glass low down and shatters one of the gunmen's shins.

Panicked, the pilot reels backward and releases his grip on the controls. Although only three or four feet off the ground, the chopper falls heavily back down to the roundabout.

Seizing my chance, I drop to my knee and fire three careful shots at the crack in the cockpit glass. My hope is to shatter it completely, but it is to no avail.

From inside, Douglas screams for the pilot to get them airborne again. The chopper slowly rises. When it is twenty feet in the air, it turns until the nose is facing west.

"Fuck!" I scream. "Time for damage control, Sean."

Resigned to the fact that Douglas has beaten me again, I sprint towards the back of the armored escort van. DI Gray is calling for help and I hammer on the sides to get her attention.

"Ma'am, it's Sean, I'm going to try to get you out."

"Oh thank God," Gray yells back. "What's going on? What's happened to the escort team?"

"Hurt, but all alive," I shout. "Cover your ears, I'm going to try and shoot the lock out."

Without waiting for a reply, I fire at the lock. Two more shots are enough for it to surrender, and I wrench the back door open.

DI Gray is pushed up against the bars of the cage frantically pointing to the floor. "Under the seat. Look! The keys."

I open the cage and offer Gray her sidearm, "Yours I believe, ma'am."

She shakes her head. "You keep it for now. Where's Mike Thurgood?"

"Outside, ma'am. He needs our help."

DI Gray tries to push past but is stopped by my outstretched hand. "He got away, ma'am. Douglas got away. I'm sorry. I tried my best."

"Forget it," Gray says. "We have work to do." She leaves to find the escort team and I turn to PC Jarvis, who is sitting in the furthest corner of the cage with his head in his hands.

"Oy Jarvis, do you want to sit there feeling sorry for yourself or do you want to make yourself useful? There are injured police officers outside that need your help."

Grateful for this shot at redemption, Jarvis gets to his feet and climbs down from the vehicle.

Outside, DI Gray is busy organizing the onlookers to help the injured officers and she tells me that help is on the way. "I've called it in, Sean."

Then, gesturing to the fast disappearing chopper, she asks, "Did Douglas give you any idea where they might be going?"

Looking west, I shake my head with frustration. "No, ma'am. I've no idea."

I'm pondering where I go from here, when we are all suddenly shocked by the sound of a shot from a high-powered rifle. The civilians tending to the injured police officers scatter for cover and DI Gray looks to me with alarm.

"What the hell was that, Sean?"

Confused myself, I look to the hill and then to the silhouette of the chopper. For a moment it continues unchecked. Then, as if hitting an invisible brick wall, it abruptly stops mid-flight.

From this distance it is hard to see exactly what is happening, but it's soon clear that the chopper is in trouble. Smoke wisps upwards from the tail rotor and, despite the pilot's best efforts, the chopper begins to buck and spin wildly like a demented rodeo bull.

Losing height rapidly, Douglas must now be wishing that he had taken my advice and surrendered. Just ten seconds after the sound of the shot, the pilot loses all control.

The helicopter plunges nose-first into the ground and explodes in a massive fireball. A mushroom cloud of burning aviation fuel and thick black smoke rises almost two hundred feet into the air.

"My God!" Gray exclaims. "Nobody could survive that."

A battered and bruised DI Thurgood gets shakily to his feet and joins us. "Fuck, was that what I think it was?"

"Yep," I say. "I don't think Clive Douglas is going to be needing that cell in solitary after all."

Sarah Gray is still just as puzzled and asks, "I don't get it. What just happened?"

Under my breath I quietly say, "I'm not sure. But if I was a betting man, I would say 7.62 mm armor piercing."

"What was that?" Gray asks.

"I was saying that I'm not sure. But it's possible that we weren't the only ones that Clive Douglas had to worry about. I think an old enemy might have just settled a score, ma'am."

"That's quite possible," she replies. "And I don't think there are going to be many tears shed at his demise. All the same, though, we should get a team up there to see if we can locate the shooter."

The comment is to DI Thurgood, who has fully regained consciousness and is remarkably steady on his feet. But after his recent treatment he is no hurry to go after the man that stopped Douglas in his tracks. "We will. First things first, though, Sarah. My guys need to get properly checked over. They're a tough bunch of lads but being rammed by a speeding bus is no joke."

In the distance we hear the approach of sirens. Sarah takes Thurgood's arm and says, "Yes. You're right. Come on, let's get you checked out as well."

■　■　■　■　■　■　■

Her final shot was made against almost astronomical odds of success and was never intended to take down the chopper.

But, frustrated with her botched second shot, Cath had wanted to send a final message to Clive Douglas that we would never stop coming after him. The recoil from the armor-piercing round was an unpleasant surprise, but Catherine was more surprised when the chopper slowed down and started to spin.

"Fuck! I hit it."

She continued to watch through the telescopic sights until the result of her efforts was a foregone conclusion.

Unwilling to watch the inevitable, she lay down the rifle and wiped the tears from her eyes. The explosion and the intensity of the fireball, however, were too much to ignore and she looked back towards the crash site.

Struggling with the enormity of what she'd done and, in an effort to justify the deaths of six men, she repeated over and over to herself, "They had it coming. They had it coming. They had it coming. It was the only way." Then, "It was the only way of stopping them and saving lives. Christ, I hope you were right about that, Sean."

Knowing it wouldn't be long before a response team descended on her location, she took a deep breath to compose herself.

"Okay, Cath. Think like a bad guy. Leave nothing behind to link yourself to this place."

Working quickly, she placed the Dragunov and the binoculars into the case, along with the three spent shell casings. Next, she gathered up the torn refuse sacks and electrical tape.

Everything was thrown onto the back seat of her car and she got in and started the engine.

"Now, no need to draw attention to yourself, Cath. Keep to the speed limit. Find somewhere to ditch the rifle. Then go home and act like nothing has happened."

As she pulled away, she said to herself, "I seriously hope this is what you wanted, Sean McMillan. Because you've got a lot of bloody explaining to do."

■ ■ ■ ■ ■ ■ ■

A fleet of squad cars and ambulances converge on our location and the civilians assisting our injured officers are pushed beyond a cordon set up to protect the crime scene.

While my uniformed colleagues go through their well-rehearsed procedures, I take a moment to look around me.

Mike Thurgood's Land Rover is on its side and is burning out of control. Flames from this vehicle have also spread to the front end of one of the stolen buses. By comparison, the second Land Rover seems to be more or less intact, apart from a crumpled side and a missing door.

What makes the entire scene truly apocalyptic, however, is the thick black smoke and flames still rising from the helicopter crash site. Although it's not yet midday, the density of the smoke is enough to fool you into thinking that it's late afternoon.

On the ground in front of me, the dead Irishman is frozen in wide-eyed shock. I don't notice DI Thurgood until he says, "I guess he wasn't expecting his day to end like this when he had his tea and toast this morning."

I shake my head. "No. I don't think he did."

"Any idea, who he was?" Thurgood asks.

"I heard Douglas call him Liam," I say.

Thurgood points to the entry wound in his throat. "Not you, I'm guessing?"

I shake my head again and he asks, "The same shooter that took down the chopper?"

"Yes, I think so. Whoever it was they saved my life. Liam here was about to blast me with his sawn-off."

Thurgood smiles and looks up towards the hills. "We've a team on our way to see what's up there. I've a feeling that they're not going to find very much, though. A quick search of the area should do it. No need to waste too much time. What do you think, Sean?"

I'm thinking about Cath and whether it had been her intention to take down the chopper and what she must be thinking now. I'm also thinking that I hope to God she has already made herself scarce.

Realizing that Thurgood expects an answer, I hastily nod agreement and say, "Yes, you're right. Why waste time and resources trying to find someone who did us all a favor?"

Thurgood pats me on the back, "Good. Now, are you okay, mate? I can get the paramedics to check you over, if you want. They are nearly done with my lads."

"No need," I assure him. "I'm fine. More to the point, how are you and your men doing, sir?"

Thurgood lightly rubs the back of his head. "All good, Sean. So far, just two cases of concussion and some mild whiplash. All things considered, we got off pretty lightly I would say."

He then adds, "That was in no small part down to you, Sean. I think this bastard would have killed Bob Wilkins if you hadn't taken that key. And I'd probably have been next."

"Just doing what I thought was right," I say.

Thurgood offers me his hand. "Well, you have my thanks anyway. I owe you one, Sean."

We shake hands and then Thurgood says, "Come on. Let's find DI Gray. The powers that be will be looking for a debrief on this debacle. Best we get our stories straight."

■ ■ ■ ■ ■ ■ ■ ■

We find DI Gray standing beside a hastily setup mobile incident unit. The unfortunate young PC Jarvis is in cuffs and DI Gray is reading him his rights.

"Police Constable Mark Jarvis, I am arresting you on suspicion of aiding an escape from custody. You do not have to say anything, but it may harm your defense if you do not mention when questioned something which you later rely on in court. Anything you do say may be given in evidence. Do you understand?"

Jarvis turns towards Thurgood in the hope of help or guidance, but his pleas go unanswered and Gray repeats the question, "PC Jarvis. Look at me. Do you understand what I've just said?"

He reluctantly nods and is led away to the back of a squad car. Thurgood says to Gray, "He's a good lad. You really think he was involved in this?"

Gray shakes her head. "No. It appears that he may have been coerced into cooperating. But until we can confirm that, we need to treat him as a suspect."

"So, what now, Sarah? How long before SCS get here?"

"They're not coming, Mike. DCI Morgan is on his way. He's going to lead the initial debrief."

Shocked, I ask, "The boss is coming here, ma'am? But surely he's–"

"He just discharged himself," Gray interrupts. "It was against my better advice, but as soon as he heard what happened, he insisted on coming."

Thurgood is also shocked that Morgan would be coming to lead the investigation. "But this is way beyond DCI Morgan's scope of responsibility. Surely, this falls within the realms of Serious Crimes?"

"It does," Sarah agrees. "But it looks like the boss has called in a few favors to keep it in-house."

"Okay, but is he well enough?" Thurgood persists. "The man looked like he was on death's door when he left us yesterday."

Slightly annoyed at the comment, DI Gray scowls at Thurgood. "If the boss says he's fine, then he's fine. He should be here soon anyway, and you can judge for yourself."

■ ■ ■ ■ ■ ■ ■

While we wait for Morgan to arrive, Gray sends out for coffee and asks us all to assemble in the waiting room of the incident unit.

A Scenes of Crime officer hands out statement sheets and pens. When he's gone, DI Gray stands up and says, "You all know the drill. Get down as much detail as you can, starting with when you brushed your teeth this morning, guys."

In a much-needed moment of levity, PC Bob Wilkins smirks and holds his hand in the air. "Sorry, ma'am. I didn't brush my teeth this morning."

Taking it in good humor, Gray nods and raises her eyebrows. "I know. I can smell your breath from here, Bob. Or is it because you didn't wipe your ass either?"

The room erupts with laughter and Gray says, "Okay, guys, settle down and get to work. DCI Morgan will be debriefing each of you."

Then, pointing to me, she adds, "And you're up first, DS McMillan. So, get busy."

■ ■ ■ ■ ■ ■ ■

Although I've witnessed it before, it's still distressing to see Kevin Morgan looking so tired and out of it. He's clearly unwell and he struggles to stand up when I enter the interview room.

"Please, sir, don't try to stand on my account."

Morgan gratefully retakes his seat and forces a smile. "It's good to see you in one piece, son. It's been quite a day from what I hear."

"Not just quite a day. It's been quite a week, sir."

He nods. "Yes, you're right. And I think we were all hoping for a bit of a rest. But such is the lot of a copper, eh?"

223

Pointing to the hospital bracelet poking from under his shirt cuff, I ask, "I hope you didn't drive here yourself, boss?"

"No," he replies with a small laugh. "I discharged myself and commandeered a driver from the traffic division.

"Mind you, with the number of drugs in my system, I think I could have flown here. Now, let's get this over with so that we can all get home for some rest."

DI Thurgood and DI Gray are also in the room and we watch in silence as Morgan reads through my statement and makes notes. When he finishes, he reads through the statements from the two inspectors and occasionally cross references them with my own until he is satisfied that he has a clear picture of events.

"Well, that's quite an ending to the story of Clive Douglas," Morgan says to nobody in particular. "Not quite how I expected it to end, but, in all honesty, I can't say I'm particularly sorry."

He clears his throat and smiles at me. "Right then, young man, this is not a formal interview or meeting. But it is a fact find following on from a serious incident that will no doubt be investigated by the Serious Crimes Squad in due course.

"So, for all our protection, I need you to answer my questions as honestly and as fully as you are able. You understand, Sean?"

"Yes, sir, I do."

Morgan smiles again and refers to his notes. "That's good. Start by telling me why you were on the escort detail today. Why were you so insistent on being present?"

Although it's a perfectly reasonable question, I still can't help feeling a little paranoid that I am under suspicion. I hesitate and Morgan prompts, "Was it because you knew something about the plan to spring Clive Douglas?"

"No, sir. Nothing like that. I just wanted to be there to make sure he got back to Yarwood. I wanted some final closure, and well …" My eyes wander to Morgan's bandaged hand. "Well, I felt somehow responsible for your injury, sir."

Morgan looks me in the eye and then turns to DI Gray. "Sarah?"

Looking at me, Gray confirms, "Yes, sir. That's what DS McMillan said to me this morning."

"So, you had no prior information or reason to believe that there would be an escape attempt?" Morgan persists.

"None at all," I reply.

"Explain then your behavior just prior to the ambush, DS McMillan. And Clive Douglas alluding to the fact that you may have rendered him some kind of assistance."

"Assistance, sir?"

DCI Morgan looks at his notes. "DI Gray refers in her statement to comments made by Clive Douglas and the fact that he initially took you with him after locking DI Gray and PC Jarvis in the transport cage. I quote from her statement: Clive Douglas said, I should probably thank you now, Sean. Just in case I don't get the chance later. When I questioned what Douglas meant, DS McMillan told me to ignore him, to which the prisoner added, 'Don't be so modest. I really couldn't have got this far without your help, Sean. We really are a good team.'

"Why would Clive Douglas say these things, Sean and why did he not leave you behind in the cage with the others?"

"Because he was getting a kick out of making DI Gray think I was in league with him, sir. You know that bastard almost as well as I do. It's what he does."

Morgan thinks about it for a moment and then nods and makes a note in his pocketbook. "So you categorically deny any prior knowledge of the escape or any personal involvement with Clive Douglas, DS McMillan?"

I look to each of my fellow officers in turn before responding. "That man put me through a living hell that nearly resulted in my death and the death of my partner. So, pardon my apparent lack of sensitivity, sir, but I wouldn't piss on Clive Douglas if he was on fire."

Struggling to suppress a smirk, Morgan waits a moment before saying, "That's a no then, Sean?"

"Yes, sir. That's a categorical no on both counts."

"But what about your warning to DI Gray?" Morgan asks. "Just before the ambush you told her that something didn't feel right and that she should warn DI Thurgood. What was that all about?"

"Like I said to DI Gray, it was just a feeling because of the way Clive Douglas was acting."

"Just a feeling, son. Nothing more?"

"No, sir. I've said already. I had no idea we were about to be ambushed. I just know the way Douglas' twisted mind works."

"Okay, let's move on." Morgan pushes a sheet of paper across the table. It's a mugshot of the big Irishman. "What can you tell me about this fella?"

I pick up the sheet and say, "I can tell you that he had it coming, sir. Other than that, I've never met him before in my life. Who is he?"

Morgan takes up the rap sheet and reads aloud: "Liam Dónall Clancy. Former enforcer for the Ulster Volunteer Force. Suspected of multiple sectarian killings both during the Northern Ireland troubles and after cessation of hostilities.

"Interestingly, though, he was never convicted of any crime and never spent a single day in prison, which suggests to me that he was protected from on high. Whatever the reason, you're probably right, Sean. He probably did have it coming."

Morgan checks his notes again and then asks, "Did you see where the shot came from that killed him?"

I shake my head. "No sir. I was staring down the barrel of a shotgun at the time. Most likely it was from the hills behind us, though. That's where the other shots seemed to come from."

"Any comment from you pair?" Morgan asks Gray and Thurgood.

"Sorry, sir. I was still locked up when Clancy was killed," Gray replies.

"And I was still seeing tweety birds," Thurgood adds. "I remember hearing the shot, but that's about it, sir."

"Okay, well, wherever it came from, it looks like you owe the shooter your life, DS McMillan."

"Yes, sir. It certainly looks that way."

"And you've no idea who it could be?"

"No, sir. None at all. I was as surprised as anyone. Judging by that last shot, though, I'd say that we are looking at a professional. The shot that took down the chopper was a one in a million. In my opinion, only a trained sniper with something specialist could have made that shot."

Gray and Thurgood nod their agreement and Morgan adds his own concurrence, "Yes, I think we can all agree on that. Clive Douglas must have upset some pretty important people for them to enlist that kind of talent to keep him quiet."

"The Network?" I suggest.

"That had crossed my mind," Morgan replies. "I don't think we will ever fully understand just how far-reaching and how powerful the Network was."

"Or possibly still is," I add.

"Indeed," Morgan concurs. "Or possibly still is, son."

There is a brief pause and then he asks, "How did you end up in possession of DI Gray's service weapon?"

"Douglas made me take it, sir. He was threatening to kill DI Thurgood and PC Wilkins if I refused."

Realizing how close he was to dying, DI Thurgood looks slightly pale, but DCI Morgan doesn't flinch. "But what did Clive Douglas possibly have to gain by giving you a fully loaded weapon?"

"It was part of the act," I say. "There were witnesses close by, sir. He was trying to make it look like I was part of his team. He also wanted me to shake his hand."

"Or he would execute Inspector Thurgood and Constable Wilkins?" Morgan asks.

"Yes, sir. But once I had the weapon, I refused and called his bluff."

"Go on, Sean. What do you mean, you called his bluff?"

"I told him that we were already onto him and that we knew where he was going."

Morgan raises his eyebrows and asks, "And he believed you, son?"

"When I heard the Irish accents, I played the odds, sir. I told him that we knew he was going to Ireland. He didn't confirm it in so many words, but he told the Irishman that we knew about them."

"Did you hear any of this exchange, Mike?"

"Sorry, sir. I was still pretty much out to it at that point. After the crack on the back of my neck, I really don't recall very much until just before the chopper went down."

"That's okay, Mike," Morgan says. "Perhaps, Constable Wilkins may have heard something. Remind me to ask when we go over his statement later. Did you get yourself looked over by the paramedics?"

"Yes, sir," Thurgood replies. "No lasting damage."

"That's good," Morgan says with a nod. Then back to me, "You say in your statement that you discharged DI Gray's firearm on three occasions during this incident?"

"Yes, sir. I fired a warning shot into the ground to stop Douglas from leaving, three rounds at the chopper, and a further three rounds at the lock on the backdoor of the armored escort vehicle."

"The three rounds fired at the helicopter—were these aimed at any of the occupants?"

"No, sir. I was aiming at the cockpit glass. I was hoping to shatter the glass to force the pilot to land."

"But this was unsuccessful," Morgan states. "The helicopter was subsequently taken down, though, by our rogue sniper, DS McMillan?"

"Yes, sir. It would appear that way."

Morgan makes some notes at the end of my statement and then puts it aside. "Okay, I think we're done here, Sean. DI Gray, DI Thurgood, do you have any questions or anything to add?"

Thurgood shakes his head and Gray says, "No questions, sir, but I would like to add something for the record."

"Go on, Sarah," Morgan urges.

"Yes, sir. I would just like to say that the comments from Clive Douglas and DS McMillan's behavior during the prisoner transport did initially give me some cause for concern."

"You were concerned that there was some element of collusion or inappropriate relationship, DI Gray?"

Before answering, Gray looks towards me. "Yes, sir. That thought did cross my mind."

"And now?" Morgan asks.

"And now there is absolutely no doubt in my mind that … that my suspicions were completely unfounded. DS McMillan's actions following the ambush were exactly what I would expect from a police officer. And I fully accept Sean's explanation that Clive Douglas was simply trying to undermine his credibility."

Morgan nods his agreement and then thanks DI Gray for her comments. "All comments duly noted and will be included in my assessment for SCS, Sarah."

I thank DI Gray for her support. Embarrassed at suspecting me in the first place, she shrugs off the thanks and quickly looks away.

Picking up on the slightly uncomfortable atmosphere, Morgan stands up. "Okay, well, if there are no further questions for DS McMillan, I'd like to stretch my legs and get some fresh air before the next interview." Then, just to me, "Why don't you join me for a few minutes before you leave, Sean?"

■ ■ ■ ■ ■ ■ ■

Outside, it is a hive of activity. Uniformed and plainclothes officers have flooded the area, and, in the distance, more emergency vehicles are visible at the site of the downed helicopter. Smoke is still rising from the wreckage, but the flames are out, and the air above us is starting to clear and freshen.

We watch the rescue crews hard at work for a moment, before Morgan says, "This has been a nasty business, Sean. Not just today, but the whole rotten mess with Clive Douglas. That man was rancid to the core and I'm sorry that I ever allowed him to get involved in one of our cases. I should have pushed back."

"None of this is your fault, sir. You couldn't have known he was corrupt."

"But that's the point," Morgan says. "I should have known or at least suspected. It's my job to be able to sniff out the bad apples. So, what does that say about me?"

"All I know, sir, is that you're a fine police officer and a great boss. We're lucky to have you."

"Maybe," Morgan says, unconvinced. "But you nearly died because of his interference in your case."

I point to his bandaged hand. "You didn't exactly get away scot-free yourself, sir. And that's partly down to me."

Morgan is quick to dismiss my comment. "No, Sean. There is only one man to blame for this. And it's certainly not you."

"Okay, but it proves that none of us were able to predict what was going to happen as far as Clive Douglas was concerned. None of that matters now, though. What matters is that we're still alive and kicking and Clive Douglas is not. We won, sir. It's over."

Morgan thinks my comment over and then takes a deep breath. "I certainly hope so, son. I'm not sure I can take another week like the one that we've just had. Come on, time you weren't here. You look as exhausted as I feel."

We walk towards Morgan's commandeered vehicle and he knocks on the window to get the driver's attention. "Get this fella home please and then come back here and wait until I've finished."

Before I get in, Morgan asks, "Have you spoken yet to DC Swain, to let her know what has happened?"

I shake my head. "Not yet, sir. With all the excitement, I haven't had the chance. I'll call her now."

"Good," Morgan says, "she deserves to know, and she'll appreciate hearing it from you first."

"I'll do it right away," I assure him. "Oh and, sir, I know that SCS will need to speak to me, but do you think you could delay them until at least the 10th? Only, I'm officially on leave now and I've made some plans to go away fishing with friends in Scotland. I know that this is important, but I could really do with a break to recharge my batteries and clear my head."

The fishing trip is a total lie, of course, but I can hardly tell Morgan that this is in fact a dream and that at this very moment I'm asleep in my apartment. Neither can I tell him that the real reason for requesting a delay is to ensure that SCS don't come looking for me between now and May 10th. If that were to happen, the timeline could be screwed completely and there would also be a very real danger of me bumping into myself on May 9th before I get the chance to wake up.

That can't happen under any circumstance, and I look to Morgan hopefully. "Is that approved, sir? I really need this break."

"Consider it done," Morgan says with a nod. "I'll delay submitting my own report for a few days. That should give you enough time for your trip. Keep your phone switched on, though, lad. Just in case."

"Yes, sir, of course. We'll be out at sea most of the time, though. So it may be difficult to get a signal."

Morgan shakes his head knowingly and then says, "Sure. Go on then. Get yourself away home. Have a good break and for God's sake keep yourself out of trouble. I'll see you when you get back."

■ ■ ■ ■ ■ ■ ■ ■

The traffic on the Gallows Corner roundabout is at a complete standstill, but my driver skillfully negotiates a path through to the A12, with the help of his strobes and siren.

In less than five minutes we hit free-flowing traffic heading back towards London and the driver turns briefly to tell me we are through the worst of it. "It should be a free run now, DS McMillan. Just sit back and relax. I'll have you home in thirty minutes."

I thank him and then ask him to raise the privacy partition. "I've a couple of confidential calls to make," I explain.

He nods without looking back and the partition silently rises and shuts with a comforting click.

Today has been tough, but it's far from over. There is one urgent matter still pending. And until I resolve it, I can't even begin to think about getting back to the real world. I reach into my jacket pocket for my cell phone and check for missed calls or messages. There is a message from my mother asking me to call and there is a message from Catherine. It was sent twenty minutes ago and simply says: We need to talk.

With no idea what I'm going to say, I take a deep breath and place the call.

The call is answered immediately. "Hey. Are you okay?"

"Yeh, yeh. All things considered, I'm good, Cath. What about you?"

There is a short pause and then she says, "All things considered, I'm absolutely bloody tip-top. I'm now an international assassin of course, but what's a few dead criminals amongst friends?"

"Yes. I'm sorry. That wasn't supposed to happen."

"Oh well, in that case, what am I worrying about?" Cath snaps sarcastically. "As long as it wasn't premeditated multiple murder, then that's okay, is it?"

There is no real way to answer that, so I don't. Instead I try to focus on something positive.

"It wasn't the intended outcome, Cath. But your actions saved lives today. Mine included. What we did has also probably saved others from suffering at the hands of Clive Douglas and his cronies. And that can't be a bad thing, can it?"

Catherine ignores my question and says, "I need answers, Sean. I need to see you."

"I know, Cath. I need you to be patient for a few more days, though. There are still a few things I need to–"

"Patient! Are you out of your tiny mind, Sean McMillan? I've just put my life and career on the line for you. Not to mention the fact that you've just turned my life upside down."

I try to cut back in, but Cath is quick to shut me down. "I haven't finished yet. I've a million and one questions about what I've just done. I want to know about a letter with my signature on that is dated four days from now. I want to know about an envelope containing DNA test results and a Polaroid photograph that I have been carrying around in my purse for the best part of fifteen years. And, most importantly, I want to know how you got your hands on it and who the hell you are."

I let her finish ranting before quietly saying, "I know, Cath. And I promise to give you the answers to all those questions and anything else that you ask me. I can't do it now, though. I need a few more days. Come to my apartment on Wednesday afternoon around 4 pm and I promise I will tell you everything."

Cath gives a bitter laugh. "You're serious, aren't you? I've just had my world turned upside down and you actually expect me to carry on for five days as if nothing has happened."

"It's not like that," I say. "I need these five days for everything to make sense. You've trusted me this far, Cath. Please just trust me a little longer."

"No, your time's run out, Sean," Catherine responds. "I'm coming to your place right now. I'll be there just after you."

"What? What do you mean? Where are you, Cath?"

"Check your rear-view mirror."

Careful not to attract the attention of my driver, I sit upright in my seat and check the mirror. Sure enough, Catherine's car is tucked into the inside lane seventy or eighty yards to the rear of us.

I sit back and say, "Catherine please, I need you to wait until Wednesday. I promise it will make sense when I see you and explain what's been happening."

"No, Sean. I need to know that what I did today was for the right reasons. I'm coming whether you like it or not. And it's up to you whether or not I make a scene outside your door."

Knowing that I am not going to change her mind without seeing her face to face, I relent and say, "Okay, fine, but tell me that you got rid of the stuff."

"You mean the sniper rifle, Sean? Is that what you mean?"

"Christ, Cath. Not on the phone, please."

"Not so fun when your career is at risk is it, boss? And yes, I got rid of it. I'm not that bloody stupid. I did what I had to do, and you'd better be prepared to do the same. I'll see you in ten minutes and don't you bloody dare reach for the Jameson bottle. I want you stone cold sober when you tell me what's been going on."

Before I can say anything else, Cath ends the call.

"Great," I mutter to myself, "what now, genius?"

■ ■ ■ ■ ■ ■ ■ ■

I've been in my apartment less than two minutes before the bell rings and Catherine impatiently hammers at the door to be let in. The last time I saw Cath face to face in this timeline was when she challenged me over her discovery of my warrant card in Ashdown Forest. The look on her face today is only slightly less confrontational than it was on that occasion.

Obviously on a mission, she pushes past, and I follow her into the living room.

"Tea or coffee, Cath?"

"I'm not here for refreshments and trivial conversation, Sean. Sit down and start talking."

I take the seat opposite her and, at the risk of angering her again, I say, "I really don't know where to begin. None of this will make any sense if I try to explain now. Give me until Wednesday and I promise it will."

Surprisingly, Catherine remains calm. She sizes me up for a moment and then says, "After I found the rifle, I was all for packing it in and getting the hell out of Dodge. So, why do you think I stayed, Sean? What was it that convinced me that perhaps there was more to you then meets the eye?"

"The letter?" I ask.

Catherine shakes her head. "Try again ... I'll give you a clue. It wasn't the DNA test results telling me that you and Maria are Ben Pinto's biological parents. No, they just did my head in. But test results can be forged or falsified. So, what was it that convinced me to trust you and to stay? What was compelling enough to make me stay and to pick up that rifle?"

We both know the answer, but she wants to hear it from me.

I nod slowly and look her in the eye. "It was the Polaroid picture of us in 2003, Cath."

She takes the picture from her pocket and places it down on the coffee table. "Clever boy, Sean." Then wagging her finger in my face. "But this is not possible. It can't be, and I refuse to believe it is."

"So, why did you stay?" I ask. "If you don't believe that's me in the photograph, or that I've somehow manipulated it to make it look like me, why did you stay?"

She struggles to answer, so I help her out. "You stayed, Cath, because seeing me in that picture today made you realize that you had found a piece of a puzzle that has been tormenting you for so many years. You stayed because, desperate as you were not to believe what you were seeing, the need to know the truth was just too strong to resist."

Rarely is Catherine Swain lost for words, but she remains silent and I continue, "You've had that Polaroid since I made you promise to keep it fifteen years ago. Do you remember that?"

She shakes her head and puts her hand across her mouth.

"Okay," I say. "What about hitting me across the head with your hockey stick. That was pretty memorable, wasn't it?"

Tears well up in the corners of Catherine's eyes and she angrily spits out, "You absolute bastard, Sean McMillan."

I nod my agreement. "Yes, I probably am a bastard, Cath. But I'm telling you the truth. Look at the picture and tell me in all honestly that you don't believe it was me in that alley fifteen years ago."

Catherine refuses to look at the photograph and turns away. I pick it up and hold it out for her to see. "Look at the photograph, Catherine. It's me. You know it is."

She slowly turns to face me. Her expression is defiant, but she looks down at the Polaroid, and the image of her fifteen-year-old-self standing next to me.

She starts to say something but stops and suddenly snatches the photograph from my hand. "How did you manage to get hold of this without my knowing about it? I don't let my handbag out of my sight ... ever!"

I think about my answer carefully before I say, "Would you believe me if I told you that you left it here in my apartment?"

"Really?" Cath asks wide-eyed. "And when exactly was that?"

Bracing myself for the inevitable fireworks, I take a breath. "Two days from now. On Sunday morning."

As expected, my comment is as well received as a dose of crabs at a swingers' convention. Catherine has had enough and angrily gets to her feet. "I was wrong, Sean. You're not just a bastard. You're also a bloody head case. How dare you sit there and take the piss out of me after everything I've done for you? How bloody dare you, Sean McMillan?"

I step forward to stop her leaving, but this of course only makes matters worse. "I'm warning you, Sean. Get out of my way, or I won't be responsible for my actions."

I don't doubt for a moment that she would quite happily remove my testicles with a rusty fork right now, but I can't let her leave like this. Risking life, limb, and the family jewels, I stand my ground. "Okay. But just let me say one last thing before you go. Please, Cath?"

She shakes her head and then says, "Just get on with it. Then get the hell out of my way."

Choosing my words carefully, I say, "I told you earlier that none of this would make sense to you today. And that's not because of anything I have or haven't said. It's because words alone will never be enough. The only way to ever make sense of this is to show you who I am."

"What are you talking about now, Sean?" Cath asks frustrated. "Either put up or bloody shut up."

"You're right," I say. "Put up or shut up. That's what I should have done as soon as you got here. And it's what I want to do now. If you really want to know who I am, Cath, follow me to my bedroom."

I don't wait for an answer. There is no need. Catherine follows me without question to the bedroom and then asks, "Okay, what now?"

I reach down to the hole in my mattress and pull out the illegal automatic pistol that will be taken from me by Clancy a few days from now.

The sight of it in my hand is enough for Cath to be concerned that things have taken an unexpected turn for the worse and that she has reason to fear for her own safety. She holds out her hands and pleads for me to give her the weapon.

"Sean, please no. This is not how it ends. Please, you don't need to do this."

Realizing that I've inadvertently scared her, I quickly apologize. "Oh, God. No, Cath. It's not what you think. You're not in any danger."

"Okay, well, why don't you put that down anyway please, Sean? I've seen enough guns for today, thank you."

I shake my head. "I'm sorry, but I can't. I need it for you to understand who and what I am."

Clearly confused, Catherine shakes her head and shrugs. "Okay, you have my undivided attention. Who and what are you, Sean?"

Knowing full well that she won't believe me, I raise my eyebrows and just spit it out, "I'm a time traveler."

"Yes of course," Catherine responds mockingly. "That would explain everything. Really, Sean? Time traveler? Is that the best you've got?"

"Well, not exactly a time traveler," I amend. "Technically speaking, I'm a dream traveler. But I'll explain more about that the next time we meet."

"So, is this a dream now?" Cath asks trying to humor me.

"It's a dream for me," I reply. "It's real enough for you, though." Then pointing to the bed, "I'm not really here. I'm lying on that bed and it's Wednesday, May 9th. Or it was at least when I left."

Catherine shakes her head. The anger and sarcasm have gone, and she is now more concerned for the state of my mental health than anything else.

"Sean, whatever is going on in that head of yours, we can get you help. Just put the gun down and come with me. I promise that I will help you to make sense of all this."

She reaches her hand out to me and smiles, "Please, Sean. Give me the gun and all of this can be over."

When she tries to come closer, I raise the weapon and press the muzzle under my chin.

"No!" Catherine screams. "Please, no. I won't come any closer."

"It's the only way," I say. "It's the only way that you can understand who and what I am."

Cath is desperately trying to hold back the tears and to stay calm, but she is failing miserably. I know how much I am upsetting her, but this is the only way.

"I'm sorry. I have to do this. But none of this is real, Cath. In a few seconds you'll understand what I mean. You'll also understand what happened after you left me bleeding to death in that alley fifteen years ago. It will finally make sense."

She tries to speak, but I shake my head. "This is not the end of our story, Cath. This is just the end of the first chapter. Remember, though, this isn't real. It's only a dream."

Done explaining, I smile and wink. Then I look up and release the safety catch. "Chin up, mate. Come see me on Wednesday afternoon. I'll put the kettle on."

Too late, Cath lunges for my arm. The 9 mm slug carves an upwards trajectory through my throat and brain. At nine-hundred-and-fifty feet per second it exits from the top of my skull and decorates the wall behind in a grisly collage of brains, blood, and bone.

Although distressing, my chosen method of dying is a conscious effort to spare Catherine from the pain of watching me die slowly in front of her. As an option, it's bloody and horrifying.

But most importantly, it's also instantaneous. I'm gone before I even hit the ground.

Present Day – Wednesday, May 9th, 2018

My eyes remain closed, and the room is completely silent. My senses, though, alert me to that fact that I am not alone. As casually as I can, I lower my arm over the side of the bed and fumble at the side of the mattress. When my hand finds my hiding place, a feminine voice from the opposite side of the room says, "I think these are what you're looking for, Sean?"

Catherine is sitting in a chair next to my desk. In one hand she is holding the Smith & Wesson taken from Stephen McConnell. In the other, she has the stun gun.

I slowly sit up and Catherine raises the revolver until it is level with my chest. "This is quite the stash of illegal weapons you have here, mate. What happened to the automatic?"

Now, fully awake, I raise my hands. "Give me a minute and I'll explain everything. Do me a favor, though, and put that down please."

Cath screws up her face and shakes her head. "No, this is fun. I'd like to see you do your disappearing act again. It was too fast for me to follow last time."

Smiling she pulls back the hammer and my heart starts to race. "Whoa, Cath. Let's just take a moment please. What happened before was a dream. This is real li–"

Ignoring me, Catherine squeezes the trigger and my words are cut off by the metallic clunk of the hammer striking home. Desperate to avoid the .38 caliber slug from tearing through my vital organs, I lunge to the side. Moments later, Catherine explodes in laughter and the reality hits that I've been had.

I allow my partner to laugh it out and then say, "Good one, Cath. I guess I deserved that."

Still chuckling, Cath smirks and says, "Yes, you bloody well did, you tit. Don't you ever pull any shit like this on me again."

Then, after a further bout of laughter, "Oh God. That was priceless. The look on your face, mate."

She reaches for a glass of wine and takes a sip. A half-empty bottle of my best red is on the desk and I ask, "How long have you been here?

"A little over an hour thereabouts," Catherine replies.

"And how did you get–"

"I picked your front door lock," Cath interrupts. "It wasn't that difficult. You really should take home security more seriously. There are a lot of bad people around, you know."

I nod and raise my eyebrows. "Thanks for the advice. How's the wine?"

Cath takes another sip and swirls the expensive Argentine Merlot around in her mouth. "I've had better, but it's passable." Then, pointing to the bottle, "I hope you don't mind me helping myself?"

"No more than I mind you breaking into my apartment," I say sarcastically. "So why didn't you wake me up as soon as you got here?"

Catherine shrugs her shoulders. "You looked peaceful and I was enjoying the wine."

Suddenly looking pensive, she reaches into her purse and hands me the Polaroid. "Times up, Sean. I've been patient. It's time now to tell me what's been going on."

Nodding my agreement, I say, "Yes, I know. And thank you for giving me these five days."

Cath shakes her head and laughs slightly, "I'm not talking about the last five days, idiot. I'm talking about the last fifteen years."

She stands up and hands me the revolver and stun gun. "The shells are in the top drawer of your desk. Go and freshen up. I'll wait in the living room for you."

■　■　■　■　■　■　■　■

Refreshed and changed into a t-shirt and shorts, I find Catherine ready and waiting for me in the living room. Her wine glass has been topped up and she has poured a large tumbler of straight Jameson for me. Noticing I'm staring at it, she asks, "Do you want me to get you some ice before we start?"

"That's not what I was thinking," I reply. "I was going to say that we can leave that, if you prefer for me to be completely sober?"

Catherine smiles and tells me to sit down. "After the last few days, we both need a drink. And if what you're going to tell me is even half as messed up as what I witnessed on Friday, it's probably better that we are both a bit sozzled."

I reach for the drink and nod. "Okay, well, if you're sure."

"I'm sure," Cath replies. "I want to hear everything, though, Sean. No lies. No beating about the bush. Give it to me warts and all. Understood?"

"Understood, mate. I'm actually happy that it's come to this and I can finally get everything off my chest. And even better is the fact that this time around there is no need to gag you or duct tape you into that chair."

Shocked, Cath asks, "Sorry? What was that? You gagged me?"

"Handcuffed and gagged you," I say with a smirk. "It's a long story. But we'll get to it. I promise."

Turn the page for an extract from…

Walk With Me
One Hundred Days of Crazy
By Ernesto H Lee

"Walk With Me, One Hundred Days of Crazy is a novel with a powerful tale of romance and one that explores the deep longings of the human heart." Ruffina Oserio for Readers Favorite.

"Walk With Me, One Hundred Days of Crazy by Ernesto H Lee is a fascinating book packed with craziness, emotions, family, and love (lots of love)." Ankita Shukla for Readers Favorite.

At forty years old, Mark Rennie was the man that appeared to have it all. As a successful commodities trader with one of the leading London trading houses, he was happy, healthy and, engaged to be married to the woman he loved. Then came the devastating news that would change his life forever. Less than two years later, his health is in tatters, his fiancée is gone, and his life is reduced to nothing more than a series of difficult choices and harsh realities. In search of answers and, in search of a drink, he walks an unfamiliar part of London. He doesn't find the answers he is looking for, but he does find Karen. With Karen, he finds hope. With Karen, he finds love. With Karen, nothing is ever going to be the same again.

Available Now

Walk With Me
One Hundred Days of Crazy

By Ernesto H Lee

Preface

"Good morning, ladies and gentlemen, this is your captain speaking. I hope you all had a pleasant flight and were able to get some rest during the night. For your information, we will shortly begin our descent, and we expect to be on the ground by 11.42 am. If you would like to adjust your watches, the current local time is seven minutes past eleven and the weather is a crisp twenty-eight degrees Fahrenheit. For any passengers that are visiting for the first time, I would encourage you to open your window blinds to take in the breathtaking scenery of the Alps as we pass overhead. It really is a sight to see. Finally, on behalf of myself and the rest of the crew, I would like to thank you for choosing to fly with us and we hope to see you onboard another of our flights soon. Thank you, and please enjoy your stay in our beautiful country."

■　■　■　■　■　■　■

Usually, what I enjoy most about flying Business Class on a long-haul flight is the ability to turn my seat into a fully lie-flat bed. My usual routine is to eat, have a couple of drinks, watch a movie and then sleep until just before landing.

On this occasion, however, I have struggled to concentrate on sleep for more than a few minutes at a time. After trying unsuccessfully for more than an hour, I resign myself to a sleepless night and turn my attention back to the inflight entertainment system.

My next four hours were spent absentmindedly surfing the various movie, TV and music channels trying to find something to keep me occupied. It is a great relief then to finally see daylight creeping through my window.

Captain Müller is absolutely right, the Alps are stunning and probably even more so at this time of the year. The morning sunshine reflecting off of the snowcapped peaks is both magnificent and oddly captivating.

Before his announcement, I was so lost in my own thoughts that I only realized how long I had been staring out of the window when Müller's German accent came to life on the PA.

I look down at my watch and am surprised to see that more than an hour has passed since I last checked it. For the life of me, I have no idea what I might have been thinking about during this time. Given the circumstances of this trip, it is hardly surprising I have been preoccupied, but to remember absolutely nothing of the last hour is extremely unusual. I can't decide, though, if remembering nothing is worrying or liberating. I rack my brains for answers for another few minutes before I finally give up and turn away from the window.

Unlike me, Karen has been sleeping soundly for almost the entire flight. Even Captain Müller's chirpy morning announcement has failed to disturb her. I lean in to kiss her on the forehead. Her breathing is slow and relaxed, and I consider for a moment to allow her to sleep for longer. But I know she will be annoyed if I do. This is the last leg of an incredible journey that we started together more than three months ago, and today of all days, she will want to arrive at our final destination looking her very best. I smile at the thought of everything we have done together in these last three months, and then I gently shake her shoulder.

"Karen, we're going to be landing soon; you need to wake up now and get ready."

She doesn't react and I shake her for a second time. This time she reaches up and squeezes my hand.

"Just a few more minutes, babe. Please, I'm so tired. I promise, just give me a few minutes more."

Her eyes remain closed while she speaks, and even though she has been asleep for almost eight hours, I know how badly she needs the rest. The cabin crew haven't yet started their preparation for landing, so I kiss her hand and gently place it back down on her pillow.

"Okay, just a few minutes more, darling. Go on, go back to sleep now."

My gesture is returned with a sleepy smile, and within seconds she is sleeping peacefully again. I take the opportunity to freshen up in the washroom before returning to my seat.

Then, all too soon, the cabin crew start their rounds and politely ask me to wake Karen up. I lean over to speak to her, but there is no need for me to touch her or to say anything. She opens her eyes and after a short pause to get her bearings, she sits up and takes a deep breath.

"I don't think I ever truly appreciated sleep until we started this thing, Mark. No matter what's going on in life, when you sleep, you can take yourself away from everything. You can build your own alternate reality, and, to a certain point, you can create your own destiny. Does that make sense, or am I rambling?"

"It actually does make sense," I reply. "It's a reality that doesn't last, but while it does last, it's a comfort. So, how was last night's reality?"

"Ironically, it was probably the best one in a long time, Mark. Do you think that's because we are near the end?"

This question brings back the seriousness of our situation and the expression on my face shows it. The look on Karen's own face tells me instantly that she regrets asking the question. She takes my hand and apologizes for upsetting me.

"Mark, I'm so sorry, that was a stupid thing to say. The words were out of my mouth before I could stop myself. I really am sorry. Please forgive me?"

I squeeze her hand and force the smile back onto my face.

250

"There is nothing to forgive, Karen. It's just a shame that you didn't bring me along for that reality. I spent the night twiddling my thumbs and listening to you snoring. I had to check under your blanket a few times to make sure it was still you and not an escaped rhinoceros. No offense, of course. To the rhinoceros, I mean."

In response, she playfully punches my arm and then shakily gets to her feet. She steadies herself on the headrest of the seat in front and I pass her handbag up to her.

"Go on, go and get freshened up. The Captain is going to be putting on the seatbelt signs soon and I doubt you'll be allowed into the country looking like a hobo. It would be such a shame if I had to leave you on your own at immigration."

"Yeh, you wish," she replies. "Even if I was refused entry, you wouldn't leave me on my own. It's not possible because you, Mr. Mark Rennie, are completely infatuated with me."

With that, she winks and then blows me a kiss before stepping into the aisle and walking slowly towards the washroom.

Knowing full well that I am watching her, she stops at the door and playfully wiggles her ass, much to the amusement of myself and all the other guys that have been following her progression down the aisle.

She steps inside and closes the door, leaving me alone once again with my thoughts. Like it or not, Karen knows me almost as well as I know myself. I'm not just infatuated with her, I am head over heels, up to my neck, batshit crazy in love with her. Despite the utter irony of our situation, the last few months have been the happiest of my life, and no matter what happens from here on, nothing will ever change that.

Chapter One

Four Months Earlier

After my initial diagnosis, I had spent nearly two weeks researching my condition and looking into who the top specialists in the UK were. My final shortlist had three names on it. After a consultation with each of them, I had sat down with my father and brother to make the most important decision of my life to date.

With his impeccable credentials and an even more impressive track record of success, I finally chose to put my faith and my life in the hands of the eminent Harley Street Consultant Oncologist, Dr. Alan Bleakley. More than eighteen months on, he now feels like a close friend, and I feel like I know the layout of his surgery better than I know my own apartment.

As with all close friends, there is an unwritten rule that no matter how harsh the message or the opinion, friends should always be honest with each other. They shouldn't be afraid to tell the truth and they should never, under any circumstance, try to sugarcoat the message in an attempt to spare the feelings of the other person.

With Alan, this has never been an issue. By the very nature of his profession, Alan Bleakley is as straight as they come when delivering bad news. Unfortunately, this is of no consolation to me, and despite there having always been a chance of this scenario, it's a bombshell none the less. After delivering the latest bad news, Alan tactfully stays quiet and allows me a couple of minutes to fully digest it, before he speaks again.

"Mark, I know we've discussed this possibility before, but I think now is the time to look at the options we discussed prior to your last transrectal MRI scan. You should really consider the—"

"Sorry, doctor, but am I missing something here?" I angrily interrupt. "You've just told me that my tumor has grown and that the cancer may also now have spread to my lymph nodes and bladder. Is there any real point in continuing this conversation? When I first met you, you confidently told me there was a ninety-one percent survival rate for prostate cancer at my age. That was pretty good odds by any measure. So, what the hell went wrong? Did I back the wrong horse?"

My outburst is completely uncalled for, but, ever the professional, Alan doesn't immediately respond. Instead, he allows another short pause for me to compose myself, during which I immediately regret speaking to him in such a way.

My reaction to the news that my cancer is now at stage four is most likely a scenario that he has witnessed many times before, and whilst I have no doubt that he has heard a lot worse from other patients, this is still no excuse for my behavior, and I offer an apology.

"I'm sorry, Alan. I didn't mean that the way it sounded. I'm truly grateful for your advice and support. I just never thought it would ever get this far. I'm forty-one years old and I have no idea if I'm going to see my next birthday. I really don't know what else to say."

"You don't need to say anything," he replies. "I do need you to listen carefully though, and then I suggest you go home and speak to your family."

I nod my agreement and then I ask him how long I have left.

"Well firstly, Mark, let's clear something up, shall we? Stage four cancer doesn't necessarily mean that we are out of options. It's very serious, of course, but it's still possible to beat or to prolong life expectancy with the right combination of therapies and surg—"

"But, how long do I have?" I Interrupt again.

My question causes him to look down at his notes and then he frowns and pushes his glasses further back on the bridge of his nose.

"Your best-case scenario without further treatment is nine to twelve months, but it could be as little as six months. However, with surgery and a more intensive application of hormone therapy and chemotherapy, there is a real chance of…"

Dr. Bleakley is still talking, but he lost me at six months and my mind wanders to a place where all that awaits me is a protracted and painful death. The way I see it, the only two options I have are to continue my unpleasant course of treatment with a slim chance of beating my cancer, or to walk away now and make the best of what little time I have left. Neither option gives me any sense of comfort or hope, and when he realizes that I am not listening, he stops talking and reaches across his desk for my hand.

"Mark, why don't you go home and get some rest. I'll ask my PA to make you another appointment in a few days' time. We can discuss then how you'd like to proceed. Would you like me to arrange for one of our drivers to take you home?"

I can still barely comprehend what is happening, but I get to my feet.

"No, that's okay, thank you. I think I'd prefer to walk for now and get some fresh air."

Alan gets up and walks me to the reception to make my next appointment. His PA is an attractive blonde in her early thirties, and despite her best efforts she is failing horribly to hide the fact that she knows the details of my latest prognosis.

On my previous visits she was chatty and bubbly, but today her smile is forced and I'm almost feeling embarrassed for her. To save both of our blushes, I turn away and pretend to check something on my cellphone whilst Alan checks for the next available appointment.

"Joanna, please check if we have a one-hour slot available on Monday for Mr. Rennie."

There is a short pause and then she asks me if 2 pm would be okay, adding, "If two is difficult for you, then we could also fit you in at four. Which would you prefer, Mr. Rennie?"

"Both are fine," I reply, "so put me down for the 4 pm slot, please. I can finish work early and I'll head straight home afterwards."

"Okay, that's confirmed for you," Joanna says. "Would you like our driver to take you anywhere?"

Alan replies on my behalf, "Mr. Rennie would like to walk to get some fresh air. Mark, please let me show you out."

I turn towards the door, but before either of us can move, Joanna informs her boss about his next appointment.

"Dr. Bleakley, Dr. McKenzie is here to see you next."

We both turn to face the waiting area and the stunningly beautiful woman sitting on one of the leather sofas. I had been so wrapped up in my own thoughts that I hadn't seen her when I came out of Alan's surgery. Now, though, I can't take my eyes off of her. She is in her mid- to late-thirties, around five-feet eight-inches tall, slim with a fair complexion and long black hair. I'm wondering about her connection to Dr. Bleakley when he puts his hand on my shoulder and my concentration is broken.

"Mark, are you sure you won't take that ride? It's no problem, the car is just outside."

I decline again and Alan walks me to the door. He shakes my hand and tells me again to speak with my family.

"This is not the end of the line, Mark. There are options. I'll see you at 4 pm on Monday, but feel free to call me if you have any questions before then."

■ ■ ■ ■ ■ ■ ■ ■

I step out into the street and Alan closes the door behind me. The time is just after three, but I have no appetite to go back to work. My boss and my colleagues are all aware of my condition, and I am in no mood for the inevitable questions, or the barrage of advice and suggestions that I know will be waiting for me. They all mean well, but for now I just want to walk and be on my own. It will be bad enough talking to my father and brother later today, without also having to explain myself a dozen times to my workmates.

Without really knowing where I am going, I slowly walk down Harley Street and take some time to reflect on the frailties of life. Less than two years ago, I hadn't a care in the world. Approaching my fortieth birthday, my career in the city was on the rise, and I was living a life that most can only dream of.

As a successful commodities trader with one of the leading London trading houses, I had it all. I had more money than I could spend. I had the flashy car, a penthouse apartment, memberships to the best clubs and, above all, I had my health and a beautiful fiancée.

I still have the material things, of course, but the things that mean the most are long gone. My body has been ravaged by cancer, and unable to cope with the challenges of my illness, my beautiful and caring fiancée turned out to be not so caring after all and is now engaged to one of my former friends.

I stop for a moment and take in the sight of the impressive Victorian and Edwardian period buildings that dominate Harley Street. It's famous as the center of private medicine in England, for those fortunate and wealthy enough to be able to afford it.

A fat lot of good that has done for me.

Despite the enormous sums of money I have thrown at my treatment, it has still not been enough.

When the odds are against you, it doesn't matter how much money you have. You still can't win.

At the top of Harley Street, I turn right onto Devonshire Street and then left onto Portland Place until I reach the crescent that encircles Regents Park. It's still early September, and although I've been walking slowly, I am sweating.

I take off my suit jacket and tie, and for a moment I consider going into the park, but then decide against it. Inexplicably, I leave my jacket and tie hanging on the railings and I turn right towards Marylebone Road. I've lived in London for more than fifteen years, but I've never been to this part of town before and this is the first time I've seen the John F. Kennedy Memorial close-up.

The memorial itself is beautiful in its simplicity. There is a bust of JFK on a tall black plinth with the simple inscription 'John F. Kennedy 1917–1963'.

I compare my own situation to his, and then completely irrationally I find myself getting angry that he was forty-six years old before he died.

"For Christ's sake, even he made it to forty-six. What the hell have I done to deserve this?"

My question is to myself, but my outburst has caught the attention of a small group of elderly American tourists who are also looking at the memorial. One elderly gentleman wearing a baseball cap emblazoned with a US Navy emblem and the words USS Arizona approaches me and puts his hand on my shoulder.

"Are you okay, son? You look a little pale. Can I help you with anything?"

His words are sincere, and I find myself blushing as his friends crowd around to offer their help. I assure the veteran that I'm okay and then I ask him about his cap.

"The USS Arizona, wasn't that one of the ships at Pearl Harbor?"

My question makes him smile and his chest swells with pride as he confirms that it was. I can tell he is itching to tell me more, but I interrupt him and ask his age. If I thought his chest couldn't swell anymore, I am instantly proved wrong as he answers me.

"Would you believe me if I told you I was ninety-two years old, son? I was just eighteen when the japs attacked us at Pearl Harbor."

I'm stunned at how well he looks for his age and I ask him a final question.

"Would you say you've lived a good life, sir?"

"I think so," he replies. "Don't get me wrong, I haven't led a perfect life and I have plenty of regrets. But, on balance, yes. I think I have led a good life. Is everything all right, son?"

"It is, thank you. You've been very helpful."

I shake his hand and then leave the veteran and his friends to mull over my last comment.

I continue to walk, but now I know what I want. I want some time alone and I want a cold pint. On Euston Road, I stop outside The Green Man pub to check my phone. It has been on silent for the last few hours and I have half-a-dozen missed calls and text messages from my father and brother asking me to call them. I message them both to tell them that I'll call them later, and then I turn off my phone and go inside the pub.

This is my first visit to The Green Man, but if I had to put a label on it, I would describe it as a contemporary British boozer. The clientele, however, are anything but contemporary. Even without needing to hear the accents, most of the drinkers have tourist written all over them. It's likely they are here simply to tick the trip to the British pub off of their bucket list.

I walk towards the bar and signal to the barman. He is a tall, good-looking young man with tightly cropped blonde hair, so it is no surprise when he greets me with a strong Eastern European accent.

I return his greeting and order myself a pint of Stella Artois. Then I take a seat in a quiet booth opposite the bar.

I watch for a few seconds as the condensation runs down the side of my glass, and then I take a large gulp and savor the taste of the cool liquid. If anyone was watching me, they might think that I'd never had a cold beer before, and they wouldn't be too far wrong. After my diagnosis, and on the advice of Dr. Bleakley, I gave my lifestyle a complete overhaul. Healthy eating, a sensible exercise regimen, no more late nights and, most importantly for my immune system, no alcohol.

In retrospect, that all seems to have been a bit of a waste of time, and whilst I'm not entirely sure if I've lived a completely good life, the words of the navy veteran have made me realize that I at least need to live what little of my life I have left.

I finish my drink and head to the bar to order a refill. While the barman fills my glass, I turn towards the end of the bar to watch the early evening BBC news. It's the usual banal rubbish, but when I hear a soft female voice ordering a drink, I turn back towards the barman to see who it is.

"Hi, Pawel, a gin and tonic please, and make it a double."

The accent is distinctly northern and not at all what I was expecting. As stereotypes go, and based on looks alone, I would have put her down as a London girl, or, at the very least, home counties privately educated. The accent is not the real surprise though, and as she catches my eye, we both awkwardly look away.

I take my drink back to my booth and put our encounter down to nothing more than an embarrassing coincidence. Despite this, I keep looking over towards her and more than once she catches me staring.

After catching me for a third time, she smiles, finishes her drink and picks up her handbag. To my great relief, she walks towards the door, but then she turns and walks back in my direction. I look down, hoping she is going to the bathroom, but she stops and puts her bag down on the bench opposite me. I look up from my drink and she asks if I'd mind her joining me.

I'd been hoping to be left alone and, gorgeous or not, her interruption is unwelcome, and my response is suitably curt.

"That really all depends on what you want. Did Dr. Bleakley send you to spy on me, Dr. McKenzie? Are you going to report back that you caught me having a sly pint?"

"Yep, that's right," she replies with a smile. "I followed you with the GPS tracker that he implanted into you earlier today. I take it that you didn't know that Dr. Bleakley is an undercover agent for MI5?"

Her response makes me blush and without waiting for an invitation she sits down opposite me.

"I'm no different from you. I needed a drink and was intending to have one before going home. I didn't follow you. I live close by. What's your excuse?"

"This is my first time in this pub. I started walking and ended up here. You haven't answered my question, though. What do you want?"

"Just some company with a like-minded soul. I'm guessing you came here to get some peace and quiet and to escape reality for a while. Well, so did I, but when I saw you at the bar, it made me think about fate and what really matters most in life."

"I'm sorry, I'm really not following you, Dr. McK—"

"Call me Karen," she interrupts and holds out her hand. "And you are?"

"It's Mark, Mark Rennie. But didn't you know that already?"

"Why would I? Are you famous?" she adds with a smirk.

Now I'm completely confused.

"Sorry, Karen, but can we start again, please? What's your connection to Dr. Bleakley, and what did you mean by a like-minded soul? Did Bleakley discuss my case with you?"

She laughs slightly and then takes me by surprise as she reaches across the table for my hand.

"That would be a massive breach of patient and doctor confidentiality, Mark. And, besides, it wouldn't mean all that much to me. Pediatrics is my specialty. My business with Alan today was completely personal."

"Okay, so, part two of my question?" I ask.

"Yep, part two, that's the real winner for both of us. I wasn't trying to listen as you were leaving the surgery, but I heard Dr. Bleakley tell you that you still have some options. I, unfortunately, am out of options."

My look betrays my surprise, and without thinking I blurt out something about how she looks so normal.

This causes her to laugh again and she thanks me for the compliment. "Thanks. It's amazing what a shitload of medication, makeup and a wig can do. Believe me, though, ovarian cancer is a bitch, and underneath this extremely expensive wig I've got the whole Britney Spears meltdown thing going on. Do you want to see?"

She jokingly tucks her fingers under the wig to lift it off and laughs again when she sees the panic in my eyes.

"For a man knocking on death's door, you really need to loosen up and live a little. What's the worst that can happen?" She says with a lift of her eyebrows.

"I'm sorry, the news today hasn't quite sunk in yet. You seem to be coping okay though. What's your secret?"

"There's no big secret. I knew deep down that my cancer was terminal. So, when Alan confirmed it today, I think I was already mentally prepared for it. The way I see it, I have two choices: I can sit around waiting for the end, or I can make the most of what time I have left."

I nod my head and tell her that I was thinking much the same thing.

"Great, so we're in agreement," she says, before calling to the barman. "The same again for both of us, please, Pawel. And two shots of the tequila gold."

"Oh no, no tequila for me," I protest. "I've got work in the morning."

Pawel looks at her for guidance, and after squeezing my hand and telling me to relax, she tells him that we'll both have a tequila. He smiles and starts to prepare the drinks, and I tell Karen that she is playing with fire.

"You do realize that with the medication I'm on, there is a distinct possibility that I'm either going to pass out or throw up?"

"Well, the same applies for me, but let's hope we don't pass out. Throwing up might not be such a bad thing though."

"And why would that be?"

"Two reasons. Number one, it will do us good to get some of that medication out of our system."

"Wonderful! And number two?"

"Number two, Mark, is that we'll have room for another tequila."

She looks at me with the wickedest of smiles and I can't help but smile back.

"You really are quite crazy aren't you, Dr. McKenzie?"

"Not yet," she replies. "But I'm hoping to get there quite soon. Now, are you going to leave me to drink alone or are we going to have some fun?"

■ ■ ■ ■ ■ ■ ■ ■

Also, by Ernesto H Lee

The Dream Traveler Series

Out of Time, The Dream Traveler Book One – published August 2018.

The Network, The Dream Traveler Book Two – published October 2018.

Finding Lucy, The Dream Traveler Book Three – published March 2019.

Fools Gold, The Dream Traveler Book Four – published – February 2020.

Standalone Novels

Walk With Me, One Hundred Days of Crazy – published July 2019.

For questions about any of his books or other enquiries, the author can be contacted at – ernestohlee@gmail.com

Printed in Great Britain
by Amazon